WHAT HAPPENS IN PARADISE

OLIVIA SPRING

Boldwood

First published in Great Britain in 2025 by Boldwood Books Ltd.

Copyright © Olivia Spring, 2025

Cover Design by Rachel Lawston

Cover Illustration: Rachel Lawston

The moral right of Olivia Spring to be identified as the author of this work has been asserted in accordance with the Copyright, Designs and Patents Act 1988.

All rights reserved. No part of this book may be reproduced in any form or by any electronic or mechanical means, including information storage and retrieval systems, without written permission from the author, except for the use of brief quotations in a book review. This book is a work of fiction and, except in the case of historical fact, any resemblance to actual persons, living or dead, is purely coincidental.

Every effort has been made to obtain the necessary permissions with reference to copyright material, both illustrative and quoted. We apologise for any omissions in this respect and will be pleased to make the appropriate acknowledgements in any future edition.

A CIP catalogue record for this book is available from the British Library.

Paperback ISBN 978-1-83633-002-8

Large Print ISBN 978-1-83633-003-5

Hardback ISBN 978-1-83633-001-1

Ebook ISBN 978-1-83633-004-2

Kindle ISBN 978-1-83633-005-9

Audio CD ISBN 978-1-83617-996-2

MP3 CD ISBN 978-1-83617-997-9

Digital audio download ISBN 978-1-83617-998-6

This book is printed on certified sustainable paper. Boldwood Books is dedicated to putting sustainability at the heart of our business. For more information please visit https://www.boldwoodbooks.com/about-us/sustainability/

Boldwood Books Ltd, 23 Bowerdean Street, London, SW6 3TN

www.boldwoodbooks.com

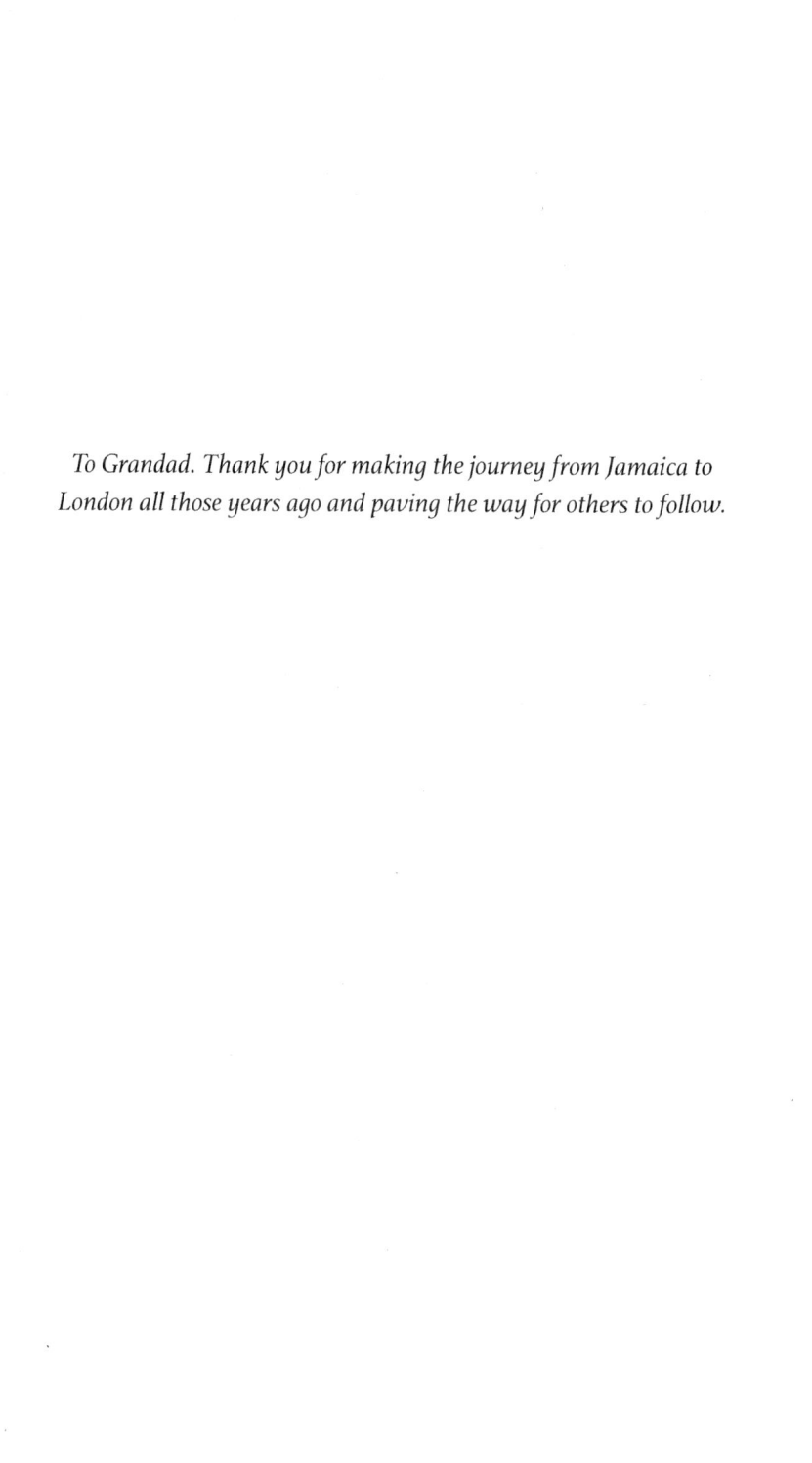

To Grandad. Thank you for making the journey from Jamaica to London all those years ago and paving the way for others to follow.

1

JASMINE

I hated firing people.

It went against my nature to make others happy.

But as I stood at the door of the hotel's laundry room, I knew that unfortunately, I wouldn't have a choice.

As I watched Miguel, the very married head of housekeeping, shagging Carolina, the new chambermaid, on the washing machine, my jaw dropped.

Although his back was facing me, I recognised his shiny bald head glistening under the bright light that illuminated the immaculately painted white room, which had multiple washing machines neatly lined up against the wall.

Whilst his navy trousers and boxer shorts were wrapped around his ankles, exposing his large, hairy arse, Carolina's blouse was unbuttoned and her eyes were squeezed shut.

The scent of fresh detergent flooded my nostrils. A laundry room was supposed to be clean and sanitary; I really hoped they planned to thoroughly disinfect every surface afterwards.

As the washing machine vibrated furiously, Carolina

bounced up and down, moaning with pleasure, whilst Miguel continued thrusting into her.

I quickly turned my back and groaned internally.

Why oh why did I have to spill my bottle of juice all over my office floor and decide to get a towel to clean it up?

This wasn't the first time I'd caught someone *in the act*. One of the main goals of my job as a 'Love Alchemist' at the Love Hotel was to bring couples together, quite literally. So walking in on awkward situations had become an occupational hazard.

But catching two co-workers going at it on a washing machine was a new one for me.

My stomach tightened. My new boss, Hazel had made it very clear that any co-workers found to be engaging in 'extra-curricular activities' were to be dismissed. Jobs at the Love Hotel were like gold dust. There was no way they'd find anywhere else to work that was as good as this and I hated to be the one to send them straight to the unemployment line.

Sweat pooled on my forehead. I reached into my electric navy-blue pencil skirt for a tissue then blotted it over my brown skin, whilst I worked out my next move.

I could stand outside and wait until they'd finished. Considering they were both about to be sacked, the least I could do was let them enjoy an orgasm before their lives went to shit.

For a second, I even contemplated creeping outside and pretending I hadn't seen them. But then I remembered that gut-wrenching feeling of betrayal I'd felt three years ago and I knew I couldn't just turn a blind eye.

Plus, if Hazel found out I knew about this illicit afternoon-delight session and hadn't said anything, she'd be furious. I'd worked too hard to get to where I was and I wasn't going to allow anything to jeopardise my career.

Nope. I had to put a stop to it. Right now.

After turning back to face them, I cleared my throat loudly, but the loud whirring from the washing machine drowned it out. No wonder they hadn't heard me come in.

Just as I was considering covering my eyes and walking over to switch the machine off myself, Carolina's eyes flicked open, then widened as she caught sight of me.

'Fuck!' she screamed.

'*Sí*,' Miguel said smugly in his Spanish accent as he continued pumping into her. 'I give it to you good!'

'No!' She pushed him back, her eyes now the size of saucers. 'Someone's here!'

Miguel froze, then spun his head around. When he saw me, horror washed over his face.

'Señora Jasmine!' He yanked up his trousers. 'It is not what you think!'

A sharp pain ripped through my heart and those painful memories came flooding back.

I quickly pushed them away. This wasn't about me. This was about my career. If I wanted to get that promotion, I had to act like a boss. I couldn't let my emotions get involved.

My phone rang. I pulled it from my pocket then looked down at the screen. It was Hazel.

Dammit. I was supposed to be going to her office to confirm that everything was in place for the VIP guest who'd be arriving shortly.

'I'll leave you two to get dressed,' I said calmly before stepping outside. 'Hazel, hi. Sorry I'm late. There's been an incident...'

An hour later, Miguel and Carolina were both being escorted from the hotel after being fired on the spot by Hazel.

I'd pulled Carolina to one side beforehand to ask if she'd felt pressured by Miguel, but she'd insisted it was consensual and that they'd just got *caught up in the moment.*

I warned her that Hazel wouldn't be sympathetic about two employees *losing control* on company property and I was right.

Once I'd told Hazel what had happened, I hadn't had to do the firing like I'd feared, but I still felt bad: for Miguel's wife and how gutted she'd be when she found out, and for Carolina, who'd only been here for three weeks.

And although I'd never do something so reckless, I could empathise a little because I knew too well what it felt like to be drawn to someone and be tempted to do something you shouldn't.

The important difference though was that I'd never get involved with someone who wasn't single. Zero exceptions.

In my case, the person I was drawn to was unattached, but there were still a million reasons why I had to keep my distance.

Anyway, I didn't even know why I was thinking about *him.* I wasn't interested in getting involved with anyone. Romance and love were something I helped our guests to find. It wasn't for me. Not any more. I was just fine with being single.

Yep. What happened with Miguel and Carolina was a warning and I'd received the message loud and clear.

As the security guard shut the door to Hazel's office, I blew out an exasperated breath.

'Don't feel bad,' Hazel said as if reading my mind. 'You did the right thing by telling me. Miguel was in a position of power. Carolina was his subordinate. Even if she insists it was consensual, it was an abuse of power. We can't have bosses screwing their underlings. *And* he's married. If this got out, it'd damage our reputation. We're the world's leading matchmaking destination hotel. We're supposed to bring couples together, not tear them apart with sordid affairs. *Jesus!*' She shook her head like a disappointed parent. 'What is it with married men? Why can't they keep it in their pants?'

Another sharp pain shot through my heart.

'Good question.' I sighed.

'You did well today, Jasmine. Please continue to be vigilant. We can turn a blind eye to our guests becoming *amorous* on the hotel's grounds, because their satisfaction in all areas is what we strive to achieve, but we need to ensure that all of our Romance Rockstars are operating at the highest levels of professionalism. We can't afford any scandals. Especially with our plans for expansion.'

'Of course.' I nodded.

Romance Rockstars was the Love Hotel's name for its employees. They didn't believe in using traditional job titles. Technically, Miguel wasn't called the head of housekeeping; he was a Comfort King. Carolina wasn't a chambermaid; she was a Comfort Champion. And for the past two years, I'd worked here as a Love Alchemist, which was a fancy way of saying guest relations manager.

Basically, I was in charge of ensuring the guests were well looked after and doing whatever I could to bring them together as a happy couple.

'Perhaps it's worth adding another reminder at the next meeting.'

'Got it,' I said, noting to add *no banging your co-worker* on the itinerary.

I couldn't exactly put a camera on everyone's genitals to see what they got up to, but somehow, I'd find a way to keep everyone's libidos in check at work because that was what I did: I got the job done.

'Excellent. So is everything in place for our VIP's visit?'

'Yes.' I nodded. 'I've triple-checked her room is spotless, I've circulated her photo to everyone and will make sure I'm there to greet her personally the moment she arrives.'

A mysterious VIP was coming to visit the hotel. Apart from showing us her photo, management hadn't revealed exactly who she was or why she was coming here, but Hazel was very clear that I had to make sure that everything went without a hitch.

'Great. And have you checked that the restaurant has a list of her dietary requirements?'

'Yes, Marco confirmed he'd received them yesterday.'

'Marco's off sick, so Alejandro will be leading tonight's service.'

'Oh.' I swallowed hard, trying to ignore my racing heartbeat. 'I... I wasn't aware.'

'Marco only left about two hours ago. That's why I called you.'

'I see. I'll head to the restaurant now to double-check.'

'Perfect. I knew I could count on you.'

'Thanks.'

As I headed towards the door, a warm sensation filled my chest. I prided myself on making sure things ran like clockwork and I was glad that Hazel was finally starting to recognise my worth.

She'd only worked at the hotel for a few months, so we were still building a relationship. Hazel was the one I needed to impress to secure the promotion I'd wanted for ages, so it was good that I was on the right track.

Seeing as she'd just complimented me, now would be a good time to ask about my progression.

'Actually, Hazel.' I turned back to face her. 'I wondered if you'd given any more thought to my promotion?'

'There might be something in the pipeline,' she replied and a wave of happiness swept through me. That sounded promising. 'I should know more in the next few days.'

'Thank you!' I said, trying to contain my excitement.

'Report back once you've spoken to Alejandro to confirm that everything's set for tonight, okay?'

'Will do.'

I closed her office door, then took a deep breath. I didn't know why my heart was still racing.

So what if Alejandro was in charge of preparing the VIP's dinner? All I had to do was check he had the info then leave. Simple. No big deal.

After popping into my office to swipe on a fresh coat of glossy nude lipstick, powder my nose and check my smooth, jet-black, shoulder-length hair hadn't gone frizzy in the heat, I took another deep breath then strode to the restaurant.

Just as I stepped through the back door, my phone chimed with a message. I was about to type out a reply when I crashed into something hard and my phone flew to the ground.

'I am sorry!' a deep voice boomed as I realised the hard thing I'd crashed into was a very muscular chest.

As his unmistakable, deep, woody scent flooded my senses, I instantly knew it was *him* I'd bumped into.

My pulse rocketed.

My lips parted.

My body tingled.

I was about to close my eyes and inhale his delicious scent again when I snapped out of my thoughts, quickly stepped back then looked up at him.

Oh. My. God.

How was it possible that he got more attractive every time I saw him?

I swallowed hard, drinking him in.

Alejandro was standing inches away from me in a crisp, white chef's jacket with the sleeves rolled up to his elbows.

His dark, wavy hair looked like it'd been freshly trimmed. His clean-shaven, olive skin looked silky smooth and his hypnotic, light-brown eyes sparkled.

The phrase *tall, dark and handsome* was made for him. This man was 6ft 2 of pure hotness. Such a shame he was too young for me.

And it was an even bigger shame that we worked together.

'Are you okay?' He said in his deep, rich, ridiculously sexy, Spanish accent, which almost caused me to melt into a puddle on the floor.

Then I remembered, I was standing here, jaw open, drooling like a teenager swooning over their favourite pop star.

I quickly closed my mouth, pulled back my shoulders, stood up straighter then cleared my throat, hoping that it would stabilise my racing heartbeat.

'I'm fine!' I said, my voice sounding like I'd just sucked on a helium balloon.

'I am sorry about your phone.'

'It's... no worries!'

I bent down to pick it up, just as Alejandro did the same, so my palm landed on top of his.

The heat from his big, manly hand sent a bolt of electricity straight through me and my knees turned to jelly. I quickly removed my palm, stood up and tried to compose myself.

'Here.' As Alejandro got up and handed the phone to me, his fingertips skimmed my hand, causing goosebumps to erupt over my skin.

'Th-thank you.'

Our eyes locked and my heart raced.

This was insane.

Alejandro had worked here for more than six months. This ridiculous crush should've gone away by now. I was a thirty-nine-year-old woman. I'd be forty soon. I shouldn't be acting like a hormonal adolescent.

'I...' I broke the silence, determined to act like a professional, but then my mind went blank. I'd come here to check something with him, but as we continued to hold each other's gaze, I couldn't remember what it was. 'I... have... needs!' I blurted out.

Ground, please swallow me up.

Alejandro's eyes widened, then he frowned.

'You have *needs*?'

'No! I mean, yes!' I did have needs and under different circumstances, I was sure Alejandro would be just the man to satisfy them, but that wasn't what I meant to say. 'I meant *requirements*. Not mine. The VIP's. I came to check if Marco had passed on her dietary requirements.'

Hallelujah! I'd finally managed to string a sentence together.

This was so unlike me. For some reason, whenever Alejandro was around, my brain turned to mush and I lost the ability to speak coherently.

'*Sí*. I have it. She is a vegetarian, but she eats fish. But not salmon or tuna, correct?'

'Exactly,' I nodded, impressed that he'd memorised the details.

'And she would like to try Spanish dishes. Something traditional, but not tourist food.'

'That's right. So perhaps no paella.'

'Understood. And she likes dessert, but nothing too creamy.'

'Yes,' I started to relax, feeling confident that he'd get the job done.

'Do not worry, Jasmine. I will make a very special menu for her. Everything is fine.'

Just when my pulse was starting to stabilise, Alejandro had to go and say my name in his delicious accent. I always loved how he pronounced it. I swore my body temperature just shot up ten degrees.

'Great!' I squeaked. I had to get out of here before I embarrassed myself even more. 'I'll let Hazel know. Thanks. Bye!' I raced to the door.

'Wait!' Alejandro called back. 'Would you like to see the menu?'

Doh. I should've asked him that.

'Yes. Of course.'

He disappeared to the office attached to the kitchen then returned clutching a sheet of paper.

'Here. I printed it for you. Two copies. In case you would like to keep one to show Hazel. I know you like to be organised.'

'Thanks.' My heart fluttered, grateful that he knew that was important to me.

'*De nada.* So,' he leant on the shiny, silver counter. 'Tell me. What do you like to do when you are not working? You like to go out, to eat?'

'Sometimes,' I replied. 'You know how much I love food!' I was always first in line when Marco, the head chef (or Cuisine King, to use his correct title) needed volunteers to sample new dishes.

'Or perhaps you prefer when someone cooks for you?'

'For everyone else's safety, it's usually better if I don't do the cooking!' I laughed. 'So yes, a meal that I haven't had to make myself is *always* a better option.'

Alejandro smiled, his full lips parting to reveal his gorgeous, perfect white teeth.

'I am happy to hear that. Maybe one evening, on your day off...' He paused as if he was considering how best to phrase the question.

Wait.

I might be out of practice (actually, there was no *might* about it, I definitely was) but I got the feeling that Alejandro was about to ask me out.

'I was thinking that maybe we could...'

'I have to go!' I jumped in. 'Busy! I have loads to do before the VIP arrives. Thanks for the menu!'

I flew out the back door like my feet were on fire, heading straight to my office, where I slumped into my chair and put my head in my hands.

That was close.

If I was honest, that wasn't the first time I'd thought that maybe Alejandro was about to ask me out.

We'd had a few near misses. Nothing major but lately, whenever we worked together, there'd been occasions where we'd exchanged lingering gazes and brushed hands.

I thought I was imagining it until my friend Stella, who was a former hotel guest, asked if there was something going on between us.

Of course I told her there wasn't, which was true. But the fact that she suspected wasn't good. At the next team meeting, I was supposed to stand up and remind everyone that co-worker canoodling was not encouraged, so I couldn't start being a giant hypocrite and the poster girl for bad decisions.

It was clear. Being alone with Alejandro wasn't a good idea. So, I just needed to avoid him.

Yes, we worked in the same hotel. Yes, I was kind of his boss and had to meet with him to discuss special meals for our guests, but it was still possible for us not to cross paths.

Right?

2

ALEJANDRO

'Did you do it?' my eldest sister Lola shouted down the phone as I walked along the hotel's private golden, sandy beach.

'*Sí*.' I rolled my eyes, then wiped the back of my hand over my forehead as the blazing afternoon sunshine heated my skin. 'She is not interested.'

When my sister had called last week and asked for the hundredth time if there were any attractive women working at the hotel, I made the mistake of mentioning Jasmine. And after Lola had finished screaming with excitement about the fact that I was finally showing some interest in another woman, she said – no, in fact, she *demanded* – that I ask Jasmine out.

I told Lola that just because I considered Jasmine to be an intelligent and attractive woman, it did not mean that I was ready to start dating again, because I was not. It was too soon.

But when my hand touched Jasmine's in the kitchen earlier, I had felt a connection, so I thought it was worth a try.

Based on the way she had run out of the kitchen, the feeling was not mutual. It was no big deal though because like I had said to Lola multiple times, right now, I was happy just to focus on my career.

'Rubbish!' Lola spat in her best British accent. Despite being Spanish like me, she had spent the last fifteen years living in London and had been married to an Englishman for eleven years. When she used words like *rubbish*, it showed. 'You're gorgeous! There's not a woman on this earth who wouldn't want to date you.'

'You are biased. You *have* to say that.' I smiled down the phone.

'No! If you looked like the back end of a bus, I would tell you!'

'*Qué?*' I frowned, not understanding. 'What is wrong with the back of a bus?'

'It's just something they say here!' She laughed.

'*Vale.*' I nodded.

'If you had a face like a monkey's arse, I would tell you. But you are beautiful and funny and kind and smart and a fantastic chef. Any woman would be lucky to have you.'

'That is a lot of compliments in one sentence. What do you want? You need me to send some more Spanish ham?'

'I don't want anything. Just your happiness! Although, I wouldn't say no to more *jamón* if you're offering!'

'We will see,' I teased. 'Anyway, it is better that she is not interested.'

'Why?'

'We work together.'

'Yeah. That isn't ideal. You shouldn't shit where you eat.'

I had only told Lola that we were co-workers. If she knew Jasmine was one of my bosses, she definitely would not be so enthusiastic about us dating. For a moment, I thought about telling her, then decided it was irrelevant because now it was clear that nothing would ever happen anyway.

'Exactly.'

'But this is the first woman you have shown an interest in since...' Lola paused. She knew it was difficult for me to talk about.

'I know. Which is another reason why it is not a good idea. It is still too soon.'

'I think it is time, Ale. Try asking Jasmine out again. It's just one date. What do you have to lose?'

'No,' I said firmly as I watched the waves ripple against the shore. 'I have a great job here. Marco has become complacent. If I continue to work hard, there will be a chance for me. Being a head chef has been my dream for so long, I must stay focused. Now is not a good time.'

'That's what you've been saying for years! You know as well as I do that tomorrow is not promised. Live your life *now*. Don't wait. I'm sure there's a way you can get promoted *and* find love. I want you to be happy again, brother.'

'I *am* happy. I am doing good work. People like my food.'

'Of course they do! You're awesome!'

Lola had always been my biggest supporter. We had lost both our parents by the time I was nineteen, so Lola became a mother figure to me and our younger sister, Evita. Usually, I took her advice, but she was wrong about dating. My career had to come first.

'*Gracias.*'

'Okay. I can tell you're not listening so I'll drop it – for now... Oh, Evita was here earlier and she said to say thanks for the money.'

'*De nada*. She already messaged. I am glad I can help.'

When I found out that Evita was considering dropping out of university in London because she could not afford to pay the fees and living costs, despite having a part-time job, I offered to send her money every month. I knew how important her degree was and she had always wanted to go to university in London, but it was not cheap. Without financial support, she would have to give up on her dream. I could not let that happen.

'You're the best!'

'I try.' I grinned. 'I must go now. We have a big VIP that I will cook for tonight and I need to impress her.'

'You'll smash it.'

'*Smash?* This is another British saying, right?'

'Yep! Break a leg!' She laughed.

'*Hasta luego.*' I ended the call, still not understanding why my sister had suggested I *smash* something and *break a leg*, but thinking that it did not sound very pleasant. I would look up the translations later, but first, I had to prepare for tonight.

* * *

'That was delicious!' Clementine, the VIP guest smiled as I stood at the table.

Hazel had sent one of the waiters, or Cuisine Champions as they are called here, to get me from the kitchen so that she could introduce me.

'*Gracias.*' I smiled.

'Alejandro is our sous-chef, or Cuisine Prince as we prefer to say, but he has a promising future here,' Hazel said.

'I agree! Remind me what I've just eaten?'

'The starter was *Salmorejo*, which is a cold tomato soup made with olive oil, garlic and bread. Normally it is also served with a garnish of ham and boiled eggs, but I removed it for you.'

'I appreciate that.'

'The main course was *Potaje*, which is like a stew with chickpeas, spinach and cod. We would normally have this for lunch, but I remembered on your requirements that you preferred to have something filling and warm.'

'It was perfect! And the dessert?'

'That was *Torrijas;* it is bread soaked in milk, dipped in egg then fried in olive oil.'

'Wonderful!' She beamed.

'*Gracias.* It was a pleasure to cook for you, Clementine. Enjoy the rest of your stay at the Love Hotel.'

'Oh my goodness!' Clementine gushed. 'He's perfect!'

'Excuse me one moment. I'm just going to escort Alejandro to the kitchen.' Hazel got up and we walked away from the table. 'You did well. Come and see me tomorrow afternoon at four. I have the ideal opportunity for you.'

'*Genial!*' My eyes widened. '*Gracias.*'

As Hazel left and I stepped into the kitchen, my heart raced.

Earlier, I had said to Lola that I was confident my time would come if I kept working hard and now it seemed like it was finally happening.

This was why I needed to focus on my career. I liked Jasmine, but getting involved would have been a distraction.

Lola was right. Jasmine had been the first woman that had interested me in a very long time.

She was smart, strong, confident and attractive: all the qualities I loved in a woman. And her sweet scent was intoxicating.

Whenever I saw her, my body always reacted. When we crashed into each other earlier and she was pressed against my chest, my body felt like it was on fire. I was relieved when she pulled away, because it was a battle to stay calm.

I thought she had felt the same pulse of electricity when our hands touched, but I was wrong. I should not be surprised that I misread the signs. I had not dated for years, so I was out of practice.

Although I was relieved that my sexual desire had finally returned, the timing was not good. That was why I needed to keep my distance.

It would be impossible to avoid Jasmine completely, but I could not allow myself to get close to her.

If she came to see me, I would avoid looking at her for too long. And I would make sure that I avoided all physical contact.

No cheek kisses. No hand brushes. *Nada*.

I had overcome some of the darkest times in my life over the past two years. I had pulled through even when I thought I would not make it.

If I could do that, I could resist the temptation of my boss.

Everything would be fine.

3

JASMINE

See. It wasn't so hard.

As I strolled along the beach, my bare feet sinking into the soft sand, I gave myself a mental high five. It'd been twenty-four hours since I'd last laid eyes on Alejandro and I'd survived.

It'd been much easier than I thought. When one of my couples had requested a lunch hamper so that they could enjoy a romantic picnic on the beach, instead of going to the restaurant to ask him, I'd just called Juan, who worked in the kitchen, and asked him to pass on the instructions.

And when I needed to see next week's menu, I'd emailed Alejandro. Admittedly, it had taken much longer for him to respond than if I'd just walked over to ask him, but it didn't matter. I'd still got what I'd needed and I kept my professionalism firmly intact.

Go, me!

I'd completely overreacted. In fact, if I timed it right, I could probably go *weeks* without having to ever lay eyes on Alejandro again.

That famous saying that if you put your mind to something,

you really could achieve it was true. I was sure whoever came up with it probably had loftier goals in mind than just avoiding the hot chef at work, but I didn't care. I was just happy that everything was under control.

I blew out a satisfied breath, slipped on my sandals then walked back to my office. Just as I was about to check that everything was in place for tomorrow's couples' activities, my phone pinged.

It was a message from Hazel, asking me to come and see her. She probably wanted to give me feedback on the VIP guest's visit.

I wasn't worried. When I'd gone to say goodbye to Clementine, she'd raved about how much she'd enjoyed her stay, said that we were all doing a fantastic job and praised my professionalism.

That was what I lived for: knowing that I'd made our guests happy. I glanced up at my office walls. Both sides were covered with thank-you cards and photos of happy couples who'd met at the Love Hotel. Which reminded me: I needed to order a bottle of champagne and a bouquet of flowers to send to Serena and Elijah who were two guests who stayed at the hotel last year.

I was thrilled when they'd called me yesterday to say they'd just got engaged, so I wanted to send them something nice to celebrate.

I couldn't take all the credit for pairing them up. It was the team of matchmaking experts that made the selections before the guests arrived.

My job was to build a relationship with the couples and anticipate what was needed to help bring them closer together.

As far as I was concerned, I had the best career in the world. I gave everything to it. I didn't really have a social life or hobbies. I worked at least fourteen hours a day to make sure every guest had whatever they needed.

I'd finally found my calling. And if my gut feeling was right, by the end of the week, I'd get news from Hazel that would demonstrate that all my hard work had paid off.

My heart raced with excitement as I headed to Hazel's office. She'd said she would know in a few days if there was an opportunity for me, but with any luck, I'd find out sooner.

'Knock knock!' I poked my head around the door to Hazel's office.

'It's my *favourite* Love Alchemist!' Hazel chirped. 'Don't tell the others I said that.' She laughed.

My heart bloomed. Praise was definitely my love language.

'Thank you.' I took a seat in front of her desk.

'So.' She leant forward. 'I've got some exciting news.'

'Ooh!' I clapped my hands together, eager to know what it was.

'A third location for the Love Hotel is about to open!'

'Wow! That's amazing! Obviously, I knew the Italian resort is opening in a few weeks and you were planning to add to the hotel's portfolio, but I didn't know it was going to happen so fast!'

Hazel had recently taken over from my previous boss, Victoria, who I adored, but had been appointed to help run the new hotel in Italy.

'The demand from around the world has far surpassed our expectations, so the board are keen to capitalise on that as quickly as possible. Renovations on the building are almost complete and they're hoping to start offering places to guests within the next six to eight weeks.'

'That's fantastic!' My eyes popped. They really weren't hanging about. 'Where is the new location?'

'Jamaica.'

'Oh! That's where my parents are from!'

'I didn't realise. The hotel gets a lot of enquiries from the US, so it made sense to have somewhere outside of Europe that was idyllic and beautiful and Jamaica fitted the bill perfectly.'

'I haven't been there for years, but I remember loving it. We went when I was a child and I've always said I wanted to go back.'

'I'm very pleased to hear that Jasmine, because Clementine, the VIP who visited us, is actually one of the directors on the board for the new hotel in Jamaica. And she didn't just come to see how we run things here. She came to check how *you* and some of our other Romance Rockstars operate. To see if you'd be a good fit.'

'For what?'

'We need someone to go to Jamaica for two weeks to help the management team there set up the operations. We need people who know how we work and embody the Love Hotel brand. Your record is flawless. You've got an eye for selecting great staff and knowing what romantic activities will delight our couples, so you're the obvious choice. If this goes well, when you return, the promotion to Love Alchemist Empress could be yours!'

I blinked then blinked again, trying to take everything in.

I couldn't believe it.

The Empress was basically in charge of all of the Love Alchemists. That role would give me even more responsibility and a big pay rise.

Technically, I'd been doing the work of an Empress for months anyway. As well as all of my normal Love Alchemist tasks, I was in charge of training new alchemists, overseeing the guest itineraries and I was also the Dining Doyenne. That involved organising special meals, for example, briefing the Cuisine team on what I needed them to create for events, picnics, romantic dates etc., which meant that as well as reporting to the Cuisine King, the team also had to report to me. I did a lot more work than I was paid for, so I was glad that I was being recognised for my efforts.

I was in touching distance of getting everything I'd ever wanted: a dream career with a great salary.

'This is... wow!' My brain was whirring at a million miles an hour. I opened my mouth to speak, struggling to find the words that would adequately convey the emotions that were racing through me. 'I don't know what to say! Thank you *so* much for the opportunity. I'm so excited!'

'Excellent! I know you and Alejandro will do a fantastic job over there.'

'I'm sorry, *what*?' My eyebrows shot up to the ceiling. '*Alejandro*? What does he have to do with this?'

'Oh, I forgot to tell you. Alejandro will be going too. We also need someone to work with the Jamaican Cuisine King. Food is a very important part of the hotel's experience, so he'll be able to help share his knowledge and ensure everything aligns with our brand values.'

The blood drained from my face and my veins turned to ice. This couldn't be happening.

'But it's a restaurant in Jamaica! Alejandro Garcia is Spanish. Wouldn't it be better to hire a Jamaican head chef? Someone who knows how to create authentic dishes?'

'Yes. Like I said, we already have a Jamaican Cuisine King, but it's not just about the food; it's about making sure the cuisine team there are shown how we like to do things as a company. They need to embody the essence of the Love Hotel. Alejandro knows how we operate and the level of professionalism we expect.'

'So wouldn't it be better to send Marco?' I said, my heart thundering against my chest. I needed to change her mind. 'After all, he is the *head* chef, I mean, Cuisine King. And he's worked here since the beginning. He's more experienced.'

'No. Marco will stay here. We were very impressed with Alejandro's menu last night. He brings an air of freshness to our brand. It's settled.' She slapped her hands excitedly on the table. 'The two of you will leave this weekend. Juliet will be in touch to make the necessary arrangements, but in the meantime, get your suitcases prepared. You're going to Jamaica!'

'Yay,' I said half-heartedly as I rose from my seat and left Hazel's office in a trance.

My stomach crashed to the ground.

This wasn't how it was supposed to be.

I'd dreamt of the moment that I finally got told I was about to get a promotion.

In my fantasies, there were fireworks, champagne, cheers of congratulations and pats on the back for a job well done.

But right now, the sensation in my stomach wasn't elation and excitement. It was pure and utter dread.

I should be over the moon about the fact that I'd get to spend two weeks in Jamaica. Yes, I knew it'd be hard work, but I was sure I'd get a least one day off a week to explore. It should be the opportunity of a lifetime.

And it would've been except for one problem: Alejandro.

Earlier, I'd praised myself for avoiding him for twenty-four hours. But if we were both going to Jamaica, that would be impossible.

We'd be travelling. On a plane for hours and presumably staying in the same accommodation. *Together.*

Neither of us would know anyone there, so we'd be forced to spend more time *together.*

How was I supposed to be in close proximity with him every day for a fortnight and not get lost in those gorgeous brown eyes?

How was I supposed to ignore his scent, muscular body, annoyingly attractive face, and that knicker-melting accent without wanting to jump him?

Oh dear God.

It was official: I was a creepy boss having inappropriate thoughts about a junior member of staff – oops, Fledgling Romance Rockstar was the appropriate term for someone whose position was more junior.

In any case, I should know better.

For a second, I contemplated throwing in the towel, but I'd worked too hard to get this far. I couldn't lose my chance of a promotion over a man.

I was stronger than that.

I was Jasmine freaking Palmer and I could do this!

Couldn't I?

We hadn't even left Spain yet, but I already knew this was going to be the hardest two weeks of my life.

4

ALEJANDRO

Madre mía.

I could not believe that in just one hour, I would be meeting Jasmine at Heathrow Airport in London to catch a flight to Jamaica.

When Hazel had called me to her office earlier this week to tell me, I was surprised. Especially when she told me that I would be going with Jasmine.

We would be travelling together, living together and working together.

This was going to be very difficult. But I could do it. I had no choice. This was an opportunity of a lifetime. I was not an adolescent boy. I could control myself.

When a woman makes it clear that she is not interested, it is important to listen. And Jasmine had shown me that she did not want to pursue anything with me, so I would respect that.

We were going to Jamaica to do important work and help the team finish setting up the new hotel. Hazel and the management were relying on me and I would not let them down. If I did well, there was a chance that when I returned, I would be given the head chef position.

Hazel said that she could not promise, but Marco had not been performing well and I knew the management were not happy. They valued professionalism and reliability, two qualities that I excelled in. And if he continued to not take his position seriously, I could be next in line.

I wheeled my suitcase out of Lola's house where I had slept last night.

There were no direct flights from Malaga to Jamaica. As the hotel had arranged for us to fly from London, I had left Spain yesterday afternoon so that I would get a chance to spend a few hours with Lola and her husband, John, before meeting Jasmine this morning.

When I arrived at the check-in desk, Jasmine was already standing in the queue and as I took in the sight of her, I swallowed hard.

The woman was a vision. She was dressed in an elegant, long, yellow dress with a smart white, linen jacket.

'*Hola!*' I smiled.

'Hi,' she said softly.

'You look very...' I paused. I was about to say she looked beautiful, but then stopped myself.

At the team meeting a few days ago, Jasmine gave a speech about the importance of professionalism in the workplace and warned against inappropriate comments and behaviour towards our colleagues.

One of the waiters had heard it was because Miguel, the creepy head of housekeeping was caught fucking the new lady.

Jasmine's message was clear. Getting involved with co-workers was not a good idea. So calling her beautiful was not a smart thing to do either.

'You look very... *summery,*' I corrected myself.

'Thanks,' she smiled. 'It's always hard to know what to wear for a long flight.'

'Right,' I said, thinking I had not given much thought to my clothes. I was a shorts and T-shirt guy.

I had barely stood next to her for two minutes, but her beautiful scent already filled the air. She always smelt so good.

'So this was a surprise,' I said to break the silence. We had not spoken since Hazel told us we would be travelling together, so it was a good time to mention it.

'It certainly was,' she replied.

'But a good opportunity. For us both.'

'It will be. If we meet their objectives.'

'We will,' I said confidently. 'You are excellent at your job. And so am I.'

'You're very modest.' She laughed softly.

'Is it not the truth? Are you not excellent at what you do?'

'I like to think so.'

'And am I not excellent at my job?'

'Your food is very nice.'

'*Very nice?*' I gasped and clutched my chest as if I had been wounded. 'A burger is *very nice*. A glass of water on a hot day is *very nice*. *Nice* is just ordinary. It is boring. Do you think I am boring?' I raised my eyebrow as I shuffled along in the queue.

'No, well, I don't really know you.'

'That will change. We will be spending a lot of time together...' My voice trailed off and Jasmine's eyes dropped to the floor. 'You may not know me well yet, but you have tasted my food, no?'

'Of course, many times.'

'And how did it make you feel?'

'It's always been delicious. Surprising. Somehow everything you make tastes different – better than I'm expecting.'

'There, that is better. I prefer *delicious* and *unexpectedly superior* to just very nice. *Gracias*.'

'You're very confident.' She smiled.

'I believe in myself. I cannot expect others to clap for me if I do not clap for myself first.'

'That's true. So have you been to Jamaica before?' Jasmine asked.

'Never, but I have heard many great things. You?'

'Once. My parents are Jamaican. They both moved to London when they were very young and they took me over when I was a child. I don't remember much.'

'You have family there?'

'My grandad. Probably other relatives too, but he's the only one I've met.'

'You will visit him when we are there?'

'I'm not sure.'

'Why?'

'Long story. Do you travel a lot?' she said, changing the subject. 'I'm assuming you've been spent time in an English-speaking country as your English is very good.'

'*Gracias*. You are right. I lived in London for three years.' My chest tightened as I thought about what led me there. 'And my sister, she is married to an Englishman,' I added quickly.

'Ah, now it makes sense.'

'I still make many mistakes, but I try.'

'Well, your English is a lot better than my Spanish!' She laughed again and I smiled.

I liked the sound of Jasmine's laugh. It was soft and infectious. She was always so serious at work, so I liked seeing this other side of her. I wondered what else I would discover about her in the next two weeks.

My eyes dropped to her full lips and I thought about how much I would like to discover how they tasted.

As we arrived at the front of the queue, I came back to my senses. Thinking about Jasmine in that way was not appropriate.

The only thing that we would discover about each other during this trip would be work-related.

She would spend the day working on guest-related tasks and I would be busy in the kitchen. At the end of the day, we would both be too tired to socialise.

Now that I thought about it, there would be no need for us to spend a lot of time together, which was good news. That meant that controlling my attraction towards her would be much easier than I thought.

5

JASMINE

We'd checked in at the airport and were now heading to the business lounge.

I'd like to say I was doing a good job at keeping my cool, but I'd be lying.

When I saw Alejandro walking towards me, my heart skipped a beat.

It was strange. My ex-husband, Kane, was always immaculately dressed. Everything he wore was designer and he took great pride in his appearance.

Alejandro on the other hand had a more relaxed style. On the few times I'd seen him in his own clothes, he'd always worn something casual and understated.

Right now, he may only be wearing a plain white T-shirt and jean shorts, but man did he know how to make them look good.

His T-shirt accentuated his muscular chest and arms and his toned legs were made for shorts.

And his smile. Every time he looked at me, my stomach fluttered.

I liked his confidence too. My ex was cocky, but in an arrogant rather than a playful way.

Kane built himself up at the expense of others. He never hesitated to put other people down to make himself feel better.

But when Alejandro spoke about being an excellent chef, I noticed it was secondary to praising me. And it came from a place of confidence and self-belief rather than just blowing his trumpet.

We'd barely been here together for half an hour and already I found myself drawn to him. I was treading on very dangerous ground.

When we stopped outside the business lounge, Alejandro's eyes widened.

'I cannot believe we are travelling business class,' he whispered.

'We work for the Love Hotel: one of the most luxurious resorts in the world. Everything they do is first class and we're going to help them set up a luxury hotel in Jamaica, so it's important that we experience what it feels like to travel in style. Consider it market research.' I smiled.

'Very true. I am glad that I will finally become a member of the Mile High Club.' He grinned.

'What?' My eyebrows shot up.

'I will finally be travelling business class – which is like first class. That is being a part of the Mile High Club, no?'

'Erm.' I stifled a giggle. '*No*. The Mile High Club is something *completely* different... It's for...' I looked him in the eye, then quickly looked away. God, he was beautiful. It was going to be difficult to explain the meaning whilst staring at him, because I knew part of me would be wishing we really could join that club. *Together*. 'The Mile High Club is for people who have sex on planes whilst it's in the air.'

'Fuck!' He laughed, then chuckled again as he realised *fuck* was a very accurate description. 'I did not realise! I told you that I make mistakes with my English!'

'It's fine! At least now you know that's not the club that you'll be joining during this trip.'

'Well, it is a long flight. Anything could happen.' His eyes darkened and a bolt of desire raced through me.

I'd never considered having sex on a plane. The toilets were impossibly small and cramped. There was barely enough room for one person, so how two people could manage getting jiggy in there was beyond me. Not to mention the fact that it was highly inappropriate and could result in being chucked off the plane or even arrested.

It was *extremely* irresponsible.

So why was I currently picturing Alejandro pushing me up against the bathroom sink and burying himself inside me?

The shrill ring of my phone brought me back to my senses. I tore my gaze away from Alejandro's hypnotic eyes and pulled out my mobile, grateful for the interruption.

It was Stella. *Thank God.*

'I need to get this,' I said. 'You go on through to the lounge. Just show your boarding pass. I'll meet you in there.'

'*Vale.*' He nodded to confirm that it was okay.

I quickly walked away from the lounge, then once I'd double-checked the coast was clear, I answered the call.

'Hi!' I said.

'Hey!' Stella replied brightly. 'I got your message. You said you were in London last night and were staying over to catch a flight today?'

I'd been so busy doing the handover with the other Love Alchemists and making sure my last group of guests returned home okay that I'd only remembered to message her when I arrived in London.

'My boss is sending me on a work trip to Jamaica. With Alejandro.'

'Oh my God! That's amazing! What time do you go?'

'In about an hour and a half. I'm at the airport now.'

'Shame we didn't get to see you. I'm so jealous! I'd love to go back to Jamaica. I know Max would like to visit too.'

'Shame we can't swap places.'

'I don't get it. Why would you *not* want to go?'

'Because, as you've annoyingly pointed out a few times, I like Alejandro. And I'm going to Jamaica to work. But how am I supposed to concentrate with him around?'

'How long's the trip?'

'Two weeks! Fourteen days of trying not to look into his eyes or swoon when he smiles. God. Listen to me! I shouldn't even be talking about him like that!'

'First up, take a deep breath. You're freaking out.'

'Of course I'm freaking out!'

'Is it really such a big deal?'

'Yes! Especially after what just happened at work.' After swearing she wouldn't tell a soul, I filled her in on the washing-machine incident that led to Hazel wanting to reinforce the no-fraternising recommendation. Although we all knew it was less of a 'recommendation' and more of a 'requirement'.

'That's hilarious! I've never tried it on a washing machine before. On a spin cycle, it must feel like sitting on a giant square vibrator. I'll have to mention it to Max and see if he's up for it!'

'You're missing the point!' I blew out a frustrated breath. 'I *can't* fancy Alejandro. There's a whole power imbalance.'

'Really? Isn't his boss the... whatever silly term you use for head chef?'

'Yes. His main boss is the Cuisine King, Marco, but he also reports to me.'

'Right. But that's at the Love Hotel *in Spain*. Will you also be his boss whilst you're away? Why can't it be a case of *what happens in Jamaica, stays in Jamaica*?'

'Someone will find out. They always do.'

'Not if you're careful.'

'It's too risky. And anyway, that's not the only reason. He's only twenty-nine. I'm forty soon! I'm eleven years older than him!'

'*And?* You know what they say: *age is just a number*.'

'We're at different stages in life. He's young and carefree. He'd want different things.'

'You don't know that.'

'Anyway, I don't even know why I'm thinking about that. It would never get to that point. Actually, what am I saying? It would never even start. I'm not going to risk my career for a quick roll in the hay. Or sand, or wherever we'd do it. Not that I'm thinking about where we'd have sex, because we absolutely won't!'

'Of course you won't...' Stella said sarcastically like she was thinking, *Yeah, right.*

'We *won't!*' I protested.

'I believe you... sort of. Look, I know how important your job is and how professional you are, so I'm sure you'll find a way to handle it. What exactly will you be doing over there?'

'They haven't given specifics yet, but basically, I'm helping to set up the guest relations side of the operations there and he'll be dealing with restaurant stuff.'

'That's fine then! It's a hotel, so it won't be like you need to share a room or bed together. And he'll be busy doing restaurant stuff all day, so you probably won't even see much of each other.'

'True.'

'You're probably just overthinking. I know because that's what I used to do. At least you're finally getting a little taste of your own medicine!' Stella laughed. 'This is karma for all the scheming you did to bring me and Max together.'

'I *helped* you realise you two were soul mates. The end justified the means. This is completely different!'

'If you say so!' She laughed again. 'But seriously, just be your normal, confident, professional self and it'll all work out in the end. You'll see. You're gonna have an amazing time. You're going to Jamaica, baby! Don't waste your time fretting, just enjoy the experience!'

'I'll try.' I sighed. 'Where are you and Max jetting off to next?' I asked.

The two of them were always travelling. Stella had recently set up her own graphic design company and could work from anywhere in the world. Max ran a beauty-product company and thanks to his team, he was able to work remotely too.

'We're going to Madrid for a long weekend with Colton and his wife to watch Real Madrid play.'

'Great! I love that you two are having so much fun together.'

'You could be too with a certain *Alejandro*...' she teased.

'Anyway,' I said quickly, deliberately avoiding responding to her crazy comment. 'I'd better go.'

'Have a safe flight and don't forget to try out the Mile High Club!' She laughed.

'No way!' I gasped.

'Only joking!' She chuckled. 'Sort of... Max and I tried it and it was fun. I'd definitely recommend it!'

'Bye, Stella.'

'Bye, Jazzy. Safe flight and text me when you land.'

'Will do.'

6

ALEJANDRO

As we stepped onto the plane and turned left to business class, I tried to stop my eyes from popping, but it was difficult. I had never been inside an airport business lounge or travelled anything other than economy.

This was a big deal for me. When Jasmine came into the lounge after her call, she seemed completely comfortable with the large buffet of free food, snacks and drinks that were on offer.

The flight attendant had just greeted us with a glass of champagne and whilst it surprised me, Jasmine acted like she flew like this every day.

'Here we are.' She stopped at a seat. Looked like we would be sitting next to each other.

After loading our hand luggage in the overhead compartments, I sat down.

Everyone had their own cubicle which was like a mini suite. There was even a door to give us privacy. I attempted to close it, but could not.

'They're locked. You'll be able to operate it once we're in the air,' Jasmine said.

'In case it was not already obvious, this is my first time.' I grinned.

'I would never have guessed you were a virgin!' Jasmine smirked.

'I have been trying to hide it.' I tried to keep a straight face.

'Don't worry.' Jasmine rested her hand on my shoulder and the heat from her palm made my pulse quicken. 'I'll be gentle with you,' she teased. I laughed then seconds later, a look of horror filled her face. 'Oh my God, I'm so sorry!'

'Why?' I frowned.

'I shouldn't have said that. It was completely inappropriate!'

'It was a joke, no?'

'Of course! I hope I didn't make you feel uncomfortable.'

'No,' I shook my head firmly. 'You made me feel more relaxed. I am used to the luxuries we provide for our guests at the hotel, but not for myself. Look at all of this.' I gestured to the set-up in front of the seat.

There was a TV, small storage compartments, a kit with skincare products, toothbrush and toothpaste and from the look of what was on one of the screens, the chair did not just recline, it folded down into a bed.

'Oh, that's good. Sorry again.'

'*Tranquila*,' I said, encouraging her to relax. 'So, I can tell you have flown in business class before.'

'Yes.' She sat in the seat beside me. 'I used to...' Jasmine paused as if she was considering whether or not to finish her sentence. 'I used to work at a luxury travel agency, so occasionally, I would visit different locations and it was important for me to get a feel for what the client would experience.'

That sounded interesting. I thought it was just because she was rich. Jasmine was always very elegant. The way that she dressed and carried herself suggested that she was used to having money. Not just because her job at the hotel paid well. I got the impression that she had a fancy lifestyle before then.

'So you used to organise trips for rich and famous people?'

'Yes. I would create personalised holidays for them based on their interests and budget, so basically organising the flight, which could be a first class seat on a commercial flight or arranging a private jet, choosing the best hotel, booking the chauffeur, helicopter or yacht, suggesting the best restaurants – basically taking care of all the logistics so that all they needed to do was just turn up and enjoy their trip.'

'Wow.' My eyes widened. Private jets, helicopters, yachts… that was a whole different world. 'That is why you are so great at your job at the Love Hotel now.'

'My experience certainly helps.'

A flight attendant came to check we were comfortable and shortly afterwards, the pilot announced that they would be preparing for take-off.

I was disappointed that our conversation had been interrupted because I was enjoying finding out more about Jasmine. But it was a long flight. There would be other opportunities to talk.

At least that was what I thought.

Soon after take-off, food was served. Of course, it was not as good as the food I liked to make, but we were on an aeroplane so that was to be expected.

After she had finished eating, Jasmine put on her headphones and watched TV, then lowered the chair into a bed, put on her sleep mask and went to sleep.

Whilst she slept, I watched multiple films. I could not sleep. Somehow, knowing she was so close to me was a distraction.

It was like there was a magnet drawing me to her. I wanted to know more about her. What made her smile. What she liked to do for fun. And whether she was single. Not that it really mattered. I was just curious, that was all.

But she was guarded. I could sense there were things she was hiding.

I knew that Jasmine had secrets.

And I had them too.

7

JASMINE

Thank goodness for business class, I said to myself as I slid off my sleep mask, then selected another film to watch.

The door on the fancy suite, plus the seat that reclined into a bed, provided me with the perfect way to avoid engaging with Alejandro more than was necessary.

And judging by the way I'd shamefully flirted when he made a joke about it being his 'first time', the less I interacted with him, the better.

I couldn't believe I'd said out loud that I'd be gentle with him. At first, I was impressed that I'd even remembered how to flirt with a guy; after all, I'd been single for three years and I hadn't been on the dating scene since I was in my early twenties. But then I realised I was flirting with a colleague and was mortified.

Thankfully, Alejandro was okay with it, but I was lucky. Imagine how creepy it'd be if a male boss said to a female employee that they'd go gentle with them. *Ugh*. I had to do better.

That was why the minute we'd finished eating, I'd put on my headphones and watched a film, then slid on the sleep mask and pretended to doze off.

If I'd dozed off for more than a couple of hours, I'd be surprised. My mind was too busy replaying every moment with Alejandro since we'd met up earlier. How good he looked when I first saw him today, our conversation whilst we queued, the look of awe when he walked into business class, the way his biceps bulged as he lifted my suitcase in the overhead locker. And the way he seemed genuinely interested when I told him a bit about my past.

I could be wrong, but I got the impression that he thought I'd grown up in the lap of luxury.

Yes, I'd flown business class before, but this was actually only my second time.

You'd think that, considering we worked in luxury travel, I would've experienced it a lot more than that, but whenever there was an opportunity for that kind of travel, Kane always took it.

We'd met when I was working at a local travel agents in London. He was one of my customers. When he first asked me out, I was in awe. He was nine years older than me and seemed so sophisticated.

He wore a fancy suit and his shoes were so shiny, you could do your make-up in them. For our first date, he took me to a posh restaurant in central London. At the beginning, he wined and dined me and treated me like a princess.

When I told him how well the travel agency I worked at was doing, he became very interested. He explained that he was a successful businessman with his fingers in many pies and said that he was interested in breaking into the travel industry. He asked, if he set up a luxury travel agency, whether I'd like to come and work there and help him out.

Naively, I thought it was the opportunity of a lifetime, so I agreed. I thought that he'd be there, working with me, side by side, that we'd do it together. But instead, he left me to do all the work.

I worked my arse off whilst he swanned in and out, going to business meetings. It was only when it started to really take off a few years later that he became interested. Especially when there was an opportunity for free travel.

When it eventually became a successful business and I started to hire staff, I thought that after a decade of slaving away, I'd finally be able to take my foot off the pedal a bit and start to enjoy the fruits of my labour, but then he betrayed me and I lost everything.

I felt a tap on my shoulder and took off my headphones. It was Alejandro. I was sure he hadn't even gone to sleep and yet he still looked gorgeous.

'Hi,' I said, trying not to stare at him for too long.

'Just checking you are good?'

'Yeah, fine, thanks. You?'

'I am good. What are you watching?'

'A romcom.'

'Which one?'

'*Bridget Jones: Mad About the Boy*.'

The fact that I knew this film was about Bridget dating a younger man in no way influenced my decision to watch it. *Honest.*

'I like those films.' He smiled and my stomach flipped.

'You've watched them?' I frowned.

'*Sí.* Why are you surprised? You are not one of these people who believes that a man cannot enjoy a romantic comedy, are you?'

Busted.

'Truthfully? Maybe I am. My ex, he...' I paused. It probably wasn't a good idea to talk about my ex with a colleague.

'Your ex did not like romcoms?' He folded his arms, his face crumpled.

'Not really,' I said, thinking I couldn't avoid answering the question.

'Now I understand why he is your ex.' He smiled. 'How can anyone dislike a romantic movie?'

'He said they were too predictable.'

'*Madre mía!*' He rolled his eyes. I liked when he said that. Sounded much sexier than just saying *oh my God*, even though I think the literal translation was *my mother*. 'Why? Because we know that the couple will be together at the end?'

'I think so.'

'But then all films are predictable! Does the superhero not always save the world? Does the good guy not always beat the bad guy in an action film? Knowing that two people will fall in love is not *predictable*. It is something wonderful to look forward to. *How* they fall in love, their journey, their love story: that is the fun part.'

I stared at Alejandro, stunned into silence. I couldn't have said it better myself.

'Wow. You're full of surprises.'

'You have no idea. I think there is a lot about me that would surprise you.' His eyes darkened.

I bit my lip as my mind thought about just how much I'd like to find out.

Then again, maybe the less I knew, the better.

So far, I'd discovered that Alejandro was sweet, very easy to talk to, ridiculously gorgeous, an amazing cook and to top off all of this, he loved romcoms.

He was dangerously close to sounding like my dream man.

This mythical creature I occasionally allowed myself to fantasise about would also be committed, loyal and a stallion in the sheets.

Judging by how committed Alejandro seemed to be to his work, there was a chance that extended to his personal relationships too. Same with his loyalty.

Which meant the only other box that would be left to tick from that list was how good he was in bed.

Something told me he'd be committed to giving a woman pleasure. That he'd take his time and want to make sure whoever he was with was satisfied.

It was just such a shame I'd never get to find out...

8

JASMINE

We'd just turned into the hotel's driveway and although it was dark, thanks to the pretty lamps illuminating the grounds, I could already see that it was spectacular.

Lush, tall palm trees lined the wide paths and swayed in the gentle breeze. In the distance, I could see a striking entrance with large, tall, stone pillars and a grand fountain in front of it.

Wow. I shouldn't really be surprised that the hotel was impressive. The Love Hotel management were excellent at creating a five-star experience.

Thankfully, I didn't have to find ingenious ways to avoid speaking to Alejandro during the journey. Within minutes of getting into the chauffeur-driven Mercedes, he'd fallen asleep. I wasn't surprised seeing as I think he'd stayed up for most of the flight to Ocho Rios.

'Alejandro,' I said softly. He didn't stir. I called his name again, but this time gave his arm a squeeze.

My cheeks heated. His muscles were even firmer than they looked.

He started to move and his eyes opened slowly.

'*Perdón*,' he apologised. His voice was even deeper than usual. 'I did not mean to fall asleep.'

'No worries! We're here.'

Alejandro squinted as he began to take in the surroundings.

When we pulled up at reception, a woman was waiting for us. She had deep brown skin and a welcoming smile. Her hair was immaculately braided and hung just past her shoulders and she was wearing a tanned-coloured, branded Love Hotel dress.

'Hi! Welcome! I'm Nadine. Jasmine and Alejandro, right?' I noticed that she had a slight American twang to her Jamaican accent.

'Spot on! Lovely to meet you, Nadine.' I shook her hand.

'*Encantado*.' Alejandro leant forward and gave Nadine two cheek kisses.

An unexpected twinge of envy hit me straight in the stomach as I wished it was *my* cheeks his lips had brushed against rather than hers.

'How was your flight?' she asked.

'Great,' Alejandro replied quickly.

'Wonderful,' I added.

'You must be tired, so let me show you to your rooms.' Nadine walked ahead, leading us into the hotel. 'So this is the main reception area, which has just been finished.'

'It's lovely!' I said, taking in the sight of the plush cream and mahogany sofas, tall, stone pillars, and high ceilings complete with mahogany beams going across them.

A selection of tropical flowers had been expertly arranged in a large, colourful vase which rested on top of a grand, mahogany table.

Next, Nadine led us from reception and through to the main

grounds which were beautifully lit. The lush gardens were so impeccably landscaped that they didn't look real.

I spotted multiple swimming pools including an extra-large one with a swim-up bar. *Very cool.*

Although I could smell the salty sea air, the lights didn't quite stretch far enough for me to see it. When they opened the hotel and had guests here, I was sure that would be lit up fully. In the meantime, it made sense to keep those lights off to save energy.

'You can't see them now, but the hotel will have floating villas that are built on the water.'

'That's going to look amazing!' I said.

'It will. Most of the rooms in the main building are finished.' We stepped into a long, tiled corridor. 'This is where you'll be staying. Alejandro, you'll be in this suite and Jasmine, this is your new home, right next door.' She handed us our keycards.

'Thank you,' I said.

'Are you hungry? The kitchen is obviously closed, but I could send for some takeout if you need something?'

'I am good, *gracias*,' Alejandro replied.

'We ate on the plane, so I'm okay too, thanks.'

'Okay. Well, I'll be back tomorrow morning. In the meantime, here's my number. Call if you need anything.'

We both thanked Nadine then waved her off.

'I'm going to head inside.' I pointed to my room.

'*Vale.*' he nodded. 'I will see you in the morning.'

We stood in front of each other, eyes locked, not saying a word. Seconds passed with neither of us making a move.

'Well, I... goodnight.' I tapped my keycard on the reader.

'*Duerme bien*,' he said.

'Hope you have a good sleep too,' I replied, quickly pushing the door open and slipping inside before I melted into a pile of goo.

The man was sexy when he spoke English with a Spanish accent. But when he spoke Spanish, I could literally feel my knickers disintegrating.

Clearly I hadn't slept enough on the plane and was feeling delirious.

My suite was just as stunning as I'd expected. Pristine, ivory stone flooring, large, solid mahogany, king-size four-poster bed with freshly pressed, bright-white cotton sheets and plush-looking pillows.

The bathroom had a huge, standalone tub, ginormous, walk-in rainfall shower, expensive marble sink, backlit mirrors, thick, fluffy branded Love Hotel bathrobes and oversized towels.

In the living room, there was a large flat-screen TV, comfy-looking sofa and armchairs complete with pretty, gold-embroidered cushions.

Colourful, tropical artwork lined the walls in every room.

I couldn't resist stepping out onto the spacious balcony. I switched on the light.

Wow. I had direct sea views, plus there was a bathtub out here (along with privacy curtains) and a cute, white bistro dining table and chairs.

That bathtub looked like it was the perfect size for two...

When my mind started to drift and think about a certain co-worker laying back in it naked, I knew it was time for me to wash away those thoughts with a shower. Then I'd go straight to bed where I would definitely *not* be thinking about Alejandro.

* * *

When my alarm went off, I was tempted to cancel it and go back to sleep, but I couldn't. Today was a big day. I was expecting to be briefed on exactly what they needed me to do whilst I was here.

I wondered if Alejandro was already awake. I also wondered what the meal set-up would be. I was starving and could really do with a big breakfast to start the day.

After stepping out onto the balcony, I inhaled the fresh sea air. This place was beautiful. There wasn't a single cloud in the sky, the sea was multiple beautiful shades of blue and the white sand was stunning.

I definitely wanted to have breakfast out here to take in the incredible views.

Just as I was about to pick up my phone and call Nadine, there was a knock at the door.

'Coming!' I called out. I thought it was Nadine, but when I opened the door, my jaw dropped.

'*Hola, buenos días!*' Alejandro smiled. 'I brought you breakfast.'

He was clutching a tray with a plate topped with a silver cloche and what looked like three glasses of juice.

'Good morning to you too and wow, thank you!' I looked at my watch. 'It's seven thirty! What time did you wake up to do all of this?'

'I could not sleep, so I thought it would be better to do something productive. I walked around the resort and was able to get access to the kitchen. There was not much there, but there was enough. Would you like to sit with me and eat outside? It is a beautiful day.'

'Oh, okay! Yes.'

Alejandro led me down the perfectly landscaped pathway which looked even more impressive in the daylight, with the lush, green grass, tropical plants and bright flowers.

When we arrived at the beach, I gasped. The views from my balcony were striking, but nothing compared to seeing it up close.

The sand was pure white and oh my goodness, the sea!

At our hotel in Spain, the sea was beautiful, but here, the crystal-clear, turquoise waters were unreal. It was so clean and transparent, you could see everything. It was like staring into glass.

And Nadine was right: the floating villas I spotted in the distance looked incredible. One day I'd love to have the chance to stay in a place that was built on the sea.

This was paradise.

And it wasn't just the scenery that made me gasp.

On the beach was a single table with two chairs, a crisp, white tablecloth and some cutlery laid out neatly.

'This is for us?' I asked.

'*Sí.*' He placed the tray on the table, then transferred everything on top before putting the tray on the sand and pulling out a chair for me.

'Oh!' I was a little taken aback by the gesture. It seemed so... romantic. 'Thanks.'

'*De nada.*' He sat down, then lifted off the cloche to reveal slices of fresh mango, banana, guava and pineapple, all neatly arranged on a branded Love Hotel white china plate.

'This looks delicious!' I stabbed my fork in a juicy piece of mango.

'I wanted to make something like pancakes or even churros, but I could not find all of the ingredients I needed.'

'I *love* churros.'

'Me too. But of course, I want to learn how to make the Jamaican breakfast. I was reading about the fritters and the ackee fruit?'

'Yes! Saltfish fritters are my favourite! They're like mini savoury pancakes with salted cod, peppers and onion. I think ackee is the national fruit of Jamaica. I remember my grandma used to make it with saltfish too.'

'I am looking forward to trying it.'

I was so hungry I literally inhaled my breakfast at lightning speed. Just as I was about to ask Alejandro whether he wanted the last few slices of fresh pineapple, I spotted Nadine walking towards us.

'Good morning!' She smiled. 'How did you guys sleep?'

'*Bien*,' Alejandro said.

'Like a baby!' I replied. The mattress was like sleeping on a cloud and the shower was heavenly.

'When you've finished your breakfast, give me a call and I'll show you your office.'

'Perfect!' I said. 'I was going to ask where it was because I have a Zoom call at nine.'

'That's right.' Nadine nodded. 'I think Hortense has some things to update you on...' Her eyes dropped to the ground. That didn't sound good.

I looked at my watch and realised it was already after eight.

'I'd better come with you now so I have time to get everything set up. I don't want to be late.' I glanced down at the table. 'Do you want me to help carry stuff back to the kitchen?' I asked Alejandro.

'It is fine. My meeting is at ten, so I have time. You go. I will take care of this.'

'Okay.' I got up from the table. 'And thanks again for breakfast.'

Alejandro smiled and my stomach flipped. It was like his mouth had a Bluetooth connection to my stomach and every time he smiled or spoke, it made it flutter.

'It's this way.' Nadine gestured, leading me down the pathway.

'Girl!' She turned to face me, her eyes wide. 'That Alejandro is *criss*. Or *handsome* as you English say!' She laughed.

'He's an attractive man, yes,' I said as casually as I could, despite being a bit taken aback by her comment. Talking about Alejandro's appearance wasn't very professional.

'You'd have to be blind not to notice that he is *fine*!' She grinned. 'Don't tell me you wouldn't want to get some *good, good lovin'* from him!' She raised an eyebrow.

'We work together, so that would be completely inappropriate,' I said firmly. Maybe because it was just the two of us she felt she could speak more freely, but it still felt wrong. It was already bad that we were discussing the fact that he was hot.

'That's not what I asked...' She gave a knowing smile. 'Don't worry, your secret's safe with me.'

'What secret? I don't have any secrets!' I protested.

'Here's the office.' Nadine ignored my comment and opened the door to a room with one desk, two computers and two chairs. 'I'll get you both keys so you can come and go as you need.'

'*Both?*'

'You and Alejandro will share this office. The others are being renovated. I've put the log in and Wi-Fi details there.' She pointed to a piece of paper on the desk. 'Have a great meeting!' She slipped out the door before I had a chance to reply.

I couldn't share this office with Alejandro. There was no time to go after her, though. I needed to shake off my jet lag and get my brain in gear for the meeting. I was looking forward to receiving more information about what my specific tasks and objectives would be for this trip.

Shortly before nine, I logged onto Zoom and started the call.

'Afternoon, Jasmine!' Hazel beamed.

'Hi,' I said, deciding it was best not to mention that it was morning over here. Spain was seven hours ahead of Jamaica, so it must be four in the afternoon over there.

A woman with dark-brown skin and black-rimmed glasses appeared on the screen. She was wearing a headscarf and it looked like she was at home because I saw an unmade bed in the background.

'This is Hortense. She will be heading up the team of Love Alchemists there.'

'Nice to meet you.' I smiled. Hortense just nodded in acknowledgement. I thought I'd be meeting her at the hotel today, but maybe she was on a later shift.

'How was your flight?' Hazel asked. 'And what do you think of the hotel?'

'The flight was good and the hotel is stunning!'

'Excellent! So, I wanted to share a little more about our expectations whilst you're there. As you know, we're keen to emulate the success of the Love Hotel in Spain, but in a more tropical setting. The matchmakers will of course do their essential work behind the scenes, but what we need to ensure is that when the guests arrive, they will have ample opportunities to bond and fall in love. Jamaica is known as one of the most romantic destinations in the world, so we need to capitalise on this.'

'I understand.'

'So we need you to work closely with Hortense to put together a programme of romantic activities for the couples to enjoy during the first week of their stay, plus have a list of options they can consider for the second week.'

'No, problem. I assume I'll have a Jamaican who knows the country inside out to help me, like Hortense or one of the Love Alchemist's she's hired?' I turned my gaze to Hortense, waiting for confirmation.

'Um... about that.' Hazel paused. 'That was the plan, but

unfortunately, the key team members, including Hortense, have tested positive for Covid. Thankfully, their symptoms aren't serious, but we've agreed it's best they stay at home until they're fully recovered.'

'Oh no! Sorry to hear that. I hope they'll feel better soon.'

'I'm sure they'll be fine. Nadine tested negative, so she will be around to help along with a couple of other staff, but I'm afraid you'll need to manage on your own for the first week.'

I tried not to show my shock.

'I understand, but my knowledge of the country isn't strong enough to know which activities would be best to add to the guest itinerary.'

'That's not a problem. Hortense has provided us with a list of suggestions to get you started. And I'm sure Nadine has some ideas too.'

'Right, okay.' I nodded, feeling a little better.

'We need to make sure that each location or activity delivers a first-class experience that our guests will love, but most importantly, you'll need to consider how well it rates on the *romance* scale. Is it something that will bring our couples closer? Will there be opportunities for them to bond and connect with each other? *That's* what we're looking for. Activities with that *spark*.'

'Got it.' I scribbled notes down on my pad.

Actually, now that I thought about it, it shouldn't be too challenging. Many of the activities on the Spanish Love Hotel couples' activity list were places I'd researched then tried out, so I'd just be doing the same kind of thing but over here. And if Hortense provided a list of suggestions, at least that would reduce a lot of the initial groundwork.

Spending my days exploring lots of cool locations sounded like a dream. I was basically getting paid to be a tourist in a tropical paradise.

Yes, the days would be long and I'd still have to work hard, but right now, I felt like I had the best job in the world.

'We thought today you two could visit Dunn's River Falls first because it's so close,' Hortense said.

'That's the famous waterfall, right?' Hazel asked.

'Yes.' Hortense coughed, then nodded. Poor woman probably wanted to be tucked up in bed rather than on this call.

I was familiar with Dunn's River Falls but had never been so that should be fun.

Hold on.

My mind drifted back to what Hortense had just said.

I could've sworn she'd said *you two*.

'Is Nadine coming with me?' My face crumpled. 'It's just that you said *you two*.'

'I did.' Hortense clarified. 'My understanding is that there are two of you from the hotel, right? You and...' Her gaze dropped and she started shuffling through some papers. 'Yes, you and your co-worker, Alejandro Garcia.'

My stomach dropped.

'I think there's been some confusion. Alejandro is a Cuisine Prince, not a Love Alchemist like me.'

'Hortense is aware of that,' Hazel interjected. 'But given the circumstances, we thought it would be a good idea for him to accompany you on the trips.'

'What?' I said loudly, before realising I should've toned down my shock.

'Do you have a problem with Alejandro?' Hazel frowned.

'No, no, he's... fine,' I said thinking that was one of the words Nadine had used to describe him. I hoped they realised that I meant *fine* as in *okay*, not *fine* as in *hot*. 'It's just that, he's here to work with the Jamaican Cuisine King, so I wouldn't want to take him away from his restaurant responsibilities to go gallivanting with me. Not that I'd be gallivanting. I'd obviously be working and researching *very, very* hard.'

Oh God. What was it about just hearing his name that made me so flustered?

'Dudley, the Jamaican Cuisine King will also be isolating for at least a week. And we feel it'd be beneficial for Alejandro to go on these excursions with you. Although he'll still be expected to work closely with Dudley to create a menu and firm up the restaurant's protocol and Cuisine Champions' training programme, he also needs to experience the culture and life outside the hotel to get inspiration. The days and nights will be long. There will be plenty of time for him to fulfil both his restaurant duties and help you with yours.'

'That's very generous of you, but I'll be fine on my own,' I said, desperate to get her to change her mind. 'Just like I was in Spain when I added several excursions to the couples' activity list.'

'We want to find events that appeal to both men and women. Alejandro can give us a male perspective, which will be useful.'

I swallowed hard.

I understood why they might want to get a male point of view. *That* wasn't the issue. The issue was the particular male they'd chosen.

First management sent me to Jamaica. With Alejandro.

Then they put me in a suite next to him.

When I discovered that we'd be sharing an office, I thought that was bad. But that was the least of my problems.

Now we'd have to go on romantic excursions. Like an actual couple.

How the hell was I supposed to go on trips designed to foster romance, with a co-worker who was also the hottest man I'd ever laid eyes on, without doing or saying anything inappropriate or worse, developing feelings for him?

This was like putting a barrel of apples in front of Eve and telling her not to take a single bite.

How was I *not* going to be tempted?

This wasn't good.

At all.

9

ALEJANDRO

I closed the office door and exhaled.

That meeting did not go how I had expected.

When Hazel had first explained that they wanted me to come to Jamaica to help the head chef set up the restaurants' operations and training, I was excited.

Marco was always dismissive when I suggested trying something new. It was only on the special assignments and meals that Jasmine had given me that I ever had the chance to put my own twist on different dishes.

With this trip, I thought I would finally have the opportunity to take on more responsibility, help shape a menu from the beginning, share my ideas and make my mark.

Based on the meeting I had just had with Hazel, thankfully I would still have the chance to do those things. But what I had not realised was that they also expected me to work closely with Jasmine.

If that was limited to working within the hotel, it may not have been so difficult. However, they wanted us to go on different excursions. Together. And not just any activities: visits that were designed to stimulate romance.

If I did not like Jasmine, this would have been fine.

But I liked Jasmine. More than I should.

She was beautiful, intelligent, strong, determined, ambitious and kind.

For a long time, I believed that in life, you were only ever lucky enough to find one person that you were drawn to so strongly. But now I was starting to realise that sometimes lightning did strike twice.

After I lost my girlfriend two years ago, I believed I would never be interested in another woman. That was it for me.

When I finally started to get through the fog of grief last year, Lola tried to encourage me to date again.

She introduced me to 'friends' whenever I would visit her in London and when she came here, she tried to set me up on the dating apps.

The women were pretty and nice. But like I said to Jasmine during our journey here, *nice* was bland. It was like food without seasoning. Even the nicest steak needed a little salt to accentuate the flavour. There was never that spark.

But I had noticed that whenever I was with Jasmine, there were more sparks than a fireworks display.

When she squeezed my arm in the car and I woke up and saw her face, I thought that I was dreaming.

I was not short of confidence. I believed in myself. I was excellent at my job. I was a kind person. I had a lot going for me. But the truth was, Jasmine was in a different league.

She was a woman who travelled first class, came from a background of dealing with the rich and famous, she was experienced and probably used to dating successful businessmen, not a man on the rise who had not reached his goals. *Yet*.

And after the meeting where Jasmine had warned everyone

not to get involved, the fact that we worked together would obviously be an issue for her too.

I was not concerned about the age gap. Jasmine would be smart enough to know that did not matter.

Anyway, everything I had just thought about was irrelevant because she was not interested in me romantically, which was fine. It was just me who found her attractive. Clearly, I was not her type.

The point was, I could manage my attraction to Jasmine if our contact and interactions were limited. But I was worried that spending more time with her would prove more difficult.

It had taken a lot of willpower, but I had managed to stay cool at breakfast. *Just.*

When I could not sleep, I decided to get up and explore the hotel. I was hungry and knew that Jasmine would be too, so that was when I decided to make her breakfast. And when I saw how beautiful the beach was, I knew she would love it too.

That was why I decided to set up the table outside.

I will admit, I may have dreamt about sitting across a table from her, just the two of us, once or twice. But being attracted to Jasmine was like salivating at the most exquisite pastries through a French patisserie window after committing to eating healthily. Jasmine was someone that I could admire from afar, but never touch.

I returned to my room to get my swimming trunks. I had to meet Jasmine in reception in twenty minutes where we would be driven to Dunn's River Falls.

That at least was something I was happy to try. I had heard many things about this place when I researched Jamaica online.

When I arrived at reception, Jasmine was already there speaking to Nadine.

'Hi,' Nadine smiled. 'Ready for Dunn's River Falls?'

'*Sí*. I am very excited to visit.'

'Is the car on the way?' Jasmine asked.

'So here's the thing...' Nadine paused. 'The chauffeur, Linford, is also out of action this week and the driver who picked you up from the airport last night is on holiday from today. But don't worry! I asked a friend to take you instead.'

The loud toot of a car horn vibrated around us and I turned to see an old, brown Mercedes pull up.

The driver wound his window down and the sound of a Bob Marley track blared from his car speakers.

'This is Bob,' Nadine said. 'He'll be your driver today.'

Bob jumped out of the car with a big smile on his face. He had light-brown skin, a salt-and-pepper beard and his big red, gold and green oversized hat covered a head full of long dreadlocks.

'*Wah gwaan?*' Bob said in a thick Jamaican accent.

'Hello.' Jasmine held out her hand to greet him. 'I'm Jasmine.'

'*Nice fi meet yuh, pretty gyal.*' He looked Jasmine up and down then smiled approvingly. I ground my jaw.

'*Hola*,' I said flatly, keeping my hands firmly to my sides. 'I am Alejandro. I am here *with Jasmine*.'

A look of mild surprise flickered in his eyes and I knew he was trying to work out whether I was with her romantically or platonically.

Good.

Seconds later, I regretted what I had said. I would like to say that I did not know why I had said I was here with her, but that would be a lie.

The truth was that I did not like watching another man admire the woman I liked. But that was my problem.

It was true that Jasmine and I were here together for work, but we were not *together* in the way that my tone had suggested.

'Mi name Bob Harley,' he said, ignoring my statement.

'Bob *Harley?*' Jasmine frowned.

'Ya mon!' Bob replied in agreement.

'Like Bob *Marley*, but *Harley* instead?' Her frowned deepened.

'Ya mon! Come.' He gestured towards the car.

I opened the door for Jasmine, then slid onto the backseat.

Her scent hit me like lightning. She smelt like summer berries and coconut and I was torn between wanting to open the window to escape the intoxicating aroma and inhaling deeply so it could flood all of my senses.

'A weh yuh come fram?' Bob said, breaking my train of thought.

'London,' Jasmine said.

'Madrid,' I answered.

'But we both live near Marbella in Spain,' Jasmine added.

'Irie.' Bob said, then turned up the 'Could You Be Loved' Bob Marley track.

It was not a surprise that like me and so many people around the world, he was a fan of the Jamaican legend's music. Although I got the feeling that his real name was not Bob *Harley* and he probably played Bob *Marley's* songs because he wanted to make the tourists happy.

'So, I am now your activities partner.' I turned to face Jasmine. She was not in the office when I had my meeting and because we had not spoken since then, I wanted to see how she felt about it.

I was sure she could not be happy about it. Even if her reasons were different to mine.

'Looks that way. I'm really sorry.' She winced. 'I'm sure you'd much rather be out shopping for ingredients and working in the kitchen.'

'I was so angry when they told me I would have to spend time visiting one of Jamaica's most famous attractions with a beautiful woman. My life sucks so bad right now!' I smirked. I had not intended to mention that I thought she was beautiful, but *madre mía*, she really was.

Jasmine was wearing a long, orange dress and even though it was only her shoulders and arms that were exposed, she still looked like the sexiest woman I'd ever seen.

I did not know if it was because of her confidence but everything about Jasmine was hot.

'Oh!' She laughed. 'When you said you were angry, I felt awful, but you're joking, right?'

'I am not joking.' I narrowed my eyes for a few seconds before my face broke into a smile. 'Of course! I am being paid to visit a place that I would pay to visit myself. But I was not joking when I said I am going there with a beautiful woman. And I do not say that to be a creep or to make you uncomfortable, because I know that after the meeting this week, employees are supposed to not notice these things. It is just a fact.'

'A fact, eh?' She raised her eyebrow.

'*Sí.* Nobody could disagree with this.'

'In your opinion.' She smiled.

'In my opinion, which of course is correct.'

'*Ya mon.*' Bob slapped his steering wheel in agreement. I did not like that he was listening to our conversation, but at least he supported my conclusion.

'Well, thank you for the subjective observation.'

'You do not think you are beautiful?' I frowned.

'I'm not sure that anyone looks in the mirror and says they are *beautiful*.'

'They do not?' I clutched my chest pretending to be shocked by this revelation. 'My sister told me it was normal.' I smirked again.

'Oh my God!' She laughed. 'Do you seriously look in the mirror and tell yourself you're beautiful?'

'No, but not because I believe it is wrong to do that. I do not do it because I already feel it *here*,' I pointed to my head, 'and *here*,' I patted my heart.

'Wow.' Jasmine's eyes widened. 'Let me move closer to the window to give you and your ego more room.'

'So to believe in yourself is to have an ego?' I rested my hand on my chin.

'No, but...'

'Is it a lie? You think that I am ugly?'

'Of course not! I mean, clearly y-you're...' she stuttered. 'You're a... a very attractive man.' Her voice trailed off and her gaze dropped to her sandals.

This was interesting.

Jasmine was always so calm and eloquent. To see her flustered was new. And I could not deny that I liked the fact that she had just said she thought I was attractive. In fact, not just attractive, but *very* attractive. Especially when I was certain that she had no interest in me.

'*Gracias*. But you must understand, when I say these things, it is not because I want to... what is it you say? Blow my horn?'

'*Trumpet*,' she corrected. 'We say, *blow my own trumpet*. Then again, you might be right. I think Americans say blow or toot your own horn.'

'*Vale*. I do not say it to *blow my trumpet*. I say it because if I do not believe I am beautiful, how can I expect someone else to believe it?'

'Hmmm.' Jasmine nodded. 'That's actually true. You're very confident for your age.'

'You say that as if I am a teenager.' I smiled.

'Compared to me, you are!'

'*En serio?*' I said.

'You're asking if I'm being serious?' Her brows knitted together.

'*Sí.*'

'Of course I'm being serious! You're what? Twenty-nine, right?'

Also interesting that she knew my age when I had never told her.

'Correct.' I nodded. 'How old are you?'

'A gentleman never asks a woman her age.'

'And who told you I was a gentleman?' I smirked.

'Oh... I...'

'I can be of course, but perhaps I am not as innocent as you presume. Age is irrelevant. In this world, there are wise people who are twenty-nine and people who are twenty-nine and stupid. And if you think I will judge you or change my opinion of you because you tell me you are thirty-one or forty-one, then you have much to learn about me.'

Jasmine stared at me, her eyes wide, her lips parted. I did not know what she was thinking, but what I said was true.

Although I did not know her exact age, I knew that she was in her late thirties because she had mentioned a few times that there was not long before she would be forty and grimaced like it was a curse, not a blessing.

My ex would have given anything to have reached that age.

The point was, I knew Jasmine was older than me, but I did not care.

I still liked her.

And the strange thing was, whereas before I was convinced that she had zero interest in me, now I was starting to question whether that was true...

10

JASMINE

As soon as Bob pulled into the car park at Dunn's River Falls, I flung the door open and bolted outside.

I needed air. It was hot and sticky, but I didn't care, because I'd added a few extra feet of distance between me and Alejandro.

My body was already on high alert when I saw him walking towards me at reception. My temperature had risen a few more degrees when he opened the door then slid onto the seat beside me. His woody scent hit me like the smell of fresh bread wafting from a bakery.

And when he called me *beautiful* in his ridiculously adorable Spanish accent, goosebumps exploded on my skin. Especially when he declared it as a fact.

That was nice to hear. When the husband I thought I'd be with forever not only cheated on me, but also traded me in for a younger woman, it'd dented my confidence.

And although I didn't tell Alejandro my age, I got the impression that even if I did, he wouldn't care. Deep down, he had to, though. Everyone said *age is just a number* but they never really meant it.

The truth was, age *did* matter. Especially for women. Unlike men, we couldn't just wake up one day in our fifties, sixties or beyond and just decide to have children. At almost forty, of course it could still happen, but as the media frequently reminded me, the clock was ticking.

Not that I necessarily wanted children. Once upon a time, I did, but Kane always said he didn't want them. Funny because less than a year after cheating on me, he got his secretary knocked up (such a cliché) and last I heard, they had another child on the way.

Anyway, after wasting so many of my years slaving away to build a business that I thought would secure my future and then having the rug pulled from beneath me, now I just wanted to focus on myself.

But if in a couple of years I decided that I was ready to date, whoever I met definitely couldn't be younger than me. The guy would want children and by that time, it'd be more challenging.

That was why age was important and why no matter how good Alejandro looked or how hot I found his unapologetic confidence, I absolutely had to get over this attraction.

'*Yuh good?*' Bob stepped out of the car.

'Yes, thank you. We need to buy water shoes, right?' I asked.

'*Ya mon!*' Bob declared.

'Okay.'

'We should get the tickets,' Alejandro said.

'*Likkle more,*' Bob added, which I remembered meant *see you later*, then he gave us his number and said for us to call when we were ready.

I wasn't convinced that his name was really Bob Harley and he wasn't the kind of chauffeur the Love Hotel would typically hire, but he seemed fun. And as stereotypical as it was for him to play Bob Marley songs throughout the entire car journey, I had to admit, I liked it.

Alejandro and I made our way to the ticket office. There wasn't too much of a queue. Nadine had said that when there were cruise ship stop offs, it could get particularly busy, especially in high season, but seeing as it was October, it was much quieter.

Once we'd bought the special water shoes that were recommended for climbing the waterfall, we went to the toilets to change into our swimwear.

As I stepped into my swimming costume, I felt self-conscious. It'd been ages since I'd worn one so publicly.

Although we had a pool at the hotel in Spain, it was for guests. Occasionally, I went for a dip in the sea that was part of our resort, but only when there was no one else around. I preferred to go to more remote places. Away from anyone I knew.

I wasn't in my twenties any more. My body wasn't as toned as it used to be and like most women, I had stretch marks and flabby bits.

That was why when I'd flirted with the idea of wearing a bikini, I'd immediately dismissed it. It wouldn't be appropriate for a work setting.

I smoothed down the front of my plain, black swimming costume, wishing that I could've at least taken a kaftan with me to cover up a little so I wouldn't be exposing this much skin.

A kaftan wouldn't have been practical, though. I just had to go as I was.

I looked in the mirror and attempted to tell myself that I looked beautiful, but felt like an idiot. I was confident at work, yes, because I knew I was good at it. But I'd never considered myself to be *beautiful*.

Clearly, when it came to my appearance, I didn't have the same level of confidence that Alejandro had.

It was easier for him though because I was sure there wasn't a person on the planet who wouldn't agree that he was incredibly good-looking. At first, when he'd asked me whether I thought he wasn't beautiful, I'd hesitated to reply. But then I realised that to deny how handsome he was would've been more suspicious.

Saying that he was a very attractive man was an understatement. The man was hotter than a bucket of spicy jerk chicken sauce.

And *that* was a fact.

Anyway, I didn't have time to think about how gorgeous he was. I had work to do.

After picking up my bag, I headed outside.

Bloody hell.

My jaw fell open.

I knew I should at least attempt to drag it up off the floor, but it was difficult, because stood just a few metres away was Alejandro.

Sorry. Let me rephrase. It wasn't *just Alejandro*.

It was a *topless* Alejandro.

God. Help. Me.

I was aware that I'd just said I shouldn't be thinking about how hot he was, but come on.

When he looked like *that*, how could I not?

I'd only ever seen him in a chef's jacket or T-shirt. Sometimes a vest. But never, I repeat *never*, with his bare chest on show.

And *wow*.

His body was so defined, it looked like it'd been carved by angels.

His golden olive skin glowed.

Then there were his broad shoulders.

His toned pecs.

His muscular biceps.

Oh, and his six-pack.

I swallowed hard.

None of the men I'd ever dated had a body like that.

My ex was nine years older than me, so when we met, he already had the makings of a dad-bod. And I didn't mind. I loved him for him.

As far as I was concerned, muscular, sculpted bodies were what models and film stars like The Rock, Michael B. Jordan and the Hemsworth brothers had. Not people in 'real life'.

But turned out I was wrong, because Alejandro could give all of those men a run for their money.

'H-hi,' I stuttered. 'You ready to go?'

'I...' Alejandro's gaze travelled from my head to toe and I winced inside. I knew this swimming costume was frumpy. 'Sure. We should put our things away.'

A weird silence hung in the air as we walked to the lockers.

We joined a tour guide and a group of other tourists and I was grateful that we were no longer alone.

The tour guide explained that if we didn't want to walk up the waterfall, we could take the stairs. He also told us that there were many different access points so we could start midway, or climb say halfway up the waterfall then take the pathway for the rest. It was up to us.

'What do you think?' Alejandro asked. It was probably the only thing he'd said to me since we'd both got changed.

'I'd like to walk up the whole waterfall. I'm not the best with heights, but I'm here for research, so I need to try it properly so I know what our guests will experience.'

'*Vale,*' he said.

'You don't mind, do you?'

'No! I love this kind of thing.'

'Great,' I said. 'This is *only* six hundred feet high. If I can do the Caminito del Rey walk in Spain, hopefully I can do this too!'

We headed down to the beach so that we could start right at the bottom.

As I took the first steps in the water, I shivered a little. It was cold but so clear and beautiful and the more we walked, I got used to it and found it was actually refreshing.

I stepped up onto the next level. At the base, it was quite flat and relatively smooth, but when I looked up, I noticed that it became a lot steeper and more uneven higher up.

There were a range of different people in our group. Looked like some were couples, others perhaps friends or family. Everyone was dressed in swimwear and from the sound of the chatter around me, most people were from English-speaking countries, although I think I heard some German being spoken too.

The next level up was too steep to climb easily. The guide explained how best to navigate ourselves and advised where to step to avoid slipping.

'I will go first,' Alejandro offered. 'Then I can help you up.'

That was sweet, but I couldn't agree. Being beside Alejandro was challenging enough. The sensation of holding his hand would probably cause me to fall off the waterfall.

'I'm okay, thanks. I'll be fine.'

I struggled up the slippery rocks and when we got to the next steep level, I saw several people in front of us, holding out their hands to help others climb up.

Alejandro went ahead and once he'd reached the level, he offered his hand.

'I'm good,' I insisted, even though I wasn't. I needed help and for a second, I even contemplated taking the hand of a stranger. Anything to avoid making contact with his big, manly palm.

'Jasmine.' Alejandro's deep voice boomed and my body immediately straightened. 'I know that you are a strong, independent woman and you can climb this rock or the highest mountains by yourself, but just because you can, it does not mean you must. Why struggle and risk slipping when you can take my hand and make it easier? There is no shame in asking for help.'

As I looked around, everyone was getting help. If I kept insisting I could climb each level by myself, but then slipped, I'd look like a fool.

Was I going to risk ending up at the bottom of the waterfall with broken bones just because I couldn't control a stupid crush or be sensible and take his hand?

'Okay.' I stretched out my hand like it was no big deal.

But as my palm connected with Alejandro's, I realised that my initial concerns were right. This was a *very* big deal.

Alejandro's palm was warm and welcoming. The sensation was like sliding a mug of hot chocolate into your hands on a cold winter's night. It was so comforting.

He helped me up effortlessly like I was as light as a feather.

'*Todo bien?*' he asked, checking that I was okay.

'Yes, I'm good. Thank you.'

My cheeks heated and in that moment, I was grateful that my feet were immersed in cool water. Hopefully, it'd help regulate my body temperature as right now, my blood was bubbling with heat.

I looked down and realised that Alejandro was still holding on to my hand. I knew I should let go, but I didn't want to.

'W-we should go,' I quickly moved my hand away. Alejandro's

face fell and my stomach twisted, but although I could've done it more gently, I'd done the right thing.

I was grateful that he'd helped me, but we couldn't go wandering around hand in hand like some loved-up couple. That was for our guests to do in the future. Not for us.

We continued making our way up and I saw more of the group holding hands.

'I read about this,' Alejandro turned to face me. 'The human chain is a tradition. Holding hands makes it easier.'

Just as I was about to protest, a woman stretched out her hand.

'Come on, you guys!' she said in an American accent. 'Join us.'

I reluctantly slid my right hand in hers and then turned to face Alejandro. I looked down at his hand. There was no other option. I'd have to hold it again. *Shit*. I could already feel the eyes of the other tourists burning into me.

'If you don't want to hold his hand, I will!' a British woman quipped.

'Ding dong!' A guy in red shorts who also sounded British, licked his lips in agreement.

I extended my hand and Alejandro took it. I couldn't read the expression on his face, but it looked like he was maybe wounded? Upset?

Once again, the sensation of having my palm wrapped in his sent shivers shooting up my spine.

Ten minutes later, Alejandro was still holding my hand, but hadn't said a word to me.

'Everything okay?' I asked, just as the chain broke apart and the guide explained something about the waterfall to a couple on my right.

We stopped and this time, Alejandro pulled his hand away. I instantly missed the warmth and the cushion of his palm.

'*Sí*,' he replied, avoiding my gaze, but I didn't believe him.

'Did I do something to upset you?' I frowned.

'You really want to know?' he asked.

'Of course.'

'You looked at my hand like it is dirty. Before, I thought you did not want to touch it because you prefer to be independent, but now I think it is because you just do not want to touch it.'

'No!' My stomach twisted. 'It's not that.' I paused. How the hell was I supposed to explain that I didn't want to hold his hand because every time I did, my whole body lit up like a fireworks display?

I absolutely could not let him know that I was attracted to him. It was embarrassing.

'Then why?'

'It's because... I was worried about being... unprofessional. We're colleagues.'

'And?' He shrugged. 'I was offering to help you, not fuck you.'

My breath caught in my throat and my eyeballs bulged.

As I pictured Alejandro laying me down on the cold, wet rocks and burying himself inside me, a tingle raced between my legs.

'I... uh, I know you wanted to help me. And I'm grateful. Sorry. I didn't mean to offend you. It looks like it's getting steeper.' I pointed upwards. 'Would you mind helping me again?'

I held out my hand. I knew that it was going to be difficult holding it again, but I'd rather voluntarily put myself through sexual torture than make Alejandro feel bad.

I knew how it felt to be rejected.

Alejandro reached out and when he put his hand in mine, my stomach somersaulted and my body tingled again.

At this rate, once this walk was over, I'd need to sit under the waterfall for an hour just to cool down.

I knew spending time with Alejandro would be hard, but this was proving more challenging than I thought.

Wish me luck.

Something told me I was going to need it.

11

ALEJANDRO

'That was actually fun!' Jasmine said as we waved goodbye to the rest of the group.

She was right. It was a fantastic experience. I loved the challenge of walking up the waterfall, the freshness of the water and the spectacular views of the nature that surrounded us.

But I had enjoyed holding her hand a little too much. I had not done that for so long that I had forgotten how great it felt.

There were many opportunities where I knew Jasmine did not need to hold on to me and I could have let her go. The truth was, I had not wanted to.

I had thought that perhaps the feeling might have been mutual, but I was wrong. She did not even want to hold my hand.

I shook my head as my mind drifted back to our car journey here when I had thought that Jasmine could like me.

Qué tonto. I chastised myself.

Just because a woman says a man is attractive, it does not mean that she is actually interested in dating him. I needed to remember that.

'*Sí*, it was very good.'

After we got changed, we went to collect the photograph we had posed for during the climb.

We joined the queue and when they handed over the photograph, my eyes widened.

'Cute,' I said.

The photo was more than just *cute*. We looked great together.

Jasmine's eyes sparkled and she looked so happy. Just like I did.

'Aww,' the American lady who was part of our group leant over to look at our photo. 'You two make a gorgeous couple. Don't they, Joe?' She turned to the man beside her.

'Sure do! You two lucked out in the gene pool. She's a doll and even though I'm straight, I have to admit that you're a fine-looking fella. If you want to hang out and have some fun, we'd be down for that, right Mindy?'

'Damn straight.' She licked her lips.

'We're not... We're just co-workers!' Jasmine's eyes widened.

'It'll be our little secret!' The guy, Joe, winked.

'We should go.' I stepped in.

'Oh my God! Won't you listen to that accent!' The woman fanned her face. 'As if he wasn't already hot enough! You're a very lucky woman!'

'Nice to meet you.' I put on a fake smile, then took Jasmine's hand and led her away from the couple. This time, she did not resist.

'Did they just ask us to join them for some sort of orgy?' Jasmine asked when we were out of earshot.

'I think so.' The corner of my mouth turned up.

'Well, that's a first!' She laughed.

'Perhaps for you.' I smirked.

'Really? You've been asked to have a foursome before?'

'A foursome: no. A threesome: once or twice,' I said casually.

'Wow. You're right. You really *aren't* as innocent as I thought. And did you take them up on their offer?' Her eyes widened.

'A gentleman never tells.'

'But according to you, you're *not* a gentleman...' she replied.

'True.' I smiled, impressed she'd remembered what I'd said in the car.

'Don't let me cramp your style. If you want to "have fun" with Mindy and Joe.'

'Thanks, but they are not my type.'

'What is your type?' she replied quickly.

'I like smart, confident women.'

'I'm guessing young and pretty goes without saying too, right?'

'Not always. If a woman is pretty, it is a bonus, but if she looks like a supermodel, but has an ugly heart, that is very unattractive. And as for her age, that is also not important, as long as she is legal. But most of my exes were older than me.'

Jasmine's eyebrows shot up to her hairline.

'What, like by a year or two?'

'No.' I shook my head. 'Usually by several years.'

Her eyes bulged. Just as Jasmine's mouth opened to say something, a loud voice boomed around us.

'Jasmine! Alejandro!' I spun around and saw Bob standing next to his car. '*Come yah suh!*'

Jasmine was still rooted to the spot.

'Are you coming?' I asked.

'Y-yes,' she stuttered.

As soon as Jasmine got inside, she pulled out her phone. From the corner of my eye, it looked like she was scrolling through emails. She let out a deep sigh.

'Something wrong?' I turned to face her.

'No!' Her voice went higher. 'All fine! So, you enjoyed the activity, yes?'

'*Sí*. Very much.'

'Good. Great. So... if you had to rate it, hypothetically speaking of course, because naturally, we went there for research, as colleagues, but if say you went there with a girlfriend... if you were one of our guests, how do you think you'd rate it in terms of... romance?' Her gaze shifted. She was acting strange, like she was nervous to ask me. 'It's to help with my report. I need a man's perspective.'

'The views were amazing and it is always nice to take a date somewhere beautiful, no?'

'Naturally.'

'And as we experienced ourselves, there are many opportunities to hold hands with each other and that is also romantic.'

Jasmine's eyes flicked away again.

'Well, that's the human chain that you mentioned. Part of it is holding hands with strangers. For safety purposes.'

'That is true, but there is something special about holding the hand of somebody you are attracted to, no? When you hold the hand of a stranger, as part of the train, for safety, you feel nothing. But when it is someone that you like, the sensation is different. Feeling their palm in yours generates a different kind of... energy. There is electricity. Fireworks. The connection is not just romantic. It can also spark... desire. *Hypothetically speaking.*' I fixed my gaze on her, interested to see her response.

'I-I wouldn't really know, but if I used my imagination, I could see how that *might* be possible.'

Her eyes drifted upwards and this time, they locked on mine. We sat there for a few moments in silence.

And there it was. That electricity. It pulsed through me. Just like it had when I had held her hand. I did not understand how she could not feel it.

'So, it's a yes, from you for this couples' activity then?' Jasmine finally spoke.

'Definitely,' I said.

'Good.' She unlocked her phone and started typing. 'I'll include your comments in my report. Thanks again for your help.'

'My pleasure,' I said, thinking how enjoyable it had been to spend time with Jasmine, even if she did not feel the same.

12

JASMINE

I switched off the computer and exhaled. I'd just finished writing up my report on Dunn's River Falls, recommending it as one of the activities for our guests.

I'd noted that Alejandro had given it the thumbs up and as much as I hated to admit it, I agreed with what he'd said about the necessity for hand-holding helping to spark romance.

That was why I spent far too much time replaying those moments of his hand wrapped in mine, when I should've been focused on work.

The way that Alejandro described the connection was spot on. I'd felt those same sparks. The electricity. The *desire*. Thankfully, I'd pushed them away.

Obviously, I hadn't mentioned in my report how good it felt having my fingers intertwined with Alejandro's. I'd kept it more neutral and spoken about the human chain instead. But the point was, if climbing the waterfall stirred up those sensations when I was only holding hands with a colleague, imagine how magnetic it'd be for a couple who'd actually been expertly matched.

Anyway, the activity was over now and I had the whole

evening to myself. Maybe I'd read on the beach or go for a swim. Alejandro was sure to be busy catching up with the tasks he'd planned before he'd been forced to come out with me, so at least I wouldn't see him.

I headed back to my room and pulled a fresh swimming costume out of my suitcase. I'd bought three which were identical to the one I'd worn earlier. Once I found something I liked, it was easier to buy multiple items. That way if one was in the wash, I still had one to wear and another as a contingency.

After changing, I headed to the beach with a towel and my Kindle.

This place really was idyllic. I still couldn't get over the sand and the sea. I put my stuff on the sun lounger then ran into the crystal-clear water.

It felt even better than it looked: warm and beautifully refreshing.

After having a swim, I dried myself off then laid on the lounger.

My stomach rumbled. I needed to think about what to do for dinner. Luckily, when we'd come back from the trip, Nadine had got some Jamaican patties for us.

Patties were similar to a Cornish pasty. Except the Jamaican patty could be filled with different varieties of meat or veg and spices baked inside a flaky pastry shell, which was usually a golden-yellow shade, thanks to being brushed with turmeric.

I opted for the jerk chicken one which was deliciously spicy and devoured it so quickly, you'd think I hadn't eaten for days.

Once I'd returned to my room and showered, I headed out to find Nadine to get a recommendation on where was best to go for dinner. But instead of seeing Nadine, I saw Alejandro heading towards me.

'Hi.' I swallowed hard.

'I was just coming to find you,' he said.

'Oh?'

'I need your help.'

'Of course, anything!' I said, then regretted agreeing so quickly without first knowing what he needed. 'What do you need?' I added.

'I have been trying to follow the recipe the chef left for the jerk chicken. I bought the ingredients earlier from a place that Bob took me to, but something is not right.'

'I wish I could help but when it comes to cooking, pasta and sauce from a jar is my area of expertise!' I laughed.

'I do not need you to cook. I need you to come to a restaurant with me. I need to taste authentic jerk chicken. Bob said he can take us to his favourite place, but I will need a second opinion. He is a local but you know the food *and* understand the standards we have at the Love Hotel.'

Shit, shit, shit.

Going to an adventurous activity like Dunn's River Falls together was one thing, but sitting in a restaurant having a candlelit meal, staring into each other's eyes was far too dangerous.

I'd barely recovered from the hand-holding earlier.

'I…' I wanted to say no. I *should* say no. It was the smart thing to do. But how could I when Alejandro had taken hours out of his schedule today to help me?

And he was right. It wasn't just good enough for the food on the menu to be authentic. It had to be top-notch quality too.

'Will you help?' He looked at me with puppy-dog eyes and my stomach flipped. How could I say no to that face?

'I wouldn't really call myself an expert, but I do understand the level of cuisine the hotel would expect. So if you think my opinion will help…'

'It will.'

'Okay. I'll come with you,' I said, then my cheeks heated as I realised that could have another meaning. 'To the restaurant,' I clarified. 'To do the market research.'

'*Gracias!*' Alejandro beamed and seeing his smile made my stomach flutter again. 'I will call Bob and ask him to meet us in half an hour.'

'Great!' I said, trying to sound enthusiastic.

I had thirty minutes to work out how to keep my hormones under control whilst sat at a table for two with a man I was growing increasingly attracted to.

I asked the universe to send me strength and willpower.

Here's hoping it delivered.

13

JASMINE

Alejandro held the door open for me as we stepped into the restaurant.

Throughout the whole car journey, Bob had raved about all of the amazing dishes we had to try. Not just the jerk chicken, but also the rice and peas, the curried goat, the saltfish fritters... He'd gushed so much, I wondered whether he earned commission.

Still, I was glad of the distraction. The more he spoke, the less I had to interact with Alejandro. And considering we still had a whole night ahead of us, the more I could minimise having to look or speak to him, the better.

'Good evening,' our waitress greeted us, clutching two menus.

'Table for two, please,' I said.

'Come.' She summoned us over and pointed to the table. '*Wah yu waan fi drink?*'

'Bob said the rum punch and Guinness punch are good. Perhaps we should try them?' Alejandro suggested.

'Okay.' I nodded. I'd always loved the rum punch my grandad used to make.

She disappeared, giving us time to look over the menu.

'Everything sounds so good!' Alejandro licked his lips and my body reacted.

Bloody hell. We'd barely been here five minutes and I was already turning to jelly. I needed to get a grip.

'It does,' I agreed.

'I made a list of everything Bob recommended. I think that we should try it all.' He handed me his phone which was open on the notes page.

'That's a lot! You know there's only two of us, right? Not a whole army!'

'True. I am just so excited to try everything! Perhaps we can try some today and then the rest next time.'

'*Next time?*' I frowned.

'*Sí*. The chef will be away for at least a week, so I will still need to research. I can eat alone of course, but going with you to Dunn's River Falls today showed me that it is better if we work as a team. We know what will work well for the hotel. And I value your opinion.'

My heart swelled. It was nice that he appreciated me.

'Thanks. I value yours too. You coming along today was helpful. It made writing my report easier.'

'I am happy to hear that.'

'*Yuh ready?*' The waitress appeared at our table, placing our drinks down and then taking out her notepad and pen. Once we'd placed our order, she left.

'The rum punch looks very colourful.' Alejandro moved the two glasses to the centre of the table.

'It is. My grandad used to always make it for family parties. I think it's a mixture of pineapple, orange and lime juice, grenadine or strawberry syrup and of course, lots of rum!'

'*Sí*. I can smell the rum from here!'

'Funnily enough, it never seemed to affect me that much. I

could drink multiple glasses of rum punch and feel fine, but if I did the same with wine, I'd be drunk. Grandad used to joke that if he cut his veins, there'd be pure white rum inside instead of blood, so maybe it's hereditary!' I laughed and Alejandro flashed his gorgeous smile.

'You want to try first?' he offered.

'No, it's your first time, so go ahead,' I said, remembering not to make an inappropriate virgin joke like I had on the plane.

'*Vale*,' he picked up the glass, took a sip and then choked. '*Madre mía!*' His eyes watered. 'It is even stronger than I thought, but I like it. You want to try?'

'Of course!' I wrapped my lips around the straw and a tingle raced through me knowing that Alejandro's mouth had sucked on it a few seconds earlier.

God. If I got a thrill just from sharing a man's straw, I really needed to get out more.

After taking a long sip of the punch, I swallowed. My eyes bulged and I started coughing.

'Bloody hell! Grandad's punch was never that potent! That's strong enough to strip paint, but it's also delicious.'

'Do you know how they make the Guinness punch?' He picked up that glass.

'Yes.' I nodded. 'It's another thing my grandad used to make. It's obviously Guinness, but it's mixed with milk, condensed milk and different spices like cinnamon, nutmeg and I think vanilla too.'

'I will try.' He took a sip. 'This is also good. So when did your grandad move back to Jamaica?'

'About ten years ago.'

'And you keep in touch?'

'Not as much as I'd like. Grandma was the glue that kind of held the family together. When she passed, we lost a lot of contact. Grandad is a bit old school. He doesn't do emails or computers or mobile phones. My mum doesn't keep in touch with him any more, but I send him a Christmas card every year and usually call him on Christmas morning because I know I can get him on the house phone, but that's about it.'

'Are you going to visit him whilst you are here?'

'I'm not sure. He lives in the middle of nowhere. It'd probably take ages to get there and like I said, he only has a house phone, which he rarely answers, so I could go all that way and he wouldn't be there.'

'But what if he *is* there?'

'If I was here on holiday, maybe I'd try, but there's so much to do here to get things set up, so I wouldn't have time. And like I said, it's in a really remote part of the countryside. I'm not sure I'd be comfortable going alone.'

I had to focus on work. I didn't want Hazel to think I was taking advantage and using this trip to visit family.

'Jasmine, it is not my place to tell you what to do, but it is never a good idea to say you will do something tomorrow, because tomorrow is not promised. You are here, in Jamaica *now*. I am sure there will be time to see him. If you do not, you may regret it. How old is your grandad?'

'Eighty-nine.'

'He is not a young man. I think you should go to see him. You have his address?'

'Yes.' It was stored in my phone so it'd be easy to find whenever I sent his Christmas card.

'That is good. We can ask Bob later if he knows how to find it. And I will come with you.'

My eyes popped.

'I... that won't be necessary. I don't want to put you out.'

'I will come with you. Unless you do not feel comfortable with me?'

'No. You don't make me uncomfortable.'

That wasn't entirely true. Whenever I was around him, my mind and body were a kaleidoscope of emotions: excitement, happiness and desire. I liked being around him a lot more than I should. And that was the problem.

But I knew what Alejandro was asking. He was checking that I didn't find him creepy and that definitely wasn't the case.

'Good. Then we will go together to see your grandad. It is settled.'

'How about your family?' I asked, avoiding commenting on what he'd just said. As much as I wanted to see my grandad, I really wasn't sure that it was feasible. 'Are you close to your parents or grandparents?'

'I do not have any. By the time I was nineteen, I had lost both of my parents. My two remaining grandparents died a few years later.'

'Oh my God!' My eyes widened. 'I'm so sorry. That's awful.'

Sadness washed over me and I almost reached out to touch his hand or shoulder to comfort him somehow, but decided it wasn't appropriate, so stopped myself.

'It was difficult.' His gaze dropped to the table, then he started playing with a serviette. 'I was only fifteen when Mum had a stroke. And then Dad had an accident. He worked in construction and one day, well... he fell and...' Alejandro swallowed a lump in his throat.

'It's okay if you'd rather not talk about it. If it's too painful...'

'Many of the recipes I use today were inspired by my parents. They were both fantastic cooks and I always loved helping them and learning everything they were willing to share. After Mum passed, I spent a lot of time with Dad in the kitchen. We became much closer. He always wanted to be a chef, but he never got the chance. That is one of the reasons I decided to try. Because I loved cooking, of course. But also to honour his memory.'

'That's really beautiful. And I'm sure he'd be super impressed.'

'He would. Mum too. My sisters are also very supportive.'

'I didn't realise you had more than one! How old are they?'

'My youngest sister Evita is twenty and my elder sister Lola is thirty-six.'

Wow. I was even older than his eldest sister.

Alejandro took a sip of his drink, then continued. 'Lola became like a mother to us. She is very protective. Sometimes *too* protective.' He smiled.

'I'm sure it's just because she cares. Are they in Madrid?'

'No. They are both in London. Evita is studying and Lola has lived there for many years.'

'Oh yeah!' I nodded. 'I remember you saying she was married to an English guy.'

The waitress brought over the saltfish fritters, fried dumplings which were pieces of fried dough, as well as some ackee and saltfish.

'This is ackee?' Alejandro pointed to the bright-yellow pieces that kind of looked like bright fried egg yolk.

'Yes.' I squeezed my eyes shut. 'It's been so long since I've had any Jamaican food.'

'Por qué?'

'Well, it's not easy to get in Spain. And as we've established, my cooking abilities are limited!'

'Everyone has the ability to cook. Especially someone like you.'

'Someone like me?' I frowned.

'*Sí.* Someone who is intelligent, resourceful and determined.'

My heart fluttered. Alejandro was always very complimentary.

'You're such a charmer.' I took another glug of rum punch. 'I bet you use those silver tongue lines to get *all* the ladies.'

'You think that I am a Casanova?' Alejandro's brows knitted together.

'Maybe not a Casanova, but I'm sure you're not short of female attention. And you're a young and attractive man. There's absolutely nothing wrong with enjoying your life. I wish I hadn't wasted my twenties.'

'Why did you waste them?'

I blew out an exasperated breath, then picked up the punch glass which was now almost empty. I should really wait until the rest of the food came before I had more to drink, but it was so addictive.

'Where do I start?' My shoulders slumped. 'Short version is, I met a guy, fell for his charms, ended up working for him, then marrying him and sacrificing my whole life to get the company off the ground. So instead of going out and enjoying myself, I was always stuck at my desk.'

'And he did not want to go out and have fun with you?'

'Oh, he went out. He travelled for work a lot and played golf. He was older so we were at different stages in our lives. I should've dated someone my own age. Won't make that mistake again.'

I drained the punch dry just as the waitress brought over our mains.

'*Gracias*,' Alejandro said as she put the plates down. 'It sounds like you and your ex-husband were just not a good match,' Alejandro said. 'His age may not have been relevant.'

'I disagree.' I shook my head. 'Anyway, so I wasted most of my twenties and thirties on him. But now I'm making up for lost time.'

'By having more fun?' Alejandro spooned some of the rice and peas and jerk chicken onto my plate before serving himself.

'By focusing on myself and building my own career,' I said, as if it was obvious. 'When we broke up, after I'd discovered he was screwing his secretary, I lost my home and my job. When an old friend put me forward for the job at the Love Hotel, I wasn't sure. I was in the middle of a divorce, so I didn't think I'd be a good advert. But when the founder, Celine interviewed me, she said that she thought my divorce could help me relate to guests who'd gone through the same thing and were hoping for a second chance at finding their soulmate.'

'That is true.' Alejandro nodded.

'And most importantly, despite my ex-husband cheating on me, I still believed in love. Well, at least for other people. And the role combined so many elements that I enjoyed, like travel, organising trips and activities, plus I knew it'd give me the chance for a fresh start in a new country. Luckily, Celine believed in me and I got the job.'

'I am sorry you had a bad experience. Your ex is clearly an idiot who did not deserve you,' he said sympathetically and my stomach fluttered yet again at another compliment. 'But at least you turned a negative chapter of your life into something more positive.'

'Definitely. I love my life in Spain.' I slid a forkful of rice into my mouth. 'And how about you? You must be living your best life! With your talents, it won't be long until you're promoted, so your career is taking off and you have the pick of women. You're probably the envy of every man.'

'I am determined to get a promotion, that is true, and I have always believed that it is important to enjoy life, but these two years I... Having fun has not been my focus.'

'I thought that whenever you weren't working, you'd be partying!'

'No. Tell me what you think of the chicken.' He picked up a piece of the chargrilled jerk chicken. The blend of spices flooded my nostrils and took me back to those days when Grandma used to season a big tray of chicken and Grandad would barbecue everything outside inside a red steel oil barrel drum.

It hadn't escaped my attention that Alejandro had avoided responding to my partying comment. Probably because he didn't want to make me feel bad about my non-existent social life.

Anyway, he didn't have to tell me about what he did in his spare time. We were colleagues and now that I thought about it, I'd probably overstepped by sharing stuff about my background too.

Note to self to be more professional.

I blamed that glass of potent rum punch for my loose tongue. The next drink I ordered would definitely be water. If I wanted to get through the rest of this dinner, I needed a clear head.

The last thing I needed was to say something stupid and embarrass myself.

And given my slip-ups so far, there was a higher probability of that happening than I would like.

14

ALEJANDRO

'No problem!' Bob slapped my hand enthusiastically and I smiled.

We were at reception waiting for Jasmine and I had just asked if he would be free to take us to see Jasmine's grandad.

During dinner last night, she had looked up the name of the town in her phone and I'd written it down in my notes app. Although she had not explained why her mum no longer kept in contact with him, I could tell from how often she spoke about him that he meant a lot to her, so I wanted to help.

One thing I was not expecting was for her to tell me more about her personal life. I had not realised that she was married. Her ex-husband sounded like a fool. Any man who had a woman like Jasmine and did not appreciate her did not deserve to keep her.

I could not believe that he had cheated. If Jasmine was my wife, I would treat her like a queen. His loss.

'Sorry!' Jasmine said as she walked towards us.

Actually, that was not an accurate description. Jasmine did not *walk*. She *glided*. She *sashayed*. As she got closer, I tried not to look at the way her beautiful hips swayed and the way her skin glistened.

'*Tranquila,*' I said, letting her know that it was not a problem. I had finished in the kitchen early and saw that Bob was already here, so I decided to go and chat.

'*Yuh luk criss, gyal,*' Bob nodded approvingly. I guessed that *criss* was patois for something like *beautiful*.

He was right. Jasmine did look *criss*.

She was wearing a long, pink, sleeveless, summer dress which showed off her great shoulders.

I was trying very hard, but the more time I spent with Jasmine, the more attractive I found her.

'How are you?' I asked, steering my thoughts back from the danger zone.

'Fine, thanks. I'm glad I didn't have another glass of that rum punch, otherwise I wouldn't have been able to go on this excursion.'

Last night, after finishing her punch, Jasmine drank water for the rest of the evening and I noticed that she was much less talkative. We still had a good time though, mostly talking about how much we were enjoying Jamaica so far and what we were looking forward to seeing.

During the car journey, Bob chatted about his kids and before we knew it, we were back at the hotel and went back to our rooms.

Now here we were again in Bob's car. We put on our seat belts and he set off. Today, we were doing some sort of river trip on a raft. I had not asked too many questions. I did not care where we were going. I was just happy to see more of Jamaica. And of course, spending time with Jasmine was a bonus.

'Bob has said that he knows how to get to your grandad's house,' I said.

Jasmine's eyes widened.

'Perhaps we can go tomorrow?'

'That's really kind of you to ask him, but I think there's an activity Hortense wants me to try tomorrow.'

'Depending on the time, we could go afterwards? Or the day after?'

'We'll see,' Jasmine said.

After what happened to my girlfriend, I always tried to avoid delaying going to visit someone important. It was too easy to say you would see them next week or next month, but sometimes that time never came.

'*Vale*,' I said, not wanting to push her.

'So today, we're going on a bamboo raft and whilst we enjoy a relaxing ride down the river, apparently they'll tell us a bit of local history and give us a foot massage using a limestone paste made from the river rocks.'

'Sounds like torture!' I laughed.

'I thought you might say that.' She smiled and I caught myself looking at her lips for longer than I should.

'What reggae artists do you like, Bob? Apart from Bob Marley of course,' I asked, turning away from Jasmine before my thoughts started wandering into unprofessional territory again.

From the rear-view mirror, I saw that Bob's eyes had widened like he was shocked that I was interested.

I knew he probably played Bob Marley, not just because he loved him like most people did, but also because he thought that was what tourists wanted to hear. But I was also interested in learning more about other reggae artists. I wanted to soak up everything here and improve my knowledge of the culture.

'*Well, mi like* Beres – Beres Hammond, Gregory Issacs, Dennis Brown, Protoje*, an wul heap ah people dem.*'

'Can you play us some of their songs?' I asked.

'*Ya mon!*' He pressed some buttons on his car stereo and then a mid-tempo reggae song started playing.

The lyrics were easy to follow. It was about a man being attracted to a woman and how he could not stop thinking of her and how much he wanted her. I would like to say that I did not find it relatable, but I would be lying.

'I recognise this song!' Jasmine said. 'I think my dad used to play it at home.'

'*Dis deh is* "Tempted to Touch" *by* Beres Hammond. *Yuh like it?*'

'*Sí.*' I nodded. 'Very much.'

Perhaps too much...

For the rest of the journey, Bob played us lots of different reggae songs I had never heard of before. I was grateful that I had the Shazam app to save them all. I would definitely be listening to them later back at the hotel.

When we arrived at the river, multiple rafts were lined up. Each one had a throne made from bamboo for each couple to sit on which was decorated with palm leaves and bright-red flowers.

Once Jasmine had spoken to the staff, we were shown to our raft and took our seats.

Sailing down the river was calming. Jasmine took photos as the tour guide explained some of the history, then started the massage.

'So,' Jasmine turned to face me, 'is this the first time you've had a foot massage?'

'No. But usually I prefer to give them instead of having them myself.'

'Really?' Her eyebrow arched. 'Are you any good?'

'Of course,' I said without hesitation.

'Wow. Are you this confident about *everything*?'

'Not *everything*. But I do not believe in this false modesty that some British people seem to have. Why pretend that you are not good at something when you are?'

'Because people don't want to come across as big-headed!'

'If I said that I am the best in the world, *that* would be big-headed, but I only said that I am good. And I am confident enough to prove it. Derek,' I called the name of our tour guide. 'Would you allow me to continue Jasmine's massage? If the lady does not mind, of course?' I looked at her.

For a second I questioned whether it was a good idea, but then I dismissed it. I was only going to show her how I gave foot massages. It did not have to mean anything.

'It'd be rude to interrupt Derek!' she said. 'I'm sure he wants to be left to do his job.'

'*Mi gud.*' Derek stopped massaging Jasmine's feet and gestured for me to take over.

'You are fine with this?' I asked again.

She paused and I could almost hear the wheels turning in her head.

'Okay – if you insist. But don't feel bad when I ask Derek to take over. He is the professional, after all.' She rolled her eyes, which only made me more determined to impress her.

I sat at her feet, making myself comfortable on the raft.

Her legs and feet were covered in limestone paste which looked like clay, but I knew that underneath, her skin was beautiful. I noticed before that she had changed the colour of her toenail polish. Yesterday, it was a deeper coral shade, whereas today, it was pink to match her dress.

When I gently placed my palms on Jasmine's feet, she flinched.

'I am sorry. Did I hurt you?' I asked.

'No.'

Even with the paste in my hands and on her feet, I could tell that her skin was soft. Just touching her feet made my heart race faster. When I looked up, Jasmine's eyes were squeezed shut.

As I increased the pressure, a low moan slipped out of her mouth and it was the sweetest sound that I had ever heard. My dick twitched. Knowing Jasmine was enjoying the sensation of my hands on her made me feel great. I wanted to make her moan again. And again.

'How is the pressure?' I asked.

'*Mmm*,' she murmured. 'Perfect.'

I continued working my hands on her feet and massaging her legs for what must have been ten minutes. I could have done it for hours, but with her eyes shut, Jasmine was missing the views.

When I stopped, her eyes flicked open.

'You're *stopping*?' Her jaw dropped. 'Why?'

'So you enjoyed it?'

'As much as I hate to admit it, you were right. You *are* very good at giving foot massages.'

'Only *very good*?' I teased.

'Okay,' she sighed. 'You are excellent. Sorry Derek.' She winced.

Derek held up his hands in surrender. I did not think that he really cared one way or the other.

Overall, the tour only lasted about one hour and a half, so it was not long until we were back in the car with Bob.

'So,' Jasmine asked, 'what would be your romance rating for the rafting activity?'

'I liked it, but I think it would be better for the couples to do the foot massage, not the guide.'

'Good idea in theory considering how great you were, but something tells me that not everyone would be as talented as you.'

'So you are saying that I *am* the best foot masseur in the

world. Is that what I am hearing?' I cupped my ear, pretending I could not hear her.

'God.' She laughed. 'You really are something else!'

'*Something else?*' I frowned.

'Don't worry, it's an English saying. I'll put the bamboo rafting as a maybe,' she said, her mouth turning up into a smile.

Multiple smiles and moans of pleasure from Jasmine all in one afternoon?

Although she did not realise, she had just made my day.

15

JASMINE

I glanced out of the office window. The rain was still coming down thick and fast.

The weather wasn't ideal because the activity I'd planned for today couldn't be done in these conditions.

'Hey.' Nadine breezed into the office. 'How you doing? We haven't spoken since after you went to Dunn's River Falls. What you guys been up to?'

'We went to visit Bob's favourite restaurant.'

'Nice!'

'And yesterday, we tried the rafting and limestone foot massage...'

My voice trailed off as I thought about how amazing Alejandro's hands felt on my feet and my legs. I swear at one point, I was on the verge of having an orgasm.

Pretty sure that I'd read somewhere that there are nerve-endings in our feet that can set you off, so it wasn't as crazy as it sounded.

I knew that I probably shouldn't have agreed to let him

massage my feet given how I felt about him, but I couldn't resist. There was just something about Alejandro that got me going.

I loved his confidence. He hadn't even hesitated for a second when I'd asked him if he was any good at foot massages. He had no concerns about asking the tour guide if he could take over. And of course the fact that he'd delivered was hot too. The tour guide's massage was decent, but Alejandro's hands were blessed.

He knew exactly where to touch and how much pressure to apply. I couldn't help but wonder what else he could do with his hands...

'Sounds like you've been having a good time!'

'I have,' I replied, thinking that although my growing attraction to Alejandro was hard to control, I was still enjoying myself.

'What's your plan for today?'

'Well, I was supposed to go to check out a few other beaches to see if they'd be good for romantic picnic settings for couples who wanted to go outside of the hotel grounds, but the weather isn't great. Looks like I'll just have to stay in the office, which isn't good because I need to keep finding activities to add to the itinerary.'

'You should come to my class!' Nadine said enthusiastically.

'You have a class? What kind?'

'A reggae dance class. It's my little side-hustle, but I'm hoping it'll grow. If you add it to your itinerary, I'll give the hotel a discount!'

'That sounds great! I'd love to hear more!'

I loved seeing women striking out on their own, so I'd really like to support Nadine if I could, but I needed to make sure it was suitable for our guests. I couldn't just add it because I wanted to be nice.

'The lesson's around forty-five minutes and I teach students how to do different reggae moves. Jamaica is famous for our music and we love to dance, so it's the perfect way to learn more about our culture.'

'That's true. When people think about Jamaica, they often think about reggae and Bob Marley.'

I smiled as two thoughts popped into my head. First, I remembered that whenever I went to events both as a child with my parents as well as later as an adult and we were the only black people there, when the other guests heard that my parents were born in Jamaica, they'd always use music as a way to connect with us.

'Ooh! We love a bit of Bob Marley!' they'd say and I'd always chuckle to myself because it happened on multiple occasions.

That led me to my second thought: when Alejandro asked what other reggae Bob liked. I'd guessed early on that Bob played Bob Marley on repeat because he also knew it appealed to tourists. Especially as Alejandro often hummed along to all the songs.

I loved that Alejandro expressed an interest in expanding his knowledge of reggae music and learning more about the Jamaican culture.

'Exactly!' Nadine nodded. 'It'll be fun and it's a great way to bring couples together.'

'I'd like to check it out. Can I come and watch?'

'It's no fun to just watch! You need to *feel* the music. And the best way to do that is to take part!'

'But can I still take part and learn the dance moves if I'm on my own?'

'You can...'

'Okay. Count me in!'

There was no way I was inviting Alejandro, though. Jamaican dance moves could be *very* sexy. And although that could be a good thing for our guests, I was not going to start rubbing my arse against Alejandro. That'd just be asking for trouble.

I'd go along to the class, try and learn a few moves. If it was too much, I'd just watch, soak up the atmosphere, then interview some couples to get their thoughts on the classes and whether they'd recommend them.

That'd be a much more productive way to spend my afternoon than just doing research in the office. *And* it'd be helping Nadine out. *Win-win*.

'Great! I'll be going straight to the dance studio after I finish running a few errands, so I'll ask Bob to take you. I'll tell him to meet you by reception around three thirty. Does that work?'

'Perfect! Do I need to bring anything?'

'Wear comfortable clothes and bring a bottle of water, a towel, lots of energy and good party vibes!' Nadine beamed.

'Will do!'

* * *

A couple of hours after lunch, I shut down my computer, I headed back to my room to change into leggings and a vest top, picked up a towel and some water and headed to meet Bob.

I was actually excited about this class. I used to love dancing. I wasn't the best in the world, but I could keep to the beat and it was a good way to exercise and stimulate those happy endorphins.

Yes. This was going to be great.

Well, that was what I thought until I stepped out of reception and saw Alejandro laughing and chatting with Bob.

At first, I told myself that it didn't have to mean anything. Maybe Bob told Alejandro he was stopping by and he came to say hello.

But then I remembered that when Alejandro was working, he always wore his chef's jacket. And right now, he was dressed in sports shorts and a vest, which of course showed his impressive arms.

'Miss Jasmine!' Bob called out enthusiastically when he spotted me.

'Hi, Bob,' I said cautiously. 'Alejandro.' I nodded in acknowledgment.

'*Yuh ready fi dance?*' Bob said.

'As ready as I'll ever be!'

'The class sounds like it will be fun,' Alejandro said. 'I was glad when Nadine invited me.'

'Wait. *You're* coming?' My eyes widened.

'*Sí*. Is that a problem?'

'Problem?' I repeated, stalling for time. I couldn't exactly say yes, could I? What possible reason could I give for not wanting him to come without either offending him or admitting that I was worried about getting too close to him? *None*. 'No!' My voice went up several octaves. 'Of course not! Like you said, it'll be... fun! Yay!'

That was a lie. It would definitely *not* be fun.

I didn't know what reggae moves we'd be learning, but something told me it wouldn't be a dance where there would be much distance between our body parts.

Something told me there'd be booty shaking and so much bumping and grinding, it'd make *Dirty Dancing* look like a children's film.

Shit.

Once we were in the car, Bob set off. Whilst he continued his chat with Alejandro about a bad storm they'd had in Jamaica before we'd arrived, my mind raced.

Maybe I'd overreacted. Not all Jamaican dances were X-rated.

There was skanking which my dad did, where you kind of marched to the beat whilst sliding your feet from side to side and doing a little kick. We could be learning something like that.

And anyway, if I wasn't comfortable with anything, I could just watch. *Simple.*

It didn't take long to get to the studio. We waved Bob off and walked in to see Nadine stood at the front of the small room. It was pretty basic with white walls, light wooden flooring and a mirrored wall.

'Hi!' I said cheerily, then glanced at my watch. The class was due to start, but there was no one else here.

'Hey,' Nadine mumbled. She didn't seem like her normal, bubbly self.

'Everything okay?' Alejandro asked, noticing that something was off.

'Not really,' she sighed.

'What's up?' My face creased with concern.

'Six people promised they'd turn up today and no one's here.'

'Well, it's still early. I'm sure they'll be here any minute. I meant to ask: do you have any photos from your lessons or a website that you use to promote the classes?' I hoped my questions would distract her and help cheer her up.

'I have some photos on social media!' Nadine's face brightened.

'Could you show us?'

'Sure!' She reached for her phone.

Twenty minutes later, Nadine had talked us through all the photos and told us that she'd set up the class after encouragement from her friends. I'd stalled for as long as I could, but there was still no sign of anyone else.

'I can't believe no one's showed up!' Nadine sighed. 'It's so hard. I really want to make a go of these classes.'

'How long have you been doing them?' I said.

'About two months.'

'Things will pick up.' I patted her shoulder gently to reassure her. I wished I could tell her that we'd add it to our itinerary, but I couldn't without seeing for myself what it was like.

'I hope so. But I have to pay to hire the studio, so when people don't turn up, I lose money.'

'We will pay for the lessons,' Alejandro reached in his pocket and pulled out his wallet. 'Tell me what we owe you.'

'I can't take your money. I invited you as guests.' She looked at her watch. 'We should get started.'

'Are you sure you're okay?' I asked. I considered suggesting we do the class another time, but she already seemed deflated so cancelling it altogether was a hard no.

That also meant I couldn't back out of taking part. It seemed like Nadine's confidence was low, so I needed to throw myself into this and show lots of enthusiasm to make her feel better.

'Once I feel the beat, I'll be fine.' She nodded.

'Okay.'

She pressed play on her phone and reggae music boomed around the hall via two large speakers.

'So!' she shouted as she positioned herself at the front of the hall. 'Are you ready to bump and whine?'

'Er...' I paused. Sounded like we wouldn't be doing any innocent skanking today.

'*Si!*' Alejandro said enthusiastically.

'Nice. So there are lots of different popular dances in Jamaica: the Bogle, the Butterfly, the Dutty Whine. But first we need to start with the basics, so let's do a little warm up.'

Nadine encouraged us to feel the beat and bob our heads in time to the music, before starting to sway from side to side.

'When dancing to reggae music, it's all about moving your

hips or *whining*, as we call it. Roll your hips in a circle.' Nadine demonstrated, then came over to me. 'More!' she insisted. 'Nice, Alejandro. You're a natural!'

I didn't even want to look and see what he was doing with his hips.

'Good. Now, Jasmine, I need you to stand in front of Alejandro, push your butt back into him and whine.'

My eyes bulged.

'I'm sorry, what?'

'Whine up against Alejandro. That's how we dance in Jamaica. The woman stands in front of the man. Open your legs a bit, relax your body, put your hands on your hips and roll them in a circle and stick your butt out so it presses against Alejandro. Come on, don't be shy!'

'I... I'm not sure if that's appropriate for us.' My heart thudded against my chest and my throat went dry.

'It's just a dance! I thought you needed to try things out to know what your guests would experience if they took the class? You are going to recommend it, aren't you? I really need your help.'

Nadine's face fell with disappointment and my stomach twisted. I didn't want to let her down. And she was right. It was only a dance. All I had to do was stick it out for one song.

She'd only booked the hall for an hour and we'd spent most of that killing time whilst we waited for the other attendees, so there wasn't much of the lesson left.

If I did what she asked for a few more minutes, it'd put a smile on her face. It was a small price to pay to make Nadine happy.

'Okay,' I said.

The track switched and another heavy reggae beat boomed from the speaker.

I shuffled over to Alejandro, avoiding eye contact, then stood in front of him.

'Closer!' Nadine instructed. 'Legs apart, hands on your thighs, move your hips and push your butt out,' she repeated the instructions.

I took a deep breath and then did what she said, slowly pushing my arse into Alejandro.

The heat from his body hit me like a truck. Holding his hand was one thing, but the sensation of feeling my bum pressed up against him was off the charts.

Alejandro was winding his hips in time to the beat perfectly and knowing we were dancing in sync felt good. This wasn't so bad. In fact, I was starting to enjoy it.

'Nice!' Nadine beamed. 'Keep it going!'

I kept winding my hips and as the baseline vibrated around the room and through my veins, I got into it more and started pushing my bum into Alejandro with more enthusiasm. He gripped my hips and grinded harder.

Fuck.

Goosebumps erupted across my skin and I felt tingles between my legs.

I tipped my head back a little, resting it on his firm chest as adrenaline pumped through my veins.

This was so hot.

Earlier, I'd been reluctant to dance with Alejandro, but now I was, I didn't want it to end.

I rubbed myself up against him and this time, when I did, I felt something hard press against me.

I say 'something', but you didn't have to be a genius to know what it was. Even though it'd been years since I'd slept with a man, I knew an erection when I felt one. And the more I moved, the harder Alejandro got.

Right now, I should pull away. I should be horrified to know that I was dancing with a colleague who had an erection, but I liked it.

I wanted more.

I wanted to feel more of him.

I wanted Alejandro to move his hands from my waist and put them between my legs.

I wanted him to bend me over and bury what felt like a very large dick inside me.

I wanted him to...

'You guys were excellent!' Nadine shouted as she turned off the music. 'You must've danced to reggae music before. Or maybe I'm just an excellent teacher!' She laughed.

Coming back to my senses, I quickly pulled away from Alejandro and stepped forward, putting several feet of distance between us.

'You're...' I could feel myself panting. I was out of breath. Partly from the dancing, but mainly because thinking about what I wanted Alejandro to do to me had got me all worked up. 'You're a great teacher, thank you.'

'Thanks!' Nadine beamed. 'What about you, Alejandro? Did you enjoy it?'

'Very much.' I felt his eyes boring into me.

'Yay! Well, that's the class done. Sorry it was so short, but I appreciate you coming along to support me. I hope you'll come again next week if you can? In the meantime, remember to practise! I've gotta run!' She grabbed her stuff. 'There's another class next door, so the owner will lock up. *Likkle more!*'

She raced out of the room, leaving me and Alejandro alone.

My first instinct was to run out of the studio with her. I needed some air. To clear my head and remove all of the illicit feelings and thoughts that were still racing through it.

But Alejandro clearly had other ideas. He stood in front of me.

'You did not tell Nadine whether you enjoyed it,' he said.

'Didn't I?' My eyes flicked to the floor. 'It was... nice.'

'There's that word again. *Nice*. Nice is boring. That dance was more than *nice*.'

'I suppose it was,' I said more decisively.

'Like I said, I enjoyed it a lot, as I am sure you could feel. I am sorry if it made you uncomfortable, but I would be lying if I said that it was not a true reflection of how I was feeling.'

Whoa.

I wasn't expecting him to say *that*.

If most guys got an inconvenient boner, they wouldn't mention it at all. They'd make excuses or a quick exit because they'd be embarrassed. But Alejandro was totally owning it.

'It's fine.' I waved my hand dismissively. 'These things happen.'

'They do not,' Alejandro lifted my chin. 'If anyone else rubbed their butt against my cock, it would not. But when it is *your* butt, everything is different. I did not intend to get hard. I have been trying to ignore my feelings, but the truth is, having *you* pressed against me felt fucking amazing.'

My eyebrows flew up into my hairline.

'Did you just...?' I couldn't believe that not only had Alejandro just admitted getting hard whilst I was dancing against him, he'd also just basically confessed that he liked me. 'I don't think you realise what you just said.' I shook my head, my eyes still wide.

'I know *exactly* what I said.' He lifted my chin. 'One thing you will discover about me is that I am honest. I believe in speaking my mind and saying how I feel. My eldest sister, Lola, always taught me to do that. If telling you the truth makes you uncomfortable and you prefer not to be alone with me again, I will understand. My only intention when I came here was to give you my opinion on whether you should add this class to the itinerary.'

'And?' I asked, although I was pretty sure I already knew the answer.

'And I say *definitely*. Because if a couple having their bodies pressed together whilst they gyrate and dance to reggae music does not help to bring them closer, I do not know what will, because it worked for me.'

And with that, Alejandro turned and walked out of the studio, whilst my entire body burned with desire.

16

JASMINE

It was now evening and I was on my way to the kitchen. Alejandro had texted to ask if I could come and try some of the dishes he'd been working on.

When I'd received his message, my immediate thought was to decline. Not because I didn't want to help him, but because I hadn't been able to stop thinking about our dance lesson this afternoon and what he'd said:

I did not intend to get hard. I have been trying to ignore my feelings, but the truth is, having you *pressed against me felt fucking amazing.*

Those words kept swirling around my brain and every time I thought about how good it was to feel Alejandro's boner, a fresh wave of tingles erupted between my legs.

He'd confessed to liking me and the more time I spent with him, the more mutual those feelings became.

That's why I didn't want to sit alone with him in the kitchen sampling food that I knew would be delicious and make me like him even more.

I mean, let's get real. The man looked like a god. He oozed

confidence. He was kind and thoughtful and caring. Those qualities alone made him a catch. But when you threw the fact that he was an amazing chef into the mix, it was a lethal combination. Especially considering the fact we'd been thrown together and forced to spend two weeks in paradise.

I was starting to think that I didn't stand a chance. Maybe I was fighting a losing battle and should just give in to my urges.

But then I remembered: I was his boss. We were here to work. I was *this* close to securing the promotion I'd worked so hard for. I couldn't throw my dream away over some man's cock. Although I was sure it'd be a very, very exquisite cock.

A fresh wave of need raced through me.

This was getting ridiculous.

If I had more time, I would've taken another shower. I'd had one as soon as we'd got back from the dance lesson, but it was a hot one. Right now, I needed to immerse myself in cold water to extinguish the dangerous flames that were burning inside me.

It'd been ages since I'd had any real sexual desire. Going through a messy divorce saw to that. Since I'd found out that my ex had been sleeping with his secretary for months behind my back three years ago, I'd had zero interest in dating another man. I just wanted to focus on me and building a career that no man could take away from me like Kane did.

But then in walked Alejandro and my body lit up like a Christmas display. When we were working in Spain, it was easier to keep those feelings under control. If ever I felt the attraction building, I'd just remove myself from the situation. But here, it was much harder to hide.

As much as I wanted to lock myself away in my room, I had to go and help him out. After all, he'd helped with my research, so it was only fair that I did the same. That was what I was here for. We both had to do whatever it took to plan the best possible experience for our guests, so I couldn't let a stupid crush get in the way of me doing my job.

I can do this.

After taking a deep breath and straightening my shoulders, I slid on my sandals then left my room.

When I walked into the kitchen, Alejandro was standing over a pot on the stove. A mid-tempo reggae song was playing from his phone on the counter and he was bopping his head happily.

'Hi,' I said softly, trying to ignore how good he looked in his chef's jacket. His hair was ruffled and his waves looked so adorable, I was suddenly overcome with the need to run my hands through them. I quickly clasped my palms together before I embarrassed myself.

'Hey.' He looked up and when he saw me, a wide smile spread across his face.

'Enjoying the music?'

'*Sí!* I need your love!'

'What?' I frowned. I knew he said he liked to be honest, but that was a bit strong.

'No!' He laughed. 'That is the song; it is called "I Need Your Love", by a man called Beres Hammond. He is one of the artists Bob recommended.'

'Oh, right!' I said, feeling like an idiot. Of course he wasn't asking for my love.

'Dinner is almost ready. Please.' He gestured to a stool beside him. 'Take a seat. I poured you a glass of some rum punch I made too.'

I did as he asked.

After lifting up the colourful glass, I took a sip of the punch.

'Oh my God, this is delicious!' I licked my lips, then took another glug. 'Not too sweet and it's strong, but not as potent as the one at the restaurant.'

'I am glad you like it.' He smiled.

A sweet scent filled the air, but it was mixed with something spicy too.

'What are you making?' I said, attempting to take my mind off the fact that there were now just a few steps between us.

At least I should be grateful that things weren't awkward. Alejandro was acting normally. I was glad the whole inconvenient boner subject hadn't reared its head again. Pun not intended.

'A mango sauce. I want to try this with the jerk chicken I have made. I still need to make dessert, but it should not take long. Would you like to help?'

'Oh no.' I shook my head. 'You really don't want me to go anywhere near anything you'd like to eat. Unless you want to be sick tomorrow! I told you before, I'm not a good cook.'

'That I find hard to believe.'

'It's *true*!'

My ex-husband loved to remind me about my culinary shortcomings. 'Do me a favour,' he used to say. 'For all our sakes, don't cook. You're a *disaster* in the kitchen. Just stick to what you're good at: warming up the food my mum makes.'

That was another sticking point. He insisted that no one cooked like his mother, so every week, she'd deliver a batch of dishes she'd made.

It was kind of her and at least it meant I never had to cook, but at the same time, I thought it was a little OTT.

A man who was in his forties shouldn't have his mum cook all his meals, surely? Her doing that made me feel a bit shit. As outdated as the concept of the wife cooking all the meals for her husband was, I felt like I should at least be able to do it if I wanted to. But knowing how much he hated everything I ever attempted to make made me feel like I was *less*.

'Come.' He gestured for me to get up. 'You are going to help me make the dessert.'

'If dessert is pouring milk in a glass or scooping ice cream into a bowl, I can definitely do *that*!' I laughed.

'You remember the orange cake that is on the menu at our hotel?'

'Oh my God! I love that cake!' My mouth watered just thinking about it. It was the softest cake I'd ever tasted.

'I am going to make a version of that, but using pineapple, coconut and a little rum instead.'

'Sounds delicious! Like a Malibu cake.'

'Could be. All of the ingredients are measured, I would like you to put them in a bowl and mix them.'

I opened my mouth to protest and then saw Alejandro raise his eyebrow, signalling that resistance would be futile.

After I'd taken another sip of my punch, I washed my hands, grabbed an apron and went over to where the bowl and ingredients were laid out.

'Does it matter what order I put them in?'

'No. But perhaps start with the dry ingredients first.'

I emptied the flour, sugar and baking powder in the bowl, then looked at the wet ingredients.

'Yogurt?' I frowned. 'And oil? Where's the butter? I thought all cakes used butter? Not that I'm an expert or anything. Just curious.'

'I prefer yogurt and olive oil. It makes the sponge lighter.'

'Oh! I didn't know that!'

I mixed them in along with the eggs, freshly grated coconut, chopped pineapple, spices and a dash of rum.

'How's that?' I tipped the bowl so he could see.

'You need to mix it a little more.' He came over.

'Like this?' I picked up the spoon and moved it around the bowl.

'No.' Alejandro stood behind me, put his hand on mine and began to stir the mixture in large, fast, circular movements.

At least I thought that was what he was doing but I couldn't be sure because my brain had just short-circuited.

As soon as his big, manly hand connected with mine, my pulse rocketed. Just like it did that time in the kitchen when he handed me my phone after we'd crashed into each other and it'd dropped.

Just like it had when he held my hand at Dunn's River Falls.

Just like it had when he gave me the foot massage.

And again when his hard-on pressed against me during our dance class earlier.

Fuck.

I willed myself to calm down and knew the only way to do that was to create some distance. *Fast.*

'I... I think I've got the hang of it now,' I stuttered.

'Sure?' he asked.

'Positive.'

Alejandro stepped back, returned to the stove and started doing something with the sauce whilst I tried to get my heart rate to stabilise.

The worrying thing was that, although I should be grateful that he was now a few feet away from me, I missed the feeling of his hand on mine.

I also missed the heat from his body when he stood behind me and the way his warm breath tickled the back of my neck when he'd spoken.

Telling myself that I was crazy, I returned to stirring the mixture.

'I think it's done now.'

Alejandro walked back over to inspect the contents and my heart raced again.

'That looks perfect,' he smiled. 'I told you. You are a natural!'

My heart fluttered and I almost asked if he was joking before reminding myself that I was supposed to be strong and confident and that when someone complimented you, you shouldn't question it.

'Thank you. Here's hoping it tastes as good as it looks!' I joked.

Okay, so I still had some work to do on the whole accepting praise thing. I was usually fine when it came to accepting compliments about how good I was at my job, but baking? This was a new one for me.

'It will. I believe in you.'

My eyes widened and my heart swelled. Two compliments within a couple of minutes was a lot to take in.

'Oh! I just realised. Shouldn't we put the pineapple juice in the mixture?'

'No.' He shook his head. 'We will do that when we take it out of the oven.'

I frowned, then nodded. Alejandro knew what he was doing.

After I greased the baking dish and poured in the mixture like Alejandro instructed, I slid it inside the oven, then sat next to him as he plated up our dinner. I drained my glass of rum punch, then poured another from the jug in front of me.

'It looks and smells delicious. I'd love to hear what you've done and how you made it.' I leant in, genuinely interested to know more.

'So with the jerk chicken, I thought that instead of serving it as a complete thigh, it would be good to slice it finely. When our guests are on a date, they will not want to worry about biting a big piece of chicken, or thinking about if it is okay to use their fingers or cutting the meat themselves. It will be a distraction. Instead, I want them to focus on staring into the eyes of their match.'

Alejandro's gaze fixed on mine and I swallowed hard.

'That's a good idea,' I said, dropping my eyes to the plate. 'And this?' I pointed to the mash.

'That is a sweet potato mash and I have created a spicy mango salsa which is drizzled over the chicken.'

'Can I try?'

'Please,' he said.

I stabbed a piece of chicken onto my fork, dipped it into the salsa, then added a bit of mash before sliding it into my mouth.

'Wow.' My eyes popped. 'This is phenomenal!' I quickly piled my fork with another mouthful. 'You have a gift.' I exclaimed. 'This is incredible. Seriously. You're a very talented man. You're an amazing cook, great dancer, you speak English fluently, what else are you good at?' I cocked my head to the side and licked my lips suggestively.

WTF?

It sounded like I was flirting with him.

I blamed the rum punch for loosening my tongue.

'Professionally, or *personally*?' The corner of his mouth turned up.

'Both,' I said, knowing that I was entering dangerous territory, but not being able to help myself.

'As you know, I love to cook, so that covers my professional talents. As for my personal ones, I am very good at exercise.'

'What kind?'

'I am a fast runner, a strong swimmer and very good at

working out. I have a lot of energy and stamina. I do not tire easily. And even when I have a long session, I can recover very quickly and start again.'

'What kind of *working out* are you referring to? The gym or something else?'

'What would the *something else* mean?' He raised his eyebrow.

'Well, from the way you phrased it, it almost sounded like you were talking about your ability in the bedroom...' My voice trailed off.

'Is that what it sounded like or what you were imagining?' His eyes darkened.

'I don't think you want to know the answer to that.' I picked up my rum punch and took a large sip, suddenly getting cold feet. I shouldn't have said that. 'Should we check on the cake?'

I got up and put my hand on the oven door. Alejandro reached out and put his hand on top of mine to stop me.

'The cake is fine. Do not think I did not notice how you just tried to change the subject.'

Busted.

My gaze flicked up and my eyes met his. Electricity crackled between us. My lips parted. Our faces were only inches apart. All it would take was for us both to lean forward and our mouths would be touching.

Which is why I quickly pulled my hand away and sat back on the stool.

'I just wanted to check that the cake didn't burn,' I said, convincing no one.

'Jasmine, I need to ask you a question.'

God, if only he knew what him saying my name did to me.

'Go on...' My stomach tensed as I sensed that I wasn't going to like what he had to say.

'Earlier, at the end of the dance class, I told you that I enjoyed your body being pressed against mine. In case it was not clear, I am very attracted to you. Sometimes, you act as if you are not interested. But then other times, like just now, when you asked about my *skills*, you seem like you are. It is a little confusing, so I would like to know: do you feel the same? Are you attracted to me?'

'Alejandro.' I paused. 'Look, I apologise. My comments or questions a moment ago were… inappropriate. I think it's best if we change the subject and focus on your work-related talents, rather than whether or not we are attracted to each other.'

It was wrong of me to flirt with him, but it wasn't too late to shut this conversation down.

'*Por qué?* We are adults. It is better to talk about these things openly, so there is no awkwardness and we both know where we stand.'

No awkwardness? That was a joke. Forget what I said earlier. Right now, I was feeling more awkward than someone who'd just wandered onto a nudist beach by mistake.

'I appreciate you expressing your feelings and I'm flattered. I really am, but I think it's better if we forget about what happened at the dance class, what you said and my comments just now. I shouldn't have drunk that punch. It clouded my judgement. I wasn't thinking clearly, but now that I am, it wouldn't be appropriate for me to answer your question.'

'I did not ask whether it would be *appropriate*. I asked if you are attracted to me or not. It is a simple *sí* or *no*.'

I sat there in silence, not knowing what to say. Of course I was bloody attracted to him. Given the chance, I'd jump him right now, but what I said was true. It wasn't appropriate. I wasn't supposed to be attracted to him. I was in a more senior position and we worked together. End of.

'I'm sorry, but I'm not going to answer that.'

Alejandro blew out a frustrated breath, then shook his head.

'Do you know what I think?'

'What?' I replied.

'I think that you *are* attracted to me, but you are scared. Scared because you have been hurt before. Scared because you are worried what people will think. But I *know* that you can feel the electricity between us. When our hands touch. When we look at each other. This kind of mutual attraction does not happen every day. So you can continue to deny it, but it will not work. This,' he gestured between us, 'is powerful, so it is inevitable that something will happen between us.'

'Wow. *Inevitable.* Really?' I rolled my eyes. 'What are you now, a clairvoyant? If you can see the future so clearly, maybe you should tell me this week's lottery numbers. Then when we win the jackpot, we won't have to work any more!' I laughed, hoping to deflect the truth.

'Working is in our blood. Even if we had money, we would still do our jobs because we are both passionate about our careers. Passion in all of its forms cannot be denied.' His eyes darkened. 'So it would much easier if you just told me how you felt. If you are not attracted to me, tell me now, then we can move on. No problem. But if you are, if you *do* have feelings for me like I believe you do, let us explore them. Life is short and it is important to enjoy it. I understand that you take your job seriously and I respect that. But we are away from management, so as long as we are careful, we can take the risk. We can be more relaxed. Here, we are more free.'

'We're not *free*!' I scoffed. 'We may be in Jamaica, but people are still watching us. We work together, Alejandro, and I'm in a more senior position. Getting involved with you would be an abuse of power.'

'*That* is why you are concerned?' He laughed. 'I am not a boy. I am a man. I am capable of making my own decisions. *I* am the one expressing my feelings to you. You are not *making* me do anything.'

'I don't think Hazel would quite see it that way. Anyway, I'm not that kind of woman. I don't have one-night stands. And if I did, I wouldn't do that with someone at work. It'd make things very awkward.'

Things were already super awkward between us, but could you imagine how much worse they'd be if we had sex? The thought of us making small talk, or seeing him hooking up with other women afterwards made my stomach clench.

'A one-night stand?' He laughed. 'You think that I just want to fuck you once and then *leave*?'

'What else could you possibly want?' My face creased. 'You're young. I'm sure you're only interested in having fun.'

'You do not know me at all.' He shook his head. 'I have never been that guy. Jasmine, you are a queen. If you gave yourself to me, I would worship you. I would treat you the way that you deserve. I would give you the world. One night would never be enough.'

I swallowed hard.

'I've— I have to go. It's late.' I jumped up from my seat and headed towards the door.

'But you have not finished your dinner. And the cake is not ready yet!'

'It's been a long day. I need to get some sleep.'

I literally sprinted out of the kitchen and out into the cool air, walking back to my room in a daze.

Alejandro had said that if I was with him, he'd worship me and give me the world.

His facial expression was serious. He looked like he meant every word and if I was being honest, I believed him.

Which only made me like him more.

I was in big trouble.

And I didn't know how the hell I was going to get myself out of it.

17

ALEJANDRO

I took the cake out of the oven and ground my jaw.

This whole situation was so frustrating. Before, I had my doubts, but now I was certain that Jasmine liked me. I could tell from the way that she looked at me and the things she said when she let her guard down.

Jasmine felt the sparks between us, but still she insisted that she felt nothing at all.

I understood her concerns about what Hazel could say and how it could affect her career. It was important that I was careful too. I did not take this lightly. It was not just my future at stake.

Evita already spent too many hours working part-time. She needed to focus on her studies and the money I sent allowed her to do that.

Lola could not afford to help out. She already struggled to pay her bills.

My sisters relied on me. I could not let them down.

After pouring the fresh pineapple juice over the cake, I sat down, turned off the music, then called Lola. She would help me to make sense of this difficult situation.

The phone rang out. I was about to hang up when she answered.

'Hello? What's wrong?' Lola croaked like she'd just woken up.

'*Mierda!*' I winced. 'Sorry. I forgot about the time difference. Everything is fine. I will let you go back to bed.'

'You've woken me up now, so talk!'

'What time is it there?'

'Five in the morning.'

'Sorry.'

'How's Jamaica?'

'Beautiful,' I said.

'Looks like it! The photos you sent made me well jel.'

'*Jel?*' I frowned.

'It's slang for jealous over here. And you looked *very* cosy with Jasmine in that Dunn's River Falls picture. Has she finally given in to your charms?'

'Not exactly. But now I do believe that she likes me.'

'That's great!' She paused. 'Isn't it?'

'*Sí.*' I blew out a breath. 'But it is hard. I have not been completely honest with you. When I told you that we both worked at the hotel, I did not tell you that she is kind of my boss...'

'What?' Lola shouted. 'Hold on. I need to get out of bed to have this conversation otherwise I'll wake up John.' I heard the sound of a door closing. 'I'm really happy that you're starting to think about dating again, Ale, but someone from *management*? That's risky, dude.'

'Dude?'

'*That's* what you took from that sentence? The fact that I used the word *dude*?'

In my defence, it was the first time I had heard her use that word.

'I know it is risky.' I sighed, finally commenting on the important part of what she had said.

'You worked so hard to get that job. And it pays really well. If you lose it, you won't be able to help Evita and you're so close to achieving your dream of becoming head chef.'

'I know, but I cannot stop thinking about her.'

Lola groaned down the phone. She could tell this was bad.

After a few beats, she finally spoke.

'And does she know that you like her?'

'*Sí.* I told her.'

'You *told* her? *Puta madre!*' She swore. 'Why did you do that?'

'You know that I like to speak my mind.'

'Yes, but there's a time and a place for that, bruv! What did she say? She could report you to HR!'

'She said that it is not a good idea. That our boss, Hazel, will not be happy. I think she is worried because two workers just got sacked for fucking.'

'What?' she shouted again. 'You didn't tell me *that*! Otherwise I never would've suggested you ask Jasmine out! I thought if she worked in a different department, it'd be fine, but now you've told me she's your boss *and* that the company sacks people that shag each other, that changes *everything*!'

'They were fucking when they should have been working. And they got caught. We would be careful.'

'I'm sure they thought *they* were being careful too! Seriously, Ale! You know I want you to find love again. I want you to be happy. But there are four freaking billion women in the world. Four *billion*! You're hot, you're a great person and you cook like an angel. There's no shortage of single women who'd kill to have a man like you. So there's no reason to choose the one who could ruin your career and everything you've worked for. Just do your job over there and nothing more. *Vale?*'

'*Vale.*' I blew out a breath.

'I'm *serious*! Don't make me fly to Jamaica and cut your dick off!'

Lola was not joking. The only thing that would stop her would be getting the money for the flight. But she was resourceful, so she would find a way.

'*Tranquila*,' I said.

'Don't tell me to calm down! I'm trying to save you from making the biggest mistake of your life!'

'Understood.' I nodded down the phone even though she could not see me. 'And you? How is everything over there?'

'Same old, same old. Evita might be coming for lunch on Sunday. Maybe we can video call? At an acceptable hour, though. Not when I'm in a deep sleep having sexy dreams about Idris Elba like I was before you decided to wake me up.'

'Why are you dreaming about Idris Elba? Should you not be dreaming about John, your husband?'

'John is aware that I dream of Idris and he understands. He said if he wasn't straight, he'd probably dream about Idris too.'

'Right...'

There was only one woman I dreamt of these days and if I was with her, there was no way I would be dreaming about anyone else. Not even a famous movie star.

'I'll text you at the weekend to let you know what time Evita is coming.'

'*Vale. Duerme bien.*'

'Sleep well too. And don't forget: keep your dick away from Jasmine! Love you!' She hung up.

As I cleared up the kitchen, I thought about what Lola had said. She was right. It was too risky. There was a strong attraction between Jasmine and me, but I could not pursue it. It was true that there were billions of other women in the world I should wait to find a connection with one of them instead.

After I lost Freya, I thought I would never be interested in another woman ever again. But I was wrong. I had very strong feelings for Jasmine. So if I was able to find two women that I liked, then in time, I would find someone else. I just had to be patient.

Right now, it was time to focus on my career. Then in a year or two, I could start thinking about a relationship.

Just as Lola reminded me, there was a time and a place for expressing your feelings and now was not the time. Jasmine had repeatedly told me that she did not wish to pursue anything so I would respect her wishes. I would not tell her how I felt about her again.

From now on, everything I said or did around Jasmine would be strictly professional.

Time for a fresh start.

I picked up a knife, cut into the cake, then slid a small piece into my mouth.

Madre mía.

It tasted like heaven. I squeezed my eyes shut. The balance of pineapple and the coconut was perfect. The rum was not too strong. I would definitely like to make this for the head chef when he returned and see if he agreed that this could be a contender for the menu.

Next, I would need to experiment with what to serve it with. Perhaps a scoop of vanilla ice cream, or some homemade coconut ice cream? That would be less overpowering than a traditional rum and raisin flavour. But maybe that would be too much coconut?

I would be interested to hear what the Jamaican chef thought.

I was looking forward to learning from him and exchanging ideas for the menu.

Jasmine would be so happy to know how well the cake she made had turned out. For some reason, she seemed to believe that she could not cook or bake, but this showed that she was wrong.

She needed to taste this cake. If this was a few hours ago, I would not have hesitated to take it to her room.

But I had just promised myself that I would keep my distance. That I would not see Jasmine unless it was absolutely necessary. So that was exactly what I intended to do.

18

JASMINE

A loud knock at the door made me jump off the bed. I'd been trying to distract myself by reading a book so I wouldn't keep having flashbacks about my conversation with Alejandro in the kitchen earlier. But seeing as my favourite genre was romance, it wasn't exactly helping to extinguish the flames of desire. Instead it was fanning them.

I could still picture the way he looked at me: the need burning in his eyes.

My first thought was that it was Alejandro at the door.

He was very determined, so although I'd told him I wasn't interested, a man like him didn't seem like the type to give up easily.

Maybe he'd come to convince me to throw caution to the wind and give in to our urges.

But then I heard his front door slam and the sound of the shower in his bathroom next door switch on at the same time that there was another knock at the door. So unless he'd developed the ability to clone himself, I knew it couldn't be him.

'Room service,' a woman with a thick Jamaican accent called out.

That was strange. I hadn't ordered room service. Room service didn't even exist, because apart from the builders, Nadine and a couple of housekeeping and admin staff, Alejandro and I were the only people who worked at the hotel whilst it was being renovated.

After tightening my dressing-gown belt around my waist, I went and opened the door. Sure enough, it was a member of staff, clutching a tray.

'Good evening,' the lady who I didn't recognise said. 'This is for you, ma'am. Have a good night.'

'Thank you, you too.' I took the tray then kicked the door shut.

There were two plates on the tray. One large, one small, both covered with silver cloches. I lifted off the first one and saw slices of jerk chicken and sweet potato mash neatly arranged on a plate, steam rising to show that it had been freshly heated. Then I lifted off the second cloche and saw a slice of pineapple and coconut sponge cake.

My heart squeezed and it was then that I spotted a piece of paper on the tray beside it. I opened it up.

Jasmine,

    You did not finish your dinner and tomorrow is an important day. You will need your strength.

    The cake is delicious – just as I know it would be. You are an excellent baker.

    Sleep well.

    A

Butterflies filled my stomach and my knees turned to jelly. I quickly placed the tray on my bed, then flopped down on the mattress.

I couldn't believe he'd sent me my leftovers and the cake. I was gutted when I'd left because I'd really wanted to see how it'd turned out. So to hear Alejandro, one of the finest chefs I knew, say that it was delicious, especially given my poor culinary track record, made me feel happier than a child on Christmas morning.

He was right. I was starving. Walking away from his food wasn't easy.

After shamelessly shovelling down the rest of my dinner, I took a sip of water, then picked up the dessert fork, ready to dive into the cake.

A flash of doubt flew into my mind. Maybe it wasn't delicious and he was just being kind to make me feel better. But then I remembered, Alejandro was a man who spoke his mind. If it wasn't good, he probably wouldn't have sent it to me at all.

I sectioned off a small piece, then slid the fork into my mouth.

Oh. My. God.

It was *divine*.

I couldn't believe that I, Little Miss Can't Cook, Won't Cook had actually baked a cake that was edible. Actually, *edible* didn't even begin to describe how tasty it was. The sponge was light and fluffy and the blend of coconut and pineapple was to die for.

Of course, I couldn't take all of the credit. This was a team effort. It was Alejandro who'd come up with the recipe, measured out the ingredients, and shown me what to do, so my contribution was minimal, but it still made me feel amazing. Like I'd really achieved something. It was a small win, but I'd take it all the same.

And it was with that feeling of pride that I drifted off to sleep.

* * *

I woke up naturally without my alarm. This would be my fourth full day here, so I was finally getting into a routine. The jet lag had gone and I was feeling much fresher.

Today was my day off, so I'd arranged to see my grandad. Bob was meeting me at reception, so after eating a banana from the fruit bowl I had in my room, I headed down to meet him.

'Miss Jasmine!' He smiled. *'Yuh never tell me say yuh bake cake? It nice yuh know!'*

'You tasted the cake?' I frowned. Then I realised that Alejandro must've have given him some.

'Ya mon!'

'I did too.' Nadine appeared beside me. 'Alejandro brought me a slice earlier and *girl*, you got skills! It was delicious!'

It was sweet of them to say such lovely things. I'd thank Alejandro later. Via text would be best.

After our conversation in the kitchen last night, clearly he'd got the message and realised it was better for us to keep our distance. That was obviously why he'd sent someone to deliver the food to my room instead of just bringing it himself.

I was relieved that he'd decided against coming with me to see my grandad today. If I was being completely honest, I was a little disappointed too, but it was for the best. It'd be fine with just Bob and me.

'I didn't really do much,' I said, thinking how kind it was for Alejandro to share the cake with them. 'I just followed Alejandro's instructions.'

'She is being modest,' a deep, sexy voice sounded behind me. I turned to see Alejandro striding towards us, looking hotter than a truckload of jalapenos in a pair of jean shorts and crisp white T-shirt. 'Jasmine is an excellent baker. I am worried for my job now!' He smiled at me.

'Th-thanks,' I stuttered. Anyone else would've downplayed my contribution and taken the credit for themselves. But not Alejandro. He knew I was insecure about my baking skills and used the opportunity to boost my confidence.

'Big up yuhself.' Bob held out his hand in a fist bump. I did the same, and grinned as our fists connected.

'We should get going. I hope you two have a good day.' I waved to Nadine and Alejandro. Bob climbed into the driver's seat.

'Enjoy!' Nadine said before leaving. But Alejandro didn't move.

'I am coming with you,' he said.

'But I thought we'd agreed to—'

'I am coming with you. As your *colleague*. Nothing more. I agreed to come because I think it is better that you have someone with you. I will not break that promise. But I want you to know that I listened to what you said last night and you are right. It was wrong of me to express my feelings. You do not have to worry about me doing that any more. I am sorry for making you uncomfortable. It will not happen again.'

Normally, Alejandro would open the car door for me. But this time, he didn't. He went straight to the passenger side opposite to where I was standing and slid onto the backseat.

Looked like he was doing exactly what I'd asked.

He was keeping his distance.

He was keeping things between us strictly professional.

I knew it was for the best. It was 100 per cent the right thing to do.

So why the hell did I feel so disappointed?

19

ALEJANDRO

I was proud of myself. After speaking to Lola last night, today I was thinking more sensibly.

It was wrong of me to pursue Jasmine. We were both here to work, not fuck.

Did I think about her when I returned to my room and went in the shower? *Sí*.

Did I dream about her? A little.

And did I think she looked beautiful this morning? Definitely.

But Rome was not built in a day. I could not just turn off my feelings completely within a few hours. The important thing was that I would no longer act on them.

'So your grandad does not know we are coming?' I said, breaking the silence.

Rather than staring at Jasmine, to make things easier, I looked out of the window.

The sky wasn't bright blue like it normally was. It was grey and cloudy. Hopefully, it would clear soon and the sun would shine through.

'No,' she replied with a little surprise in her voice. Perhaps she was expecting me to flirt or say something suggestive, but like I had said to her earlier, I was just here today as a colleague. 'He doesn't have a mobile, only a house phone, and he rarely answers that.'

'And it is a small town that we will go to, *sí*?'

'Yes, it's in the countryside.'

'That is good. If he is not at home, then it will be easier to find him. It is unlikely that he will go far.'

'I hope so. It'd be a shame to travel all that way for it to be a wasted journey.'

'Whatever happens, it will not be a waste. You will know that you tried to rebuild that connection. And it will be an adventure. You will get to see another part of this beautiful country.'

'I like your way of looking at it.'

When I turned to look at Jasmine, she was smiling and my chest instantly expanded. If I was going to keep my thoughts professional, I needed to keep my eyes on the views outside.

As Bob continued driving and introduced us to some songs by a Jamaican reggae artist called Protoje, Jasmine told me more about her memories of her grandad.

'I loved that he used to always call me half pint.'

'Like the milk?'

'Yes! Because I was short. Obviously because I was only a little girl. But even when I grew taller, that was still his nickname for me.'

'Do you mind me asking why your family lost contact with him?' If I was going to meet him, it would be helpful to know the reason.

She took a deep breath.

'If it is too personal, you do not have to tell me.'

'No, it's okay. It's just… my mum was close to my grandma, so she was really upset when my grandad got married again, not long after my grandma passed away. She felt like it was a betrayal.'

A concrete lump formed in my throat and my heart thumped.

Jasmine could not know this, but what she had just said hit a nerve because those were feelings that I had wrestled with.

For so long after Freya passed, I never thought that I could ever think about dating another woman. It seemed like it would be a betrayal of our relationship. Like I was being unfaithful to her and her memory. But with time and lots of conversations with Lola, who was Freya's best friend, I was slowly starting to feel like I had to move on. That Freya would want me to be happy again.

'How soon did he remarry?'

'A year later.'

'I see. And was he happy?'

'He seemed like he was in a photo I saw. We didn't go to the wedding. He was adamant that it wasn't planned, that they just fell in love, but Mum was devastated and said that we had to cut all ties with him. I was heartbroken.'

'How long ago was this?'

'About five years ago. He always sends me a card and photo on my birthday, which is sweet. But it's not the same. I miss Granny, but she's gone, so there's nothing I can do. Grandad is still here and I want him to be happy. I miss him.'

'I understand,' I said. I was glad Jasmine had agreed to make this trip and really hoped that she would get the chance to see him.

Jasmine turned to look out of the window. I sensed that she needed some time to gather her thoughts, so I decided not to speak.

The further Bob drove, the greyer the sky became. Then it started to rain.

It was to be expected. When I looked online, it said that October was one of the months with the highest rainfall. I was glad that at least we'd missed the peak months for hurricanes in August and September.

'The rain's coming down quite hard,' Jasmine called out to Bob. 'Are we still okay to drive out to the countryside?'

'No problem, mon!' Bob said.

But as we continued driving, I understood Jasmine's concern.

The windscreen wipers were on the highest setting, but they could not clear the rain away fast enough and the longer we drove, the less stable the roads looked.

We were no longer driving on motorways or modern, tarmacked roads. We were climbing a steep mountain, deep in the countryside where the roads were just muddy tracks.

'We're really high up!' Jasmine looked out of the window and winced. 'Is this the only route?'

'Mi waan tuh tek anedda road, buh di rain washed eh weh laas week!'

'I'm sorry...' Jasmine paused. 'Did you just say you wanted to take another road, but that the rain washed it away last week?'

'Ya mon. Dat a wah mi seh!' Bob confirmed.

I looked at Jasmine and saw the panic all over her face.

'So when there's a lot of rain, for example, like how heavy it's raining now, roads just... *wash away*?'

'Ya mon,' Bob said casually.

'Oh my God!' Jasmine gripped the edge of the seat.

Her eyes bulged and her body tensed. I thought that she was scared when we were climbing Dunn's River Falls, but now she looked terrified.

My first instinct was to reach out and hold her hand, like I did before, but then I remembered: *boundaries.*

I could not touch her any more. It was agreed. I had made a promise to myself. And I had told her I was only here as a colleague. I could not go back on my word.

'We will be fine,' I said softly, hoping that would reassure her.

There may have been a chance that could have helped. But when we spotted a minibus coming towards us, trying to squeeze down the same narrow stretch of road and I saw Jasmine throw her hands over her eyes, I knew it would take more than a few words to calm her.

'There's no way we can *both* stay on this road. It's too tight! We're going to go off the edge!' Her voice was full of panic. 'Look at the drop! Oh my God! We're going to die!'

When I leant over to look out of her side of the window, I instantly understood her concerns. She was right. Bob's car was already dangerously close to the edge. There were no barriers. And even with the rain lashing against the window, I could see that the drop was steep. If we went over the edge, there was no way we would survive.

Mierda.

The road was muddy and slippery. I could not see how either Bob or the minibus would be able to reverse safely.

'Rhaatid!' Bob shouted as the minibus got closer. His tone of voice was unusually downbeat and shocked, so I knew he was saying something like *damn*. This was not a good sign.

But it was when Jasmine jumped over to my side of the car and gripped my arm that I was certain we were in big trouble...

20

JASMINE

Of all the ways I thought I would die, I never imagined it would be from falling off the edge of a Jamaican mountain.

But yet, here we were: inches away from plummeting what had to be at least a hundred feet. It was hard to tell exactly because the rain was coming down so fast.

When I'd first raised my concerns to Bob, he was his usual *no problem, everything is irie* self.

Then when he saw how close the minibus was and started swearing, I knew he was worried too.

Watching as the car got closer and closer to the edge was torture. That was why I'd leapt over to Alejandro's side of the car, grabbed his arm and buried my head in his chest.

If I only had minutes left on this earth, at least I didn't want to be alone.

As I gripped onto his muscular arm and breathed in his delicious scent, I instantly felt better. Still terrified, but better. This was a more pleasant way to meet my end.

Bob beeped his horn furiously and cursed the man in the

minibus who was still moving forward, determined to squeeze past, even if it meant we'd go tumbling off the cliff's edge.

'I should call my parents!' I bolted up. 'To say goodbye!' I pulled out my phone. There was zero reception. 'No!' I screamed in frustration. I didn't want to go like this. It was too soon. There was still so much I wanted to do with my life.

There were dozens of countries I wanted to explore. Hundreds more experiences I wanted to have.

And I wasn't going to lie. I hoped that maybe in a year or so, once I was settled into the new role I was still hoping to secure, that I could start dating again.

I'd hoped that I could find a hot, sexy, kind, funny man to be with.

To kiss.

To fuck.

I couldn't believe I was going to kick the bucket without having kissed another man since divorcing my husband.

This was so sad.

'Wah di raas wrang wid yuh?' Bob shouted at the man as our car skidded.

I gripped Alejandro's hand and looked up at him.

Fear was etched across his face.

Normally, in a situation like this, he would've tried to reassure me or held my hand. But I could tell he knew the situation was dire too.

Alejandro knew this was it. This really was the end.

We probably had seconds left.

If were lucky, a few minutes. Tops.

Shit.

That was when it hit me.

I could either waste my last breath panicking and miserable as I waited for the Grim Reaper to tap me on my shoulder. Or I could let Alejandro take my breath away and leave this earth with a bang.

A minute ago, I'd said that I'd wanted to live so I could find a hot, sexy man to kiss. But I had one right here. One that told me last night that he wanted me.

I'd walked away. Told him it could never happen. And that was true.

But now everything was different. Now we were about to perish, it didn't matter about the position of power, unprofessionalism stuff.

Life was short and I had minutes left to live it.

Before I had the chance to change my mind, I leant forward and crushed my lips onto Alejandro's.

His eyes bulged.

Realising what I'd just done, I quickly pulled away.

'Sorry! I should've asked first! It's just that, we're about to die and I didn't want to go without kissing you. Do you mind?'

Alejandro looked at me in a daze like he couldn't believe what I'd just said.

'I...' He paused. 'I do not mind...'

That was all I needed to hear.

I pushed my mouth on his once again.

God, his lips were so soft. I moved my mouth hungrily, but then realised that Alejandro wasn't engaging.

I was kissing him, but he wasn't kissing me back.

Now I didn't know what was worse. Death from falling off a cliff or dying from the embarrassment of kissing a guy you thought was into you, but realising mid-snog that he wasn't.

This wasn't how it was supposed to be!

All the times I'd fantasised about locking lips with Alejandro, it'd been wild and passionate. But this was quite literally mortifying.

'Sorry.' I pulled away. 'I thought you said you liked me, but I understand it must be confusing because I told you last night it was inappropriate and now here I am kissing you. It's just that... I want to live! I don't want to die with regrets!'

Alejandro dragged his hand over his face.

'Fuck,' he muttered, before swearing to himself repeatedly in Spanish.

I was just about to tell him it was no big deal when he grabbed the back of my head, then pressed his lips onto mine with full force.

Good Lord.

The next thing I knew, my lips had parted and Alejandro's tongue was flicking hungrily against mine.

A feral groan flew from my mouth.

This was *exactly* how I'd imagined what kissing Alejandro would be.

Our mouths moved desperately against each other's. As the kiss became more wild and frantic, I ran my hands through his hair, then down his broad, muscular back.

What felt like a million volts of electricity surged through me. My body temperature rocketed and my blood turned to molten lava.

If kissing was an Olympic sport, this man would be taking home the gold medal.

Alejandro's hands roamed down my back, then moved across to skim the side of my breasts and as his fingers began to flick my nipple, which was now harder than stone, another feral moan of pleasure escaped my lips.

This kiss was... explosive, passionate and *hot*.

This kiss was *everything*.

I'd definitely made the right decision. This was the perfect way to go.

Alejandro's hand dropped to my legs then slid up my dress.

'Fuck, yes.' I moaned into his mouth as he continued devouring me with his lips.

Ordinarily, I'd be bothered about the fact that we weren't alone in the car. But this felt so good, I didn't care.

If we kept on going like this, it wouldn't be long until we were fucking on this backseat. The jerking movements wouldn't be good considering we were teetering on the cliff's edge. But our fate was already sealed, so if we were going to go out, we might as well go out on a high.

Everything I'd worried so much about just hours ago, like being professional, presenting the right image and getting my promotion didn't matter any more.

It was funny how you got a new perspective and realised what was really important when your life flashed in front of you.

Just as Alejandro's fingers slid underneath my knickers, Bob cried out.

'*Ya mon!*'

Alejandro and I both pulled away quickly and when I looked ahead, we were driving down a clear road.

The rain had stopped and the minibus was nowhere in sight.

'Where did the bus go?' Alejandro called out, clearly as shocked as I was.

'*Mi did tell 'im tuh dressback!*'

'So he reversed?' I asked.

'*Ya mon!*'

'So we're not going to die?' I added, my throat suddenly feeling dry.

'*Nuh!*' Bob laughed. '*Everyting irie!*' he repeated.

But as I glanced sheepishly at Alejandro and quickly pulled down my dress which had been hitched up around my waist, I knew that everything was not *irie*.

Not in the slightest.

Of course, I was glad that we'd survived. That was amazing.

The thing that was far from amazing though was that I'd just kissed the man I worked with.

The guy that was off limits.

The guy who was technically a junior member of staff.

We'd kissed. He'd touched my breasts.

He was seconds away from touching my pussy and doing God knows what else in the backseat of a car being paid for by my employer. And I'd encouraged it, all because I thought it was our last moments on earth.

But now we were very much alive.

As for my career, after that reckless act, it was doomed.

Fuck.

I thought that going off the edge of a cliff was my biggest problem.

Turned out that now we'd survived, I was in even bigger shit than I could've ever imagined.

21

ALEJANDRO

I had fucked up.

I told myself that I would not cross the line with Jasmine. I said that I would keep things professional between us.

But instead, I had kissed her.

Well, technically she kissed me.

The important thing was, *we kissed*. And because I had gone against my word and put my career at risk, I should regret it.

Right now, I should feel disappointed in myself for not being able to resist my urges, just hours after making a commitment to control them.

But although I knew I should not have done it, the truth was, I was not sorry that it happened.

How could I when it felt so incredible?

Kissing Jasmine was everything that I had wished for and more.

Her lips were softer than butter. Her taste was sweeter than the most delicious dessert. And her skin. *Madre mía*. I did not have words to describe how silky it was.

Feeling her lips on mine and the sensation of our tongues

flicking against each other's was enough to make me hard. But when I touched her nipples, which were like stone, I nearly lost my mind.

And I could not even think about how much my cock strained against my shorts when my fingers slid up towards her pussy.

Knowing that, if we had not been interrupted, I would have got to slide my hand into her panties and really feel her was enough to make me explode.

Something told me that I would be visualising what would have happened in my fantasies tonight and for many more nights to come.

'I... I'm so sorry about...' Jasmine stuttered, a look of horror and embarrassment etched over her face. 'I thought we were going to... I thought we were about to go off the edge of the cliff. I shouldn't have...'

'*No pasa nada.*' I waved my hand dismissively to let her know it was not a problem. That was not completely true, because I was not sure that I would *ever* recover from that kiss, but I did not want her to feel bad. 'It is common for people to act differently when they believe it is the end of their life.'

Once again, I was not sure if that was true, but it sounded like it could be.

When Jasmine gripped my arm, I knew she must be terrified. But I did not ever think that she was so scared, it would lead to her kissing me.

To say that I was shocked would be an understatement. That was why when it happened, I froze.

Of course, like Jasmine, I was afraid. But as my fate was out of my hands, I did not worry about it. I just thought, *what will be, will be.* That is why at first, it felt wrong for me to reciprocate the kiss. Jasmine was doing it because she was anxious, not because she really wanted me. If another man was sitting here with her, perhaps she would have done the same.

But then I saw the hurt and rejection in her eyes when I did not kiss her back and I did not want to make her upset. If this was what she needed to calm her, I could not refuse.

That is not to say that it was a purely selfless act. Of course I wanted to kiss her too. I had dreamt about it for months. So I ignored the voice of reason in my head that was telling me not to and kissed her.

And like I said, I did not regret it. But it was clear from Jasmine's reaction now that she did.

Bob pulled over to take a piss, so I was left alone with Jasmine.

'Sorry again.' She turned to face me. 'I acted completely unprofessionally. I only kissed you because I thought we were going to die and... it's been a while since... I haven't kissed a man since my divorce and I suppose I didn't want to leave this earth without... anyway. It's no excuse. I hope you can forgive my lapse in judgement, but if you feel you need to report me to HR, I completely understand.' She hung her head.

'Of course I will not report you!' I replied, surprised that she could even think that. Especially considering I had made it clear that I was very attracted to her. 'I kissed you back.'

'Under duress.' She scoffed. 'You looked horrified.'

'I was just surprised. I was not sure if I was having another fantasy. Once I realised that I was not dreaming, I think it was very clear that I enjoyed every moment of kissing you.' I growled.

Jasmine bit her lip. She was about to say something else but then Bob returned to the car and announced that we were not far away.

We spent the rest of the journey in silence, with only the sound of Bob's music blaring through the speakers. The rain had completely stopped now and to avoid the awkwardness, I fixed my gaze on the window, taking in the sights of the endless green fields and variations of trees along the dusty roads.

Bob pulled in front of a small house.

'*Wi deh yah,*' he said.

'This is it?' Jasmine asked.

'*Ya mon.*' Bob nodded.

'Oh. Okay. Thanks.' Jasmine opened her car door. 'Well, here goes.'

'You want me to come with you?' I asked.

'Um,' she hesitated. 'Let me go and knock to see if he's here first.'

'*Vale.*' I nodded.

'Wish me luck,' she said.

'Good luck,' I replied, hoping that she would not need it.

22

JASMINE

I stared at the computer screen. I was in the Jamaican Love Hotel office and there was something I was supposed to be researching, but I'd completely forgotten what.

This wasn't the first time that had happened this morning. I'd been at my desk for almost an hour and got zero work done. Why? Because I couldn't stop thinking about *that kiss* yesterday on the way to my grandad's house.

It'd played on repeat all night in my mind.

My brain alternated from feeling the humiliation and shame of what I'd done and the possible ramifications to pure, unadulterated lust and desire as I relived just how hot it was.

The sensation of Alejandro's lips on mine was electric. It was like I'd been in a coma for years and he'd given me the kiss of life. Every atom in my body reacted like a jack springing out of its box.

I'd been desperately trying to get those memories out of my head, but it was proving impossible.

After hours of being unable to sleep, I was tempted to use my vibrator, but then worried that Alejandro would hear the buzzing through the wall. I needed to invest in one of those modern, silent ones.

So anyway, here I was spending time that I should be working, daydreaming about Alejandro's lips being pressed on mine.

When we'd arrived at my grandad's house, I was relieved. Firstly, because we'd made it there safely, but secondly, because I knew seeing him would make everything else fade into insignificance. There was no way I'd be able to focus on a kiss when I was reunited with my beloved grandfather. But despite ringing several times, there was no answer.

I waited for a while. But with nothing to do but think, my mind had returned to that irresponsible kiss. I started freaking out, so called Stella in a panic. I only managed to get a few words out, telling her that something had happened between me and Alejandro before the phone cut out. Seeing as we were in the middle of nowhere, it wasn't a surprise that reception was so bad.

Then I remembered she said she was going to Madrid for a long weekend, so I decided I shouldn't burden her with my indiscretions, and didn't call back.

Just as I was contemplating whether I should wander down the street to try and find Grandad, one of the neighbours arrived home and said Grandad was attending a wedding out of town and would be gone all day, so I'd left. Now that I thought about it, I should've left a message or a note with the neighbour, but after what happened in the car, I wasn't thinking straight.

This time though, when I got into the car I had the sense to tell Bob and Alejandro I was going to sleep. If we were going to have any more hairy, cliff-edge incidents, I'd rather not be awake to witness them. And I wasn't going to lie: I couldn't bear the thought of a car journey where I might have to look at Alejandro.

I knew that if I did, I'd start imagining the softness of his lips, the way my body reacted when he touched my nipples and when he...

The sound of a video call ring on my computer jolted me out of my thoughts. That must be Hazel. She said she'd be calling for an update. But of course, I'd been too busy fantasising about Alejandro slipping his fingers inside my knickers to remember.

'Hazel, hi!' I said brightly as I accepted the call and her face flashed up on the screen. 'How are you?'

'Ugh,' Hazel sighed, squeezing her eyes shut in despair. 'I'm in the middle of dealing with *another* employee crisis.'

'Oh, no!' I said, genuinely concerned. 'What's happened?'

'I've had to fire two more staff for inappropriate behaviour. Caught them shagging in one of the bedrooms. *Honestly!* It's like an epidemic! I've managed hotels all around the world and never seen anything like it! Does no one know how to just do their job any more without engaging in extra-curricular activities? Gosh, I wish there were more employees like you, Jasmine. At least I know I can trust you to never let me down.'

I swallowed hard as I tried to mask the guilt and shame crawling across my skin. Thank God mindreading wasn't a thing, otherwise she'd know that just minutes ago, I'd been fantasising about fucking my colleague.

My stomach twisted.

Hazel thought I was a model employee that didn't engage in extra-curricular activities with my co-workers. Little did she know that less than twenty-four hours ago, I had my tongue stuck down Alejandro's throat whilst he flicked his thumb over my rock-hard nipples and was about to let him stroke my clit on the backseat of a car with the driver present.

Shit.

For a second, I wondered if somehow, Hazel knew. Bob wouldn't say anything, would he?

No. He was too laid-back to tell tales. And I *think* he was too busy concentrating on the road and how to keep us alive to realise that Alejandro and I were playing tonsil hockey.

At least I hoped so...

'Goodness!' I said, trying to play it cool and avoid commenting on the fact that she thought she could trust me. 'Who was it?'

'One of the female Cuisine Champions and the Water Warrior.' She rolled her eyes.

At first, I thought the names were silly. I mean, why not just say waitress and the pool guy? But I quickly realised that the titles mattered. They added a sense of pride and importance to everyone's roles.

'Oh, that's a shame. Did they do it during working hours?' I asked, not really certain of what else to say.

'The horny idiots did it straight afterwards! That's how I found out. I noticed that the girl's awful car was still parked in the car park but her shift ended an hour earlier. So I made enquiries. And someone said they saw her heading in the direction of one of the old rooms.'

'Well, at least they did it outside of working hours and didn't use one of the renovated guest rooms.'

'That's not the point!' Hazel slammed her hand on the desk. 'They should *not* be fraternising together at all. We have to uphold standards! Without standards and rules, where would we be in life? Tell me, Jasmine!'

'Um.' I hadn't realised she actually wanted me to answer. I thought it was just a rhetorical question. 'Of course, standards are very important.'

'*Exactly!* Thank God, you understand! Anyway, how are things there? What new activities have you found to add to the list?'

'Well, I discovered an authentic reggae dance class that I think could be a fun way to bring couples together.'

'Good. What else? Have you visited any of the other locations recommended by Hortense?'

'I was looking at a place she suggested called Rick's Café – a cliffside bar restaurant in Negril. Apparently, it has an incredible view of the sunset.'

'Great!'

'People also like to go there to jump off the cliffs into the water below the café. Which *could* be good for thrill-seekers.'

'You must go and check it out.'

Just as I was about to reply, I heard the office door open. I looked up and saw that it was Alejandro.

Oh God.

He looked so good, I wanted to weep.

His hair was slightly damp, like he'd just stepped out of the shower. His golden skin glowed and when he smiled at me, my stomach did more backflips than an Olympic gymnast.

Why did he have to be so bloody attractive?

'Alejandro!' I said loudly to announce to Hazel that he'd just walked in. 'I'm just on a call with Hazel.'

Alejandro opened his mouth to speak, but before he could say anything, Hazel interjected.

'Alejandro!' she called out. 'I was going to call you next, but now I don't have to. Come here.'

He walked behind the desk and as his delicious scent surrounded me, I tried to keep my composure.

'*Hola*, Hazel. *Cómo estás?*'

'*Muy bien*,' she replied. 'So, I was just talking to Jasmine about a place called Rick's Café.'

'I know it!' he said excitedly. 'It is famous for the cliff-jumping of course, but they also serve traditional Jamaican food and interesting cocktails.'

'That's settled then!' Hazel clapped her hands together. 'The two of you must go. It'll be good market research. See what you can find out there too, Jasmine. See if they do anything special to foster romance.'

'Got it.' I nodded. 'I'll do some research and make arrangements to travel there tomorrow.'

'No!' Hazel slammed her hand on the desk. I really wished she wouldn't keep doing that. It always made me jump. 'Go today.'

'It's actually in Negril, so it'll take a while to get there.'

'I think it takes about three hours,' Alejandro added.

'That's fine! What's the time in Jamaica right now?' Hazel asked.

'Just after ten,' I said, my stomach tensing.

'If you set off now, you can head there for a late lunch to sample the food, then you'll have plenty of time to observe the safety of the diving before sunset, then your driver can take you back afterwards.'

'No problem,' I said enthusiastically despite the fact that I was groaning inside.

I was struggling to get that electrifying kiss out of my mind. The last thing I needed was to sit on the backseat again with Alejandro beside me for a three-hour car journey.

Then she wanted us to go to have lunch? That'd mean staring into each other's eyes and making conversation.

And if that wasn't enough, we'd have to watch a romantic sunset together.

Sweet Jesus.

Although I knew it wasn't her intention, it felt like Hazel was deliberately trying to drive me into Alejandro's arms. Or more realistically, drive me to climb onto his lap.

Give. Me. Strength.

23

JASMINE

So far, our journey to Negril had been a little awkward. Alejandro and I barely spoke. We stared out the windows, taking in the sights of the lush greenery, scrolled on our phones or chatted to Bob about the different reggae tunes he was playing. At least the music kept the atmosphere upbeat because he liked to sing along to the songs and his happiness was infectious.

'What music do you like?' Alejandro said.

At first, I thought he was asking Bob as we hadn't spoken for ages, but then I realised that we both knew that reggae was Bob's favourite and when I turned to face Alejandro, his eyes were fixed on me.

'Um...' I paused, thinking that I kind of preferred the journey when we weren't talking because then I wouldn't have to look at him and be reminded just how attractive he was. 'All sorts. Pop, reggae, hip hop, jazz, soul. Anything happy with a good beat or melody.'

'But what is your *favourite*?' Alejandro insisted. 'What do you listen to the most?'

'Probably 90s and 00s soul.'

'Like who?'

'Ah.' I chuckled. 'You probably wouldn't know the artists.'

'Why do you think that?' He frowned.

'Well, because you're young and maybe they weren't popular in Spain.'

'Hmm.' He rested his finger on his chin. 'Have you heard of the Beatles?'

'Of course!' I rolled my eyes.

'Or Bob Marley?'

'Come on!' I scoffed, thinking that was a stupid question. 'Even if I hadn't, I definitely would've by now!' I laughed, thinking about how many of his songs Bob played in the car.

'But you were not even alive when their music was popular.' He raised his eyebrow as if to make a point about my reference to him being too young.

'Touché.' I held my hands up. 'Sorry, I didn't mean to sound patronising. I just... you're absolutely right.'

I shouldn't have made that assumption. Of course it was possible to like music from a different era to when you grew up, but it just seemed unlikely; that was all I was trying to say.

'I also like 90s and 00s soul,' Alejandro said.

'Really?' I replied. 'Like who?'

'Mary J. Blige, Lauryn Hill, Destiny's Child...'

'No way!' My eyes widened. 'Mary and Lauryn are two of my favourites!'

'They are amazing,' he agreed. 'My sister used to listen to them a lot, so I started to enjoy their songs.'

I had no idea.

'And I love Lucy Pearl too,' I added, expecting him to ask who they were like some people did whenever I used to mention them, even at the height of their fame.

'*Sí.*' He nodded. 'It was a shame that they only did one album.'

My jaw dropped.

Alejandro really *did* know and like the same kind of music.

A lot of people could have named Destiny's Child. I mean, *hello*: that was Queen Beyoncé's group, so there probably weren't many people who didn't know about them.

Lauryn Hill and Mary J. Blige were also pretty successful. But like he'd just said, Lucy Pearl only did one album, which I played to death and I was also sad that they didn't do more music together.

'It really was a shame. What was your favourite track?' I said. It wasn't a test question. I genuinely wanted to know.

'That is difficult.' He rubbed his hand over his jaw. 'Obviously, the popular ones like "Dance Tonight", but I also liked "Good Love" very much.'

This was insane.

Was this man in my head right now? Had he hacked my playlist? I adored that song and the way it spoke about finding everlasting love.

'That's *also* one of *my* favourites!' I smiled and our eyes locked.

We stared at each other in silence. Never in a million years had I imagined that a man who was so much younger than me, grew up in another country and spoke a completely different language would share the same taste in music that I did.

His eyes really were beautiful. I loved how sometimes they were brown, but then other times they turned lighter, almost verging on green. How was that even possible?

I bit my lip and the sensation snapped me out of my trance. I shouldn't be staring into his eyes like this. It was making me think about things that I shouldn't.

Like how amazing he was.

Like how he wasn't just beautiful on the outside; he was also so kind and considerate. Making me breakfast on the first morning. Encouraging me to see my grandad. Bringing food to me after I walked out of the restaurant.

And looking into his gorgeous eyes was also making me think about things like how good that accidental kiss was and how much I wanted to do it again...

'"Don't Mess With My Man"!' I blurted out, then winced. It sounded as if I was warning another woman not to try anything with Alejandro. But that was ridiculous because he wasn't my man. And it didn't matter if maybe a part of me wished that in some other universe, it could be possible, because it was never going to happen. 'The song!' I corrected myself. 'I like that song too.'

'I understood what you meant.' He smiled and my traitorous stomach fluttered. 'I like it too. I have a playlist with a lot of their songs, Mary J. and other great artists. I can share it with you if you want?'

'I'd love that!' I beamed.

'Have you heard of ¿Téo?' he asked.

'No.'

'He is American with Columbian heritage and sings in Spanish and English. I like his songs. I can send those too.'

'That'd be great! I really like discovering new artists. Can't wait to listen! Maybe I'll send you some links to songs I like too?'

'*Sí!* Great idea.'

A warm feeling flooded my belly. Right now, I felt like I was one of the guests staying at the Love Hotel because sharing a playlist was one of the daily tasks we asked them to do.

I'd come up with the idea when I joined because I thought it would be a good way to help the couples bond.

Basically, every day, I asked them to add at least five songs that reflected their feelings about their partner, so that by the end of the experience, they'd have a soundtrack of how they both fell in love.

And it worked. I'd lost count of the number of guests who'd commented about how much they loved the playlists.

But at the time, I never imagined that I'd be the one sharing music with a man. And definitely not the younger man that I worked with.

It was fine, though. This wasn't the same thing. We were just two colleagues who surprisingly both shared a passion for music who'd decided to exchange playlists, that was all.

We weren't doing it to *bond*.

And we definitely weren't doing it to *fall in love*.

That would be silly. I'd already made a mistake kissing Alejandro in the car. So I definitely, absolutely, 100 per cent should *not* want to do it again.

At least that's what common sense was telling me.

But the question now was whether I was going to listen…

24

JASMINE

We'd arrived at Rick's Café. The red, gold and green circular plaque on the wall glowed in the sunshine.

After waving Bob off, we walked through towards the cliffside. I'd expected it to be popular and it really was.

In addition to the people standing by the edge in their swimsuits and trunks getting ready to jump, there were adults of all ages spread across every part of the grounds: by the pool that was located next to the bar, on both levels of the main building and in front of the stage which was presumably used for concerts.

'Wow. There are a lot of people!' Alejandro said, reading my mind. 'I am not surprised. They have won many accolades.'

'Really?' I asked. I'd planned to research the place this morning, but I got distracted thinking about a certain Spanish man's delicious lips...

'*Sí*.' he nodded. 'When I checked their website, it said that they were voted one of the top one thousand places to see before you die and one of the best bars in the world. I think they were also voted one of the sexiest bars in the Caribbean too.' His eyes darkened.

'Oh, right, yes.' I bit my lip. 'I can see that. Maybe it's a combination of the sun and the music.' I tilted my head to the dance floor area in front of the stage where there were a couple grinding to a reggae song which was playing loudly.

'I am going to get changed,' Alejandro announced.

'You're going to *jump*?' My eyes widened.

'*Sí!* I could not come here and not try. You do not want to?'

'I'll sit this out. I'm not great with heights at the best of times. I pushed myself to do Dunn's River Falls and the Caminito del Rey in Spain for our guests, but there were barriers there. Jumping voluntarily from a cliff's edge is a completely different story. I'm just here to observe.'

Just as the words left my mouth, I heard collective gasps from the crowd around us and saw people pointing towards the sky.

When I followed their gaze, I saw a man scaling a thin, willowy tree and standing on a platform at the top of a tree.

'*Genial!*' Alejandro cheered.

'I can't believe you're excited about the fact that a man is about to plunge from a very, very, high tree!' My eyes popped.

'Do not worry. He is sure to be one of the professionals. I read that they dive from around eighty-five feet into the water.'

'Bloody hell.' I gulped. Just thinking about it made my stomach bottom out.

Seconds later, the diver plunged into the water. I joined the crowds at the cliffside, my heart racing, hoping he'd be okay. Thankfully, soon afterwards, he emerged triumphantly from the water and everyone cheered.

'See! It is fine,' Alejandro said. 'Of course, normal people do not dive from the tree. They can jump from the side of the bar. There are three different heights: ten feet, twenty-five feet and thirty-five feet, so you do not have to do anything too scary. You are sure you do not want to try?'

'Positive,' I said without hesitation.

'*No pasa nada*. Perhaps you can take photos or a video for me?'

'Of course,' I agreed.

'*Gracias*. I will go to change now.'

After I'd gone to the bar to get some water, I spotted Alejandro by the cliffside and swallowed hard. His muscular chest and arms were even more chiselled than I'd remembered and the closer I got to him, the stronger the urge to run my hands all over his body became. *Shit*.

'Hey,' he said breezily. 'I will not be long. Can you look after my bag?'

'Okay.' I slid his rucksack on my back.

'*Gracias*. And remember to watch me and take pictures. I want to send them to my sisters.'

Watch him? That wouldn't be difficult. Whenever he was around, I could barely take my eyes off him.

'Will do,' I said casually.

I found a space that gave me a view of the various jumping levels and the sea below, then pulled out my phone. Alejandro hadn't given me his mobile to take photos, so I'd just have to take them on mine.

Based on how busy it was, I thought it'd take a while for Alejandro to get to jump, but soon afterwards, he'd moved to the front of the middle level. He looked up, his head swivelling from left to right as he tried to find me.

'I'm here!' I shouted. When he spotted me, his face broke into a smile, causing a basket of butterflies to erupt in my stomach. He waved and I did the same.

I quickly snapped some photos and he gave me a thumbs up before stepping forward to the edge, then jumping without an ounce of hesitation into the crystal-blue water.

My heart leapt into my throat, but my nerves subsided when I saw Alejandro rise to the surface of the water then lift his arm out to punch the air in triumph.

'You did it!' I cheered as I angled the phone to capture him swimming over to the ladder and climbing up it.

Seeing the way his wet trunks clung to his arse and capturing his muscular back sent my pulse racing. I wondered if he had any idea just how sexy he was.

I ended the recording quickly, scared that I'd accidentally let out a groan of pleasure, then slid my phone back into my bag.

Minutes later, Alejandro appeared beside me.

'That was incredible!' He beamed. He was glowing even more than usual. His brown eyes sparkled and his smile was wide. 'Seriously, you should try it!'

'I don't think I'm brave enough.'

'Do you have your bikini?'

'I have my swimming costume, but I bought it in case I wanted to go in the pool, not to *jump*.'

'It is up to you, but we are here, now. What if our bosses choose to add this to the itinerary and they ask you to work at the new hotel in Jamaica and you have to bring guests here? You will feel better knowing that you have tried it, no?'

That was true. I always liked to try activities so that I could share my own personal experience with our guests.

'I don't know...' I paused. 'I'm nervous.'

'If it helps, I will jump with you. I can hold your hand. Keep you safe.'

My heart fluttered. I didn't know why him saying that he'd keep me safe made me melt, when I was capable of looking after myself, but it did.

'And we can do it from the lowest level?'

'*Por supuesto*,' he nodded, confirming that'd be fine.

'Okay.'

After I'd got changed, I put our phones and credit cards in a waterproof bag, slid it over my neck then followed Alejandro to the first level.

My heart thumped loudly in my chest. I couldn't believe I was really going through with this.

Part of me hoped there'd be a queue to psyche myself up, but when we were able to walk straight to the edge, I reasoned it was probably better to just get it over and done with before I chickened out.

'Ready?' Alejandro asked, holding out his palm.

'Not really, but I'll give it a go!'

I slid my hand in his and fireworks exploded within me. There was something about being close to Alejandro that made me feel fearless. It was like he had some kind of superpower that instantly made me feel calm and completely safe.

The feminist in me wanted to cringe for thinking this, but somehow, when I was holding his hand, it was like I was capable of doing anything.

'After three: one, two, three, let's go!' he shouted and we both leapt off the cliff.

I'd love to say I played it cool, but I didn't. I screamed my head off like I was running from an axe murderer.

Yet, as we floated through the air before our bodies plunged into the water, adrenaline rocketed through my veins. It was then I realised that as well as being one of the most terrifying things I'd ever done, it was also one of the most exhilarating.

'You okay?' Alejandro asked as we surfaced from the water, still holding my hand.

'That was amazing!' I wiped the water from my eyes. 'Let's do it again!'

No one was more surprised than me to hear those words fly from my lips.

Miraculously, I voluntarily jumped into the water two more times. Each jump was just as exhilarating as the first. Who knew I was an adrenaline junkie?

Alejandro had asked if I felt brave enough to try the next level up, but I decided it was best to quit whilst I was ahead.

'I'm *so* thirsty!' I said as we returned to main area. 'Let's get some drinks and sit by the pool. What would you like?'

'Jamaican Viagra,' Alejandro said casually.

'Sorry, what?' My eyes flew from their sockets.

He was so matter-of-fact about it. I mean, I knew we'd had a connection and I definitely felt even closer to him after he helped me do that jump, but asking for Viagra was a bit presumptuous.

Firstly, I was surprised he thought I'd be able to just walk up to a bar and ask for it and secondly, judging by what I'd felt during our dance lesson, I wouldn't have thought that he needed it.

'I said I would like the Jamaican Viagra,' Alejandro repeated. 'It is a cocktail they have here.'

'Ohhhhh!' I blew out a breath.

'You thought I was asking you to go to a bar and ask for the *real* Viagra?' He laughed.

'Well, yeah...'

'No!' He smirked. 'I do not need any help getting hard.' Alejandro licked his lips and my pulse raced.

'Yes.' My eyes met his. 'I thought so.' Alejandro held my gaze. 'I better get the drinks. Looks like there's a queue,' I added quickly, desperate to break the spell and shut down the electricity that was pulsing between us.

'*Vale*,' he said. 'I will find us some seats.'

When I got to the bar and scanned the menu, I saw that Alejandro was right. There was indeed a cocktail called 'Front End Lifter AKA Jamaican Viagra' which was beer blended with white rum, rum cream, clear syrup and oatmeal topped with chocolate syrup.

There was also a drink called 'Sex With Rick'. Shame they didn't do a 'Sex With Alejandro' version, because I'd order that in a heartbeat.

God. I groaned internally. Trying to keep my thoughts PG was so hard. See what I mean? *Hard.*

The more time I spent with Alejandro, the more I wanted him.

In the end, I opted for the 'Jamaican Me Crazy' cocktail as it accurately described how I was feeling about my co-worker right now.

I sipped my drink and groaned with delight. It had three types of rum, banana liqueur and pineapple juice and slipped down very easily.

I spotted Alejandro by the pool area which was surrounded by different seating including dark wooden slated sun loungers and comfy-looking daybeds. There was a large *Rick's Café 1974* sign over a sheltered area. It was impressive that it had been around for over fifty years.

'Hey,' he said as I rested the drinks on a table between the two sun loungers he'd found. 'Which cocktail did you get?'

'Jamaican Me Crazy,' I said.

'That is funny!' Alejandro smiled and my stomach flipped. If only he knew how true it was.

An hour later, we were on our third cocktail and had moved to the stage area to watch a live reggae performance.

As the heavy baseline boomed around us and the alcohol zipped through my bloodstream, I felt the urge to dance. The vibe here was infectious. The atmosphere was buzzing with energy, laughter and happiness. I couldn't remember the last time I felt so free and so… alive.

'Should we dance?' Alejandro said. 'The music and the vibes are too good to waste by just sitting down.'

'I don't know if that's a good idea...' I took a long sip of my cocktail.

'Why?' Alejandro's eyebrows knitted together.

'Because last time, you got, y'know...'

'Hard?'

'Yes.' I tried to suppress a grin as I relived the moment.

'That is true. And if we dance together now, I cannot promise that it will not happen again. You are a beautiful woman and I am only human.' He smiled. 'But I understand if you would prefer not to take that risk.'

My whole body sparked.

I didn't know if it was the fact that he'd called me beautiful or because he'd mentioned the word *risk* which made it sound more exciting, but I felt so drawn to Alejandro.

I should absolutely *not* dance with him.

I should absolutely *not* want to feel his erection pressed against me.

And yet... it was all I could think about.

'Well, Nadine did say we should practise...'

'Exactly,' he said. 'And you know that she will ask us if we have.'

'Definitely. Plus it'd be a good way to test how good her lessons actually work in the real world. Without her supervision.'

'Very true.' Alejandro stood up and held out his hand.

Without hesitation, I took his hand as he led me out to the dance floor.

Alejandro stood behind me and gripped my hips and within seconds, I had my arse rubbing up against him.

We quickly found our rhythm and as I grinded into him,

Alejandro pulled me in closer, his solid body pressed firmly against mine.

It wasn't long before I felt his hardness and this time, when I did, I groaned with pleasure, pushing my head back.

'Fuck, Jasmine,' Alejandro said into my ear. 'I know we agreed before to keep things professional, but I want you.'

Jesus. Christ.

The combination of the provocative dancing, feeling his boner, and the sensation of his warm breath tickling my neck as he told me that he wanted me sent my mind and body into a meltdown. I pushed my arse into him again, then wound my body down, then back up again, revelling in the feel of him.

Just as I was about to do it again, Alejandro spun me around to face him.

'Did you hear what I said?' he growled, his eyes the colour of charcoal. 'I want you. I need to know what you're thinking. Should I walk away and call Bob to take us back, or are you going to let me kiss you?'

Oh Lord.

Now there was no way I could resist, even if I wanted to. Which for the record, I didn't.

He'd just asked if I was going to let him kiss me. That was like asking a kid if they wanted to open their Christmas presents a day early.

Ever since that first kiss, there wasn't a second that passed that I hadn't wanted to do it again.

'We can't leave yet,' I said. 'The sun will start setting soon. We have to stay and see it.'

'You still have not answered my question.' He pulled me closer and lifted my chin.

'Yes,' I said, my heart thundering louder than the reggae beat.

'Yes, what?'

'Kiss me.' I didn't know who the hell I was and what had come over me, but I wanted him. I was overcome with desire and was powerless to stop it.

I didn't get a chance to give it any more thought though because in one swift movement, Alejandro dipped his head and crushed his lips onto mine.

A loud groan of pleasure shot from my mouth and sheer relief washed over me.

Finally.

It felt like forever since our last kiss, but I was glad our lips had been reunited. As his mouth moved hungrily over mine, everything felt so right. Like this was what we were supposed to be doing. Like his lips were made for mine. Like kissing was their only purpose.

As the kiss deepened, I ran my hands through his hair, then down his back, pushing him into me.

God. He said he wanted me. But I wanted him. And I didn't want to just stop at kissing. I wanted to feel *all* of him.

Our tongues tangled together, flicking, teasing and dancing with each other, sending my heart rate through the roof.

My nipples were rock hard, the crotch of the swimming costume I was still wearing under my dress that had dried out ages ago from the sun was now sodden. Every nerve ending was heightened with pleasure.

'Fuck.' Alejandro pulled away slowly. As I opened my eyes, I saw him wince. 'You have no idea how much I want to bend you over and fuck you right here, right now. But there are too many people.'

'So if there were *less* people, you'd still fuck me on this dance floor?' I teased, thinking how crazy it was that I probably wouldn't object.

'No!' He laughed. 'I just mean... come.' He ushered me to an area further away from the stage that was quieter. We sat at a table. 'I have dreamt about fucking you for months and if we do this, I do not want an audience or to be arrested, which is exactly what would have happened if we had continued. Because believe me when I tell you Jasmine, the things I would like to do to you would not be suitable for other people's eyes.'

Pleasure zipped down my spine.

'Really?' I cocked my head to the side. 'What would you like to do?'

'First, I would—'

'Look!' A smiley woman with short, dark hair joined our table and pointed. 'The sun's setting!'

My head snapped towards the sea and I saw she was right.

The view was gorgeous and I knew I didn't want to miss it.

But part of me wished she hadn't interrupted us at that moment.

Because every part of my body was yearning to know exactly what Alejandro was about to say.

I wanted to know exactly what he wanted to do to me.

And truthfully, I didn't just want him to tell me what he'd dreamt of doing.

I wanted him to *show* me.

25

ALEJANDRO

Perhaps the 'Jamaican Viagra' cocktail really did have some kind of powers, because for the past few hours, I had been fighting to stop my dick getting hard.

My desire for Jasmine was at critical levels before. But when I saw how brave she was, conquering another fear and jumping from the cliff not once, but three times, my attraction to her intensified.

And when she pushed her butt against me, I knew I was fighting a losing battle.

The logical part of my mind knew it was not a good idea. That I needed to think about my job, my promotion, and helping my sister pay for her education, but logic was powerless against lust.

Every flick of Jasmine's hips, every bottom thrust knocked reason straight out of my brain.

Which was why I broke my promise to keep things professional and told her that I wanted her.

Fighting my feelings had become exhausting. I was tired of battling against what I was certain was the inevitable. Our connection was inescapable. The only option now was to put ourselves out of our misery and surrender.

'Oh my God, look!' Jasmine said, snapping me out of my thoughts. 'The sunset is gorgeous!'

She took my hand, instantly causing my body to light up, then led me to the cliffside to get a better look.

The sky was a fiery, golden colour. Yellow and orange shades blended together as the sun began to dip below the surface. I was not surprised everyone was taking photos. Jasmine was right. It was beautiful.

'Now I can understand why so many people come here to watch the sunset.'

'Me too.' She rested her head on my arm. It was only then that I realised we were still holding hands. It had felt so natural that I had not given it a second thought. 'It's so romantic.'

'It is.' I turned to face her and she looked up at me. Our eyes locked and our faces inched together.

I dipped my head and kissed her softly on the lips, just to see how she responded. When Jasmine kissed me back, I knew we were both finally on the same page, so I deepened the kiss, devouring her like I was a man who was about to eat his last meal.

As our tongues flicked against each other's, our hands started to wander. She wrapped her leg around me, pushing me into her and my erection strained against my shorts.

Fuck.

I was not sure how much longer I would be able to resist her.

Jasmine pulled away slowly and when I opened my eyes, I saw hers were still closed but her facial expression was one of pure joy and pleasure.

'Wow,' was all she said and I knew exactly what she meant. There was enough electricity in that kiss to light up the whole of the Caribbean. 'I should... I was supposed to...' She winced as if she'd lost the ability to talk or think clearly. I knew the feeling.

Just as she was about to open her mouth to speak, her stomach rumbled loudly. We both burst out laughing.

'Should we get some food?' I said. I could not believe we had been here for hours and not eaten.

'That would be a very good idea.' She nodded.

We sat down and ordered a selection of dishes including beer-battered shrimp, rum BBQ spare ribs and a dish called 'Ital' which was roasted vegetables with herbs and spices in an olive-oil sauce. Jasmine said she remembered her grandmother making it and wanted to try it so we did.

After we had eaten our mains, we tried the sweet potato pudding and traditional rum cake.

I was glad that I had come here. Not just because I had the chance to spend more time with Jasmine (and kiss her multiple times), but also because the menu and the dishes we had tried had given me a lot of inspiration.

Another cocktail later and Jasmine and I were back on the dance floor, our bodies rubbing against each other.

This time, neither of us even attempted to fight our feelings. I was so hard that if we kept dancing for much longer like this, I was in danger of burning a hole in my shorts.

Just when I was about to ask if I could kiss her again, the DJ announced that the café would be closing soon.

'I didn't realise the time!' Jasmine looked at her watch. 'I should call Bob to meet us.'

'*Vale.*' I nodded, disappointed that our evening was about to end. I had no idea how I was going to survive the three-hour car journey back to our hotel without wanting to kiss or touch Jasmine on the backseat.

When we left the café and saw Bob standing outside, we both

froze. He was always happy, but this time, his grin was huge and his eyes looked glazed. I could not see his car, which was strange.

'Miss Jasmine!' he shouted. 'Alejandro! *Wah gwaan, bredrin?*'

I frowned, not understanding what he had said.

'*Wah gwaan* means what's up and *bredrin* is like saying friend,' Jasmine explained.

'Oh.' I nodded.

'But I think it's us who should be asking him *wah gwaan* because he doesn't seem like himself...' she said quietly. 'Bob, we're ready to go now. Are you okay?'

'*Yuh wan fi go back tonight?*' He swayed as he attempted to step forward.

'Yes.' Jasmine's face crumpled. 'That's what we agreed, remember?'

As he got closer, the stench of alcohol hit me.

'*Mi sorry, but mi cyaan drive tonite.*'

I was glad he had been honest and told us he could not drive instead of pretending he was okay and putting everyone's safety at risk.

'Shit,' Jasmine said, then led me away from Bob. 'He's clearly off his face. We'll need to find someone else to drive us back.'

'We are three hours away from our hotel. That is a long way.' I rubbed the back of my neck, considering whether or not to say what I was thinking. 'We could stay over,' I suggested. 'Then Bob can drive us back in the morning.'

'Stay over?' Jasmine gasped like I had just suggested we jump off the cliff naked. 'That's not a good idea.'

'It is late. Do you really want to spend time trying to find a licensed taxi driver? And they may want cash. Do you have enough to pay for a three-hour taxi journey, because I do not. Staying at a hotel is a valid company expense. It is the most sensible option.'

Jasmine chewed her lip in silence, probably trying to decide what to do next.

For me, it was clear. A hotel was the best option.

Was a little part of me hoping that our rooms would be close together and that Jasmine may decide to visit me in the middle of the night to continue our kiss? I would be lying to say that had not crossed my mind. But I still thought staying over made sense.

'Okay.' Jasmine blew out a breath as her fingers flew across her phone screen. 'Looks like there are some hotels nearby, so we can go and check their availability.' She walked over to Bob. 'We're going to get a hotel room. I mean, *two* hotel rooms,' she corrected. 'Are you coming?'

'Nuh,' Bob shook his head. *'Mi gwaan sleep inna di cyar.'*

'You sure sleeping in the car will be comfortable?' Jasmine frowned. I liked that she cared about whether he'd be okay. Most bosses would not be concerned about a taxi driver.

'Ya, mon! Everyting criss!'

'*Vale*.' I nodded. 'So you will sleep in your car until the morning and then when it is safe, you will drive us back?'

Bob nodded. Once we had walked him back to where he'd parked, made sure he was locked in his car and resting on the backseat, we headed for the closest hotel.

'I am sorry, sir,' the receptionist said. 'We are fully booked.'

'You don't have anything at all?' Jasmine pleaded.

'Nothing at all,' she shook her head. 'There is a big wedding happening tomorrow, so we've been booked for months.'

'Okay, thank you.' Jasmine sighed as we left. 'It's fine. There's another hotel not too far away.'

But when we arrived there, that was fully booked too.

'I feel like Mary and Joseph asking if there's any room at the inn! At this rate, we're going to need to sleep in the car with Bob.'

'There is another hotel here.' I pointed to the map on my phone screen. 'We can try there.'

When we arrived and asked for two rooms, it looked like the receptionist was about to laugh in our faces at the idea that we thought we could come to a hotel in a popular area and expect them to have availability.

'I'm very sorry but we're fully booked. Wait...' The receptionist paused. 'Actually, my mistake.' She tapped away on her keyboard, frowning at the screen. 'We do have one room available. It's smaller than most of our standard rooms. Looks like we had a last-minute cancellation.'

'We will take it!' I said quickly.

'Sorry, but we need *two* rooms. Do you have another one available, please?' Jasmine asked.

'No, sorry, ma'am. It's just the one room. You're welcome to try the other hotels in the area; there's two nearby.'

'We tried those.' Jasmine blew out a frustrated breath. 'They were full. Do you have a licensed taxi driver who could take us to Ocho Rios?'

'I'm sorry, but the drivers we use don't go that far at this time of night. So?' the receptionist asked. 'Do you want to take the room?'

I thought we definitely should.

Now I had to see whether Jasmine agreed...

26

JASMINE

This couldn't be happening.

I couldn't believe Bob had got drunk or stoned or whatever he was and couldn't drive us home and that now I was at a hotel.

With Alejandro.

Where there was only one room left.

And we both knew what that one room meant there would only be one bed.

We were fucked.

Bad choice of expletive, but accurate.

After the way we'd been bumping, grinding and kissing today, there was no way we'd be able to survive being in such close proximity together all night, never mind sharing a bed without fucking.

Kissing him and dancing provocatively was one thing. Screwing was a whole different ballgame. There was no going back from that.

Earlier, I'd yearned for him. When he'd said he wanted to bend me over and fuck me right there, part of me wished that he would've. I wanted him to show me all of the things he'd dreamt of doing to me.

But that was the rum talking.

I mean, yes, of course, I'd be lying if I said I didn't *still* want that. But we can't have everything we want, can we?

We'd had a great time today. I'd already crossed too many lines with Alejandro and now it was up to me to make sure things didn't go any further.

First up on the *keeping things strictly professional from now on* agenda should be *not* sharing a room.

'We will take the room,' Alejandro interrupted and I swallowed hard. 'Is that fine for you?' He turned to face me.

The truth was, no. It was definitely *not* fine. Not because I didn't trust Alejandro, but because I didn't trust myself.

I'd just tried giving myself the pep talk to keep things professional, but it appeared to have gone in one ear and out the other.

I knew we absolutely shouldn't spend a night here together in one room, but right now, we were fresh out of options.

Even if I was in England or Spain, two countries I'd lived in for years, I wouldn't feel comfortable flagging down a random taxi driver in the middle of the night to drive me three hours away. So there was no way I was going to do that in a country that I barely knew.

Unfortunately, Alejandro was right. Staying overnight in this hotel really was the most sensible option.

'Okay.' I nodded reluctantly.

As I handed over the company credit card and we filled out the paperwork, I told myself that I was probably overreacting.

Despite joking about it before, I knew Alejandro was a gentleman, so I was sure he'd volunteer to sleep on the sofa and offer me the bed.

Plus, with all the dancing we'd done today, we'd be far too tired to even think about doing any horizontal gymnastics.

I took the keycard and we headed to the room on the ground floor. Although the hotel couldn't compare to the Love Hotel, it seemed clean and pleasant enough. The hallway leading to the bedroom had brown tiled flooring and plain white walls with various paintings lining them.

'So I will sleep on the sofa,' Alejandro said, breaking the silence.

'Thank you.'

See. Just like I thought. Everything would be fine.

I tapped the keycard on the door, stepped inside, then slid the card into the holder on the wall. The lights came on and as I took in the room, my stomach lurched.

'Where's the sofa?' I said, my voice filled with panic.

'Looks like there is not one here.' Alejandro's face fell. 'The receptionist did say that the room was smaller than their normal ones.'

He was right. She did say that. I just hadn't taken that to mean *this* small.

The small double bed almost took up the whole room. That was how tiny it was.

'This isn't good,' I muttered.

'I can sleep on the floor if you are not comfortable sharing the bed.'

'Thanks, but no. Your back will be killing you tomorrow.' I couldn't do that to him. It wouldn't be fair. 'We'll just have to... share the bed. Look, I know things got heated earlier, but it's best if we draw a line under it. We shouldn't take things further. We should just go straight to sleep.'

'*Vale*,' Alejandro said. 'Do not worry. I will keep to my side. I am not a teenage boy. I can control my urges.'

'Me too,' I added. 'I mean, not the teenage boy bit, but you know, controlling my urges. I'm sure there are extra pillows in the cupboard. We'll just put them down the centre of the bed. To avoid any body parts touching.'

'You mean, like they touched on the dance floor for most of the night?' Alejandro raised his eyebrow.

Touché.

'We'd had a lot to drink. And at least we had clothes on.' I attempted to make sense of my comment. 'This is different.'

'Of course.' Alejandro nodded.

'I'm going to the bathroom.' I left the room, closed the bathroom door behind me then exhaled. This was going to be difficult.

Luckily, the hotel had vanity kits with toothbrushes and toothpaste, so once I'd brushed my teeth and washed my face, I returned to the room.

Alejandro awkwardly shuffled past me to the bathroom and I used that opportunity to take off my dress. Obviously, I didn't have any nightclothes to change into, so I'd have to sleep in my underwear. My dress wouldn't be comfortable. I'd make sure that I wrapped the white bedsheets around me multiple times though to create an extra barrier and avoid my skin touching Alejandro's.

After diving under the sheets, I remembered I was supposed to get extra pillows to put in the centre of the bed. I leapt out from the covers and raced over to Alejandro's side to the dark wooden wardrobe.

There were no pillows inside, so I could only assume they were in the cupboards at the top.

Just as I stretched up to try and reach, I heard the bathroom door open and Alejandro returned to the bedroom in just his boxer shorts.

Oh. My. Good. Lord.

What was that saying? He looked like a snack?

In this case, Alejandro didn't just look like a snack; he looked like an all-you-can-eat buffet.

My eyes roamed over his chest, then lingered between his legs.

'You want some help?' he asked, breaking me out of my indecent thoughts.

'Yes. Please.'

He came and stood beside me, reached up, pulled down two extra pillows, then handed them to me.

Our eyes locked and my whole body tingled. Our faces were only inches apart and the bed wasn't that much further. It would be so easy for us to *accidentally* fall onto it. And for Alejandro to *accidentally* thrust his dick inside me.

A fresh wave of tingles raced through me. I attempted to tell my body to calm down, but I could feel my resolve weakening.

'We should...' I tilted my head towards the bed.

'Sleep?' Alejandro said. It was almost like he wanted to know whether I wanted something else to happen.

Of course I did, but I wouldn't let it.

'Yes. Sleep!' I broke the spell then returned to my side of the bed where I quickly climbed under the covers, then positioned the two pillows in the centre of the bed.

Given how small it was, that didn't leave much room for movement, but it'd be fine.

Once Alejandro had climbed in the bed, he turned off the light. I felt him moving around a lot, trying to get comfortable.

'Do you mind if I...' He wriggled again. 'With the pillows, I do not have a lot of room. Perhaps I can turn them onto their side, instead of laying them flat?' he asked.

'Okay. Go for it,' I said.

I felt the pillows move. Alejandro put them on their side, but the one he'd positioned lower down immediately fell over. 'I've got it!' I reached out for the pillow and repositioned it, but it fell again and when I tried to retrieve it, my hands landed on something hard.

'Fuck.' Alejandro groaned. 'Your hand. It is on my cock.'

'Oh shit!' I leapt up, yanking my hand away. 'I'm so sorry! I was just trying to... the pillow.'

'I wish I could say that I was sorry that you touched me, but I am not. I wish you would do it again,' he growled.

This was the point where I was supposed to say something along the lines of *don't be ridiculous!* And rehash the same spiel about it not being a good idea, *blah, blah, blah*. But I was *exhausted*. Tired of trying to keep things professional. Tired of fighting my feelings for this man.

I'd tried everything I could to stay away from him.

I'd tried doing the right thing. But it was as if the universe was deliberately pushing us together.

All this torture and denying myself a little pleasure wasn't good.

There must be loads of studies that prove that when you deprive yourself of something you want, it only leads to you wanting it more, right?

A friend of mine went on a diet and when she finally caved and allowed herself a slice of cake, she ended up binge eating the entire cake in one go and then licking every single crumb off the plate. But I reckoned if she'd allowed herself a little taste of dessert heaven every once in a while, her actions wouldn't have been so extreme.

I'd deprived myself from having sex for too long.

I'd deprived myself from enjoying Alejandro for months when it was obvious we were both desperate to get naked together.

And let's be real. We'd already spent most of today with our tongues down each other's throats and dry humping, so we might as well go all the way.

We were away from the resort. No one knew us here. No one would find out.

Fuck it.

'Like this?' I lifted my hand up and moved it back to where it was a few moments ago. Right on top of Alejandro's long, thick and now very erect dick.

'*Dios mío!*' Alejandro groaned.

'Do you like that?' I gripped him tighter, then worked my hand up and down his length.

'Like?' he said. 'Jasmine, there is not a word in the dictionary that will explain how amazing it feels to have your hand on my cock. But I need to make sure you understand what I would like to happen now. I would like us to fuck.' He growled. 'You are fine with this?'

'Yes,' I said, sliding my hand down inside his boxer shorts so that I could grip his firm dick. All that fabric was getting in my way. 'Let's fuck. But just for tonight, okay? Once we go back to the hotel tomorrow, we go back to being colleagues.'

'I…' He hesitated. I slid my hand up and down his length again and he groaned.

'So?' I asked.

'You already know I want to fuck you. I just want to make sure you are sure.'

'I'm sure.'

The words had barely left my lips before Alejandro threw off the sheets and we both tossed the pillows in the air and off the bed.

After climbing on top of me, our mouths fused together and we kissed each other hungrily, like it was the first time all over again. As our tongues flicked against one another, I reached for Alejandro's boxer shorts and started tugging them down. He pulled away.

'Not yet,' he said, then leapt up and switched on the light.

I squinted and was going to protest and suggest we do it with the light off, but then he dragged me to the edge of the bed, slid off my knickers, then knelt down on the floor in front of me and spread my legs.

'*Dios mío*, Jasmine.' He shook his head in disbelief. 'I knew your pussy would be incredible, but it is even more beautiful than I imagined. That is why I turned on the light. I needed to see you bare. And I want to see your face when I make you scream my name.'

Before I even had a chance to register everything he'd just said, Alejandro buried his face between my legs and licked me slowly, from my clit down to my entrance.

'Oh, Jesus!' I cried out. My hips rocked upwards and a bolt of lightning rocketed through me.

Alejandro flattened his tongue against my clit then lapped against it. Every stroke sent a new wave of desire shooting through my veins.

'Fuck.' He lifted his head. 'You taste like the most exquisite dish on the menu.'

Alejandro returned to lavishing my pussy with attention, circling my clit with laser-sharp precision, each lick threatening to set off my orgasm. How had I lived on this planet for almost forty years and not experienced pleasure like this before?

Any man that had ever bothered to eat me out had either done it reluctantly or lazily, making it feel like a chore. But Alejandro? He was licking and now sucking my sensitive nub like it was a Michelin-starred meal that he couldn't get enough of.

'More. Please.' I reached for his head and pushed it deeper into me.

When he thrust two fingers inside me, I cried out with ecstasy.

'Oh God, I... I... can't,' I panted, pushing his head into me again as I felt the wave building inside me. 'I'm going to... I... I...'

Alejandro picked up the pace, pumping his fingers in and out as he circled my clit faster.

This felt so good, I didn't want it to end, but I was powerless to stop it. My orgasm ripped through me like a tsunami. Every atom of my body came alive. The sweet sensations travelled at lightning speed from the tips of my toes up all the way up to my brain, which I was sure had just short circuited.

'Oh fuuucckkk!' I screamed so loudly, anyone would think I was being murdered. But this wasn't pain I was feeling. It was the most incredible pleasure. 'Oh God, Alejandro.' I lifted my hips off the bed and squeezed my eyes shut. 'Alejandro... fuck!'

As my hips crashed back on the mattress, my chest heaved and my heart raced.

Wow.

I had no words.

Best. Orgasm. Ever.

Alejandro stopped circling me and slid his fingers out; I instantly missed feeling them inside me.

When I slowly opened my eyes, I saw him licking his fingers and groaning like he was devouring the most delicious sauce.

'You even taste incredible. I could eat your pussy all day,' he growled. 'But right now, I need to fuck you. I need to feel what it is like to be inside you. Please Jasmine.' His face looked pained.

'Do you have a condom?' I asked.

'Sure.' He rushed over to his rucksack. His dick strained against his boxer shorts, causing them to tent.

Seconds later, he was back in front of me. He went to pull down his shorts, but I leapt up.

'Please.' I reached forward. 'Let me.'

I'd dreamt about this moment for so long, I wanted to savour it. I peeled his shorts down, oh so slowly and when his dick sprang free, my jaw dropped.

'Jesus!' I gasped. I'd felt him hard when we'd danced and knew he felt big, but nothing could've prepared me for *fully erect Alejandro*.

His dick was long *and* thick. I wasn't sure how all that was going to fit inside me, but I didn't care.

I grabbed the condom from his hand, slid it over his length, then laid back and admired the god standing in front of me.

'So you are sure you are fine with this?'

'I appreciate you checking, but I'm sure. So just in case it's not clear, put your dick in me right now. *Please*,' I added, not recognising myself and how I'd just spoken to him.

'You asked so politely.' He smirked. 'So how could I refuse?'

Alejandro straddled me before lining his dick up at my entrance then slamming inside me.

'Oh God!' I cried out again.

'Should I stop?' he asked.

'No!' I gripped his arse.

Alejandro slammed into me again and this time, I was more prepared. As he pumped in and out of me, my eyes rolled into the back of my head. The sensation of him filling me up was... mind-blowing. The deeper he thrusted, the more I wanted.

Our bodies moved perfectly in sync and just as I thought I couldn't feel any more turned on, Alejandro leant forward and started sucking my nipple. My back arched and arousal rocketed through me.

No way.

There was no way this man was going to make me come a second time. And so quickly? It was impossible.

As if he heard what I was thinking and wanted to prove me wrong, he brushed his thumb over my clit and started stroking it.

He did not come to play.

My hips bucked upwards and Alejandro pummelled into me again.

'Are you close?' he panted as I looked up at him.

God, he was beautiful. His sculpted, golden chest glistened with sweat and if he hadn't turned my body into a volcano, I would love to lift my head up and lick it right off him.

'Yes,' I said, struggling to speak.

'Let go. Come for me, Jasmine. I do not know how much longer I can last. You feel… incredible.'

He picked up the pace, fucking me, harder, faster whilst still circling my clit and then it happened again: the wave started building with me and I felt the explosion.

'Oh, oh, oh… my… Ale… jandro!' I screamed like a wild animal. Just as I collapsed on the mattress, his body stiffened and a loud grunt flew from his mouth as he thrust: once, then twice, before he emptied himself inside me then stilled, his chest crashing on top of mine.

Our bodies heaved against each other, slick with sweat.

Neither of us spoke for what must've been several minutes. We couldn't. I was too overwhelmed.

I was trying to get my head around the fact that not only had I had sex with Alejandro, but that he'd given me not one, but two orgasms in one night and what I knew without any shadow of doubt, was the best sex of my life.

Eventually, Alejandro pulled out, then lay beside me.

'That was…' He smiled, then shook his head. 'Wow. Fuck!'

'Yeah.' I ran my hand over his chest, still not quite believing that we were here, naked after he just fucked my brains out. No wonder I was finding it impossible to string a sentence together.

'Any regrets?' he asked.

'No,' I said quickly.

I knew that answer was irresponsible. I should regret it. Right now, I should be worrying about the consequences of what we'd just done. But that wasn't what I was thinking about.

Right now, only one word came to my frazzled head. A request that came straight from between my legs.

And that word was: *more*.

27

ALEJANDRO

I rolled off Jasmine and collapsed on the bed. My chest was heaving and slick with sweat.

I could not get enough of this woman.

It was only ten in the morning and we had already had sex. *Twice*. And something told me that even if we had did it a hundred more times today, I would never tire of her.

Jasmine was a goddess. I always believed this could be true, but now we had been intimate, I knew it for sure. Not only was she intelligent, kind and ambitious, she was the sexiest woman I had ever met.

When we discovered that there was no sofa in the room and that we would have to share a bed, I admit that I was worried that I would not be able to maintain the necessary boundaries. And when I saw her reaching up for the pillows in just her black, lacy underwear, I nearly came in my boxers.

At that moment, I wanted to carry her onto the bed, peel off her panties with my teeth and bury myself inside her.

But of course, I had resisted. I told her that I was not a

teenage boy and that I could keep my cool; however, I was not sure whether I was trying to convince Jasmine or myself.

When her hand brushed my cock, I knew I was in trouble. My willpower was already hanging by a thread and the sensation of her warm hand touching me there was too much to bear.

Everything that happened afterwards was so incredible, I was sure it was a dream. Finally seeing Jasmine's bare pussy, tasting her, seeing her face as the orgasm that I gave her ripped through her body... and just thinking about the moment she screamed my name made me hard.

And when I was inside her, it felt so incredible, I had to battle not to come straightaway. After dreaming about this moment for so long, I could not disappoint her or myself. So I held on for as long as I could and when I came... *Madre mía*. I have never experienced pleasure like that in my life.

I was relieved that she felt the same and that I had made her orgasm multiple times. It was possible that Jasmine was more experienced than me, so making sure I satisfied her was important.

After we had finished, I thought perhaps she would want to sleep, but she wanted more. So we fucked again on the bed, then when we recovered and got up to shower, we had done it there too.

We had only slept for a few hours when I woke up to go to the bathroom and when I returned, Jasmine was awake. Before I knew it, we were kissing again and I was inside her.

Now, two hours later, we were here on the bed together, recovering from the most recent round.

Sleeping with Jasmine was a big deal for me. Not just because I was so attracted to her, but because I felt that finally, I had moved on.

After grieving for Freya for so long, it was like I had been given another chance at happiness.

I could not remember the last time I felt so at peace.

'We should order breakfast.' I brushed Jasmine's hair from her face. She was so beautiful.

'So we get energy to go again?' She smiled.

'You are insatiable.' I leant over and kissed her. 'I love it! But, no. As much as I would like to stay in this bed and fuck you all day, we have used all of the condoms. And we will have to check out soon.'

'We can get more condoms and pay for a late checkout.' She tilted her head playfully.

'I like that idea. If we stayed here, we could be more free.'

'Exactly.' Jasmine ran her hand over my chest, causing my body to spark. 'It's Saturday, so technically we're off duty until Monday. We could spend the weekend here, *together*, before we have to go back to reality. I mean, we're hours away from the Love Hotel, so no one needs to know. What happens in paradise, stays in paradise, right?'

Even better.

Jasmine had made it clear that once we got back to Ocho Rios, that would be the end. I always knew that fucking her once would never be enough, so the idea of enjoying two more days together was fantastic.

'What about Bob?' I asked.

'I'll speak to him. Obviously, he'll need to be paid for his time if he has to drive back and return to pick us up on Sunday, but I'm sure he'll be fine. Even if we have to cover the cost ourselves, it'll be worth it...'

Her hand slid downwards and gripped my cock. As she stroked it gently, I knew there was no way I was saying no.

When her hands were on my dick, Jasmine could ask me to do anything and I would agree.

Which was why last night, I had agreed to just fucking her, even though deep down, I already knew I wanted more.

'Deal,' I said. 'But first, breakfast, then we will buy condoms.'

'And then?' She licked her lips.

'We will come back to bed and I will make you scream my name again.'

28

JASMINE

After gulping down my second cup of coffee, I tried and failed to stifle a loud yawn. I was shattered. My eyelids weighed ten tonnes, every part of my body ached and my vagina felt like it'd been scrubbed with a metal scourer.

But it was *totally* worth it.

Given the chance, I'd repeat last night and this morning with Alejandro again in a heartbeat.

I stood up from the dining table and as I tried to walk, the soreness between my legs hit me again. As sadistic as it sounded, I loved the fact that I could still feel the after-effects of how Alejandro had stretched me wide open as he fucked me over and over again.

'Do you think they would mind if we took some food for Bob?' Alejandro said, breaking me out of my thoughts. 'I know hotels prefer guests not to take anything from the dining hall, so I will pay. He must be hungry.'

My heart fluttered. That was one of the things I loved about Alejandro. He was so considerate.

Just to clarify: when I said it was one of the things I *loved* about him, I didn't mean literally. It was just a turn of phrase. Obviously, it was way too soon for that. We were just having fun.

'They'd probably be fine if we offered to pay.'

'I will ask.' He got up and headed over to a waitress.

As soon as Alejandro approached, her whole demeanour changed. Her eyes brightened, her head tilted and maybe I was imagining it but she even pushed out her breasts. Then she laughed and touched his bicep.

Whoa. Hands off, lady.

Touching guests was completely unprofessional.

My subconscious burst out laughing. Who was I to talk about being unprofessional? *Hypocritical, much?*

I'd just spent all night in bed, fucking my co-worker, and I was about to go shopping for a box of condoms so we could continue shagging each other's brains out. I was hardly in a position to sit on my high horse.

A sharp pain shot through my chest. What the hell was I doing? I really shouldn't be extending my stay here with Alejandro. I should be feeling guilty for crossing the line.

I should be making excuses for my shameless behaviour. Blaming it on the sunshine and those rum cocktails and vowing not to do it again.

This was a bad idea for so many reasons. For starters, *look at him.* Everywhere we went, women's eyes followed, just like they were right now. That waitress practically had her tongue hanging out. He could have any woman he wanted, so even without the work and age issues, this could never be anything long-term. I was glad we clarified that it was just sex whilst we were away from Ocho Rios, before we did the deed.

She smiled at him again, then disappeared. Alejandro returned to the table.

'All good?' I asked, fighting the pangs of jealousy that were stupidly swirling around in my stomach.

'*Sí!* Kadesha will prepare a box of food for me to take away.'

'*Kadesha*, eh?' I raised an eyebrow.

'She is a sweet girl.'

'She certainly seemed to take a shine to you...'

'Are you *jealous*?' A wide, satisfied smile spread across his face.

'No!' I said defensively. Now it was Alejandro's turn to raise his eyebrow. 'Okay. Maybe a little...' I hung my head, embarrassment flooding through me.

Alejandro lifted my chin.

'You have no reason to be jealous. Like I told you, she is a sweet *girl*. But you, Jasmine. You are *all woman*.' He leant forward and kissed me passionately on the lips. He didn't seem to care that we were in a hall full of people, and frankly, I didn't either. His kisses were just too good. When his lips were on mine, it was like nothing else existed.

The sound of someone clearing their throat loudly jolted us out of our kiss and we pulled away.

When we looked up, Kadesha was standing there clutching a box and she didn't look happy. After giving me a look so dirty, I felt the need to shower, she turned to Alejandro.

'Here you go,' she said sweetly. 'And if you need anything else, give me a call...'

'*Gracias*,' Alejandro replied. 'I have everything I need.' He took my hand, lifted it up, then kissed it softly.

Kadesha's smile dropped and she stormed off.

My stomach flipped. With that small action, Alejandro had made a very clear statement. He'd said that he wouldn't be calling her (although I didn't even see him take her number) and that he was happy with me. *Swoon.*

'Thank you,' I said.

'For what?'

'For making me feel... so good.'

'*Cariño*.' He flashed his gorgeous smile, and when I remembered that was Spanish for *sweetheart*, my stomach fluttered. 'I am just getting started.'

'What's in the box?' I asked, trying to stop my libido from spiralling again as I imagined how else he could make me happy.

'Let us look.'

When he opened the box, I burst out laughing.

'What is funny?' he frowned. 'There is a great selection of food.'

'Typical chef!' I said. 'Of course the first thing you saw when you opened the box was the food. But my eyes went straight to *that*!' I pointed to the top right-hand corner of the inside of the lid, where Kadesha had boldly written her name and telephone number.

'Oh...' Alejandro's eyes widened. 'I did not see that.'

'I reckon Kadesha would be very sad to hear you'd missed it.'

'It is not important. The only woman I am interested in is you.' And as he leant forward and kissed me again, something told me he was genuine.

We left the breakfast hall and headed to reception.

'Hello, ma'am.' The receptionist smiled. I hated being called ma'am. Made me sound about a hundred, but I knew she was just being polite. 'How may I help you?'

'We were just wondering if we could extend our stay for one more night?'

'I can check. What's your room number?'

Once I gave her the number, she tapped into the computer.

'I'm sorry. That room is booked for the next week.'

'Do you have anything else available?' Alejandro asked.

'I'll take a look for you, sir.'

'Please.' He smiled. 'Call me Alejandro. Sir makes me think of my grandfather!' he joked.

'Ohhh!' Her eyes popped. 'So *you're* Alejandro!'

'*Sí...*' He frowned. 'Why?'

Knowing people had been talking about him didn't surprise me. Like I'd said before, someone who looked like him was hard to ignore.

'A number of our guests heard your name being called out several times last night...' She smirked and my cheeks heated with embarrassment. Clearly, I was much louder than I thought.

'I see,' Alejandro said, trying to keep a straight face. 'If I get my wish, I cannot promise that they will not hear it being called again...' He faced me, his eyes the colour of charcoal, then licked his lips.

'You're a *very* lucky lady.' The receptionist smiled at me. 'We actually have a larger room available.'

The price was eyewatering, so there was no way I could expense that without raising questions. Just as I was about to reach for my credit card, Alejandro handed over his.

'I will take care of this,' he said.

'We can go halves,' I insisted.

'No.' He lifted my hand off the reception desk gently. 'Let me spoil you. You deserve it.'

Someone better bring a mop and bucket because I just melted into a puddle. The receptionist also swooned.

After my experiences with my ex, I'd vowed to be firmly independent, but somehow, I knew that Alejandro hadn't offered to pay to show off or because he wanted to 'own' me. He was doing it because he genuinely wanted to treat me.

Once everything was arranged, Alejandro offered to take the box of breakfast goodies to Bob, then get the 'supplies' we needed whilst I went back to have a nap.

But just as I stepped inside the room, I felt my phone buzzing.

When I pulled it out, I saw I'd had five missed calls. Three from Hazel and two from Stella.

A message flashed up from Hazel.

> I've been trying to call you! How was the café yesterday?
>
> I saw there was a charge on the company credit card last night for a hotel. Did you stay over?
>
> Good news: the management will be back at the hotel from Monday.
>
> Looking forward to receiving a full report on your findings ASAP!

My stomach sunk. This wasn't good. I should reply straight-away but my mind was spiralling, so instead, I dialled Stella's number. I'd noticed earlier that she'd called yesterday too, but obviously, I'd been busy...

Thankfully, she answered on the first ring.

'Hi! Everything okay?' she said. 'Not sure what happened before when you called on Thursday, but after it cut out, I tried ringing back and tried again yesterday. You said something happened between you and Alejandro?'

'Yeah.' I sighed and flopped onto the bed. 'On Thursday, I was calling because I needed to tell someone we'd kissed because I thought we were going to die.'

'What?' she gasped.

'Long story. Anyway, I thought the kiss was bad enough but since then, we... fucked.'

'Finally!' Stella squealed.

'*That's* all you have to say?' My jaw dropped.

'I've been telling you for *ages* that I knew it was going to happen! It was never a question of *if*, but more like *when*. Congrats! So? How was it? Was it just as good as you'd imagined?'

'Better.' I laughed, my shoulders relaxing as I replayed all the many delicious moments. 'The man is a sex god. I mean, his dick is magnificent. So is his tongue. And his *hands*. He made me come five times.'

'Five?' Stella shouted.

'Yes! Five! And the crazy thing is, I don't think it was even an effort for him. He could've gone all night and morning if we didn't run out of condoms!'

'That's amazing! I'm so happy for you! I know you were worried about his age, but that just shows there are benefits to having a toy boy. I read somewhere that guys in their twenties have a quicker recovery time. So once you've finished one round, it doesn't take them long to get their engine, or rather dick, revved up again!' She cackled.

'You're not wrong!' I grinned, then remembered Hazel's text and my stomach twisted again. 'But I'm worried my boss is going to find out. She's already messaged to ask about the hotel charge on the credit card. She must get alerts every time there's an expense.'

'Oh...' I heard the concern in Stella's voice.

'I mean, it *is* a valid expense,' I added, as if already trying to plead my case. 'The taxi driver was off his head and couldn't drive, so we thought it'd be safer to stay overnight rather than trying to find an authorised taxi to drive us three hours back. I didn't think we'd end up having to share a room where there was only one bed.'

'Classic!' Stella said excitedly. 'So is that how it happened then? You woke up and felt his dick pressed against you and you jumped on it?'

'We didn't make it until morning. I don't think we were even in the bed for more than five minutes...'

'Love it!' She laughed again.

As I recounted how my hand had accidentally brushed over Alejandro's manhood, Stella squealed. And when I gave her the full details of our sexscapades, she screamed so loudly, my eardrums almost burst.

'So he's gone to buy more condoms, then we'll move into the other room which Alejandro paid for and head back to our hotel tomorrow to face reality. And maybe the sack.'

'It doesn't need to come to that. Like you said, it was a valid company expense to stay over and Alejandro has paid for tonight's stay so you'll be fine. You've only got another week left there, right? And if all the management will be back on Monday, you'll both be rushed off your feet, so it'll be easier to keep your distance. Then you can hook up on the plane and get all that sexual frustration out of your systems before you go back to Spain. You'll be fine! Just enjoy the time you have together this weekend and forget about what happens next. A wise woman once told me to do the same with Max and she was right!'

'That was different. Max wasn't a junior employee!'

'True, but the principal of enjoying yourself still stands. It's been years since you've had sex, right?'

'Thanks for the reminder!'

'All I'm saying is, you've got years of orgasms to catch up on and judging by his performance so far, Alejandro is the man to deliver them!'

I heard the door open. Alejandro walked in carrying a large bag.

'I'd better go. Enjoy the rest of your stay in Madrid and I'll call you soon to hear more about it!'

'Thanks and enjoy the orgasm avalanche!' She chuckled.

'I will!' After ending the call, I went over to Alejandro and kissed him gently on the lips. 'Wow. How many condoms did you buy?' I glanced down at the bag and laughed.

'Just a thousand.' He laughed. 'Only kidding. I bought some things I thought you might need like new underwear, a change of clothes, a bikini and some toiletries.'

'Oh my goodness, really?' I wrapped my arms around him. 'Thank you.' This man was incredible.

As his lips met mine and I got lost in his kiss, I knew immediately that I was going to take Stella's advice.

I wasn't going to worry about replying to Hazel or my responsibilities.

Instead, I was going to enjoy every second of this weekend with Alejandro.

As Stella had so eloquently put it, bring on the orgasm avalanche.

29

ALEJANDRO

'Wow!' Jasmine gasped as she took in the views in front of her.

After spending some time 'testing' the four-poster bed in our new room, we had finally made our way to the shower, got dressed and headed outside of the hotel.

Now we were standing barefoot on the famous Seven Mile Beach in Negril and it was just as impressive as I had heard.

As the name suggested, the stunning, white, sandy beach stretched for miles and the crystal-clear waters were so transparent, you could see right down to the bottom.

'I understand why this is known as one of the best beaches in Jamaica,' I said, continuing to admire the scenery.

'Definitely! It looks like a postcard.'

'Shall we walk?' I held out my hand.

'Love to!' Jasmine took my palm.

'So, are you having a good time?' I asked.

The real question I wanted to ask was whether what happened between us last night and this morning meant she had changed her mind about us just hooking up for the weekend, but I did not want to come on too strong and scare her.

'I'm having the time of my life! I'm in paradise, walking along a beautiful beach, with a gorgeous man who should be entered into the *Guinness Book of Records* for delivering the most orgasms in...' she looked at her watch '...in a twelve-hour period. I have no idea how you're so good!'

'I am glad that I satisfied you.' I smiled, feeling ten feet tall.

'But seriously though, how are you so good? Did you go to some sort of female-pleasure masterclass or is it because you've slept with lots of women?' She laughed and my face fell.

I sucked in a breath, taking in the fresh, salty sea air. Her question caught me off guard.

'No. I have not slept with a lot of women.'

'I find that hard to believe! I've seen the way they throw themselves at you. Like Kadesha did at breakfast.'

'I have not dated anyone for years. And before that, I was in a relationship for almost three years.'

'Really?' Her eyes widened.

'*Sí*.'

'Why did you break up?'

My stomach clenched. I paused and my gaze dropped to the sand as I tried to build up the strength to tell her. Even two years later, I still found it difficult to talk about.

'She...' I swallowed the lump in my throat.

Jasmine stopped walking and stood in front of me, her face etched with concern.

'It's okay.' She squeezed my hand. 'You don't have to tell me if you don't want to. I find it difficult sometimes to talk about my divorce, so I know how hard break ups can be. Forget I asked.'

'We did not break up,' I said and Jasmine frowned. 'She... died.'

Jasmine's jaw dropped and her eyes bulged.

'Oh my God!' She put her hand over her mouth. 'I am so

sorry!' Jasmine threw her arms around my back and squeezed me tight. My body melted into hers.

Now that I had told her, it was actually a relief. No one at work knew and the closer I got to Jasmine, somehow it felt like I was carrying a secret that weighed heavy on my shoulders. Telling her about an important part of my past felt right.

It was hard enough when people asked about my parents. But telling them I had lost my girlfriend too only made things even more difficult.

There was even a time that I blamed myself. When I wondered if I somehow made bad things happen to those around me.

When I mentioned this to Lola, she insisted that was not true, explaining that if it was, that meant she was also to blame because she was close to Freya too.

In the end, I realised that this was just life. We loved and we lost. And when things happened, both good and bad, often they were out of our control.

It was a shame that knowing that did not lessen the pain.

I pulled away, then sat on the sand. Jasmine positioned herself in front of me and took my hands in hers.

'Her name was Freya. It was a skiing accident,' I said, knowing that it was natural that she would want to know what happened. 'She loved to ski. Her family went every year since they were kids. I was supposed to go with her, but I got a last-minute opportunity to work at a great hotel in London, which was where we were living at the time. She was the reason I moved to London. Freya was my sister's best friend. They were the same age. They went to uni together.'

'Oh,' Jasmine said and I realised that I was just vomiting random sentences. I was just so used to the questions people often asked, like how we met and why I moved to London, that I just started listing off all the responses at once.

'Anyway, so I was supposed to go with her and I did not. If I was there, maybe I could have done something. I could have saved her.' A sharp pain shot through my chest.

'I'm sure it wouldn't have changed things,' Jasmine said softly. 'Her family were there. They would've done everything they could. And although I didn't know her, I'm sure Freya wouldn't want you to carry around that kind of guilt. She'd want you to live your life.'

'You are right. She was always supportive of my career and believed I would become a top chef one day. She wanted the best for me. But even knowing that, it has been hard. Lola always tells me that Freya would want me to date again, but it has always felt like I was being unfaithful to her memory. Until last night.' I fixed my gaze on Jasmine.

'Wait.' She paused, her eyes widening. 'Am I the first woman that you've slept with since...?'

'*Sí.*' I nodded. 'I have come close before. Lola tried to set me up with someone about a year ago when I came to visit. But when we got to the bedroom, I could not go through with it. And since then, I had no desire to be with any other woman. Until you.'

'That... that means a lot.' She squeezed my hand. 'Last night must've been a big deal. I wish I'd known, so that I could've checked on you. Made sure you were okay.'

'I am good. No, more than good. You made me feel incredible, Jasmine.'

Our eyes locked.

What I said was true. Whenever I had tried to move on in the past, it had always seemed wrong. I was convinced it was too soon. But with Jasmine, everything felt right. It was as natural as breathing. I no longer felt that guilt.

Last night was not just incredible because of the sex. It was a breakthrough because it showed that there was life after Freya. I finally felt like I was ready to start a new chapter in my life, which for a very long time was something I feared would never be possible.

'I'm glad to hear it. And I appreciate you telling me. I know it must be hard to talk about.'

'Usually, I find it difficult. But you are easy to talk to. I feel like I could tell you anything.'

That was one of the many things I loved about Jasmine. She always knew how to put people at ease and genuinely cared about making others happy. I had noticed it with the hotel guests and everyone she worked with. That was why she was so popular and amazing at her job.

'Thanks. That means a lot.'

'So now you know that I am not the Casanova you seem to think I am. I will be honest: it has been so long for me that I was surprised I remembered what to do!' I smiled, trying to lighten the mood. I did not want to make Jasmine sad.

'Same here!' Jasmine laughed and my heart instantly swelled with happiness. 'It's been a long time for me too. But turns out that sex is just like riding a bike.'

'Riding a bike?' I frowned.

'Sorry! It's another English saying. It means once you learn how to do something, you don't forget. It's not literal. Although my vagina does kind of feel like I've taken part in the Tour de France! It's very sore downstairs!' She laughed again.

'*Lo siento*,' I apologised.

'Oh no! I'm not complaining! In case you couldn't tell from my screams, I was very, *very* happy.'

'Good,' I said then laughed as I remembered what the receptionist had said about other guests hearing Jasmine calling my name.

I liked to know I was doing a great job at work, but hearing that I had satisfied Jasmine in the bedroom made me feel fantastic.

A guy came over and asked if we wanted to buy some souvenirs, but when we said no, he left.

'Do you want to sit here for a bit longer or continue walking?' Jasmine asked.

'We can carry on walking.' I stood up and held out my hand. She took it and I led her over to the sea where the water gently lapped against the shore.

And as we walked along the beach, hand in hand, staring in awe at the bright-blue, cloudless sky, watching the palm trees gently swaying and feeling the soft sand under our feet, I wondered once again whether I was dreaming.

Being here, in paradise with Jasmine, was perfection. It was everything I had wished for and more.

My only wish was that it could last for longer than just this weekend.

30

ALEJANDRO

Everyone had moments in their lives that they would never forget. For some, it could be the day they got married or when their first child was born.

But I knew from the moment that I had sex with Jasmine that my life would never be the same again.

This weekend was incredible. I was glad that we decided to stay longer. I thought our first night there was mind-blowing, but Saturday and today were out of this world.

It was not just the sex, which just seemed to get better and better, but also how comfortable I felt around Jasmine.

As well as going for walks along the beach, we had exchanged playlists then spent hours talking about our favourite songs and introducing each other to new artists.

I could not believe it when she told me the music that she liked and discovered that we also had that in common. The more I got to know her, the more I knew it was not just about her beauty. We connected in so many other ways too.

We spent so much time together, I would have expected that by now, I would need my space. But although we still had about two hours until we arrived back at Ocho Rios, I was already wondering how we could find a way to see each other again without the management finding out.

Right now, we were in Bob's car. Our bodies were only inches apart, but it was not close enough. My hands were aching to touch her. I wanted to lean over and kiss Jasmine, but we could not. Although Bob did not seem like he would report us to management, we could not take the risk. We needed to make him and everyone else at the hotel believe that we were still nothing more than co-workers.

It would be difficult, but we had to try. I had already avoided two calls from Lola because I was worried that somehow, she would know I had done what I had sworn not to do: put my career and my sister's tuition at risk because I could not keep my dick in my pants.

Instead, I had texted her to let her know I had been 'busy' and would call when things were calmer. I could not avoid her forever, but I wanted to enjoy these moments with Jasmine without any negativity.

Tomorrow, when the Jamaican management returned, I would need to be professional and sensible. But until then, I would do whatever felt right.

'You okay?' Jasmine asked.

'*Sí*. Just thinking. You?'

'About going back to reality?' Her shoulders fell a little.

I nodded.

'Same here.'

Bob's phone rang and a Jamaican woman's loud voice blared from his mobile. I could not follow what she said. Bob ended the call.

'*Mi ave tuh mek ah lickle stop,*' he announced.

I frowned.

'You have to stop somewhere?' Jasmine helpfully translated.

'*Ya.*'

'Okay. Take as long as you need.'

About twenty minutes later, Bob pulled up outside a house and said he would be back soon.

It was now around eight thirty at night and the only lighting on this road seemed to come from the houses.

Jasmine and I both looked out of the window, our gaze following Bob as he stepped inside the house.

As soon as the front door closed, our eyes moved to each other. Thanks to the light from the front of the house, I was able to make out Jasmine's beautiful face. Her lips were parted. Her eyes were wide and sparkling.

She did not need to speak. I knew what she was thinking, because I was thinking the same.

Our heads inched forward, cautiously at first, but then what could not have been more than two seconds later, our faces launched forward and our mouths crashed together.

The kiss was wild and passionate.

'Oh God,' she moaned into my mouth.

My cock instantly thickened, desperate to be inside her.

The sound of voices brought us back to our senses and we both sprung backwards; our heads flicking to the car window.

Bob was waving to the woman and on his way back to the car. I instantly wished he had taken longer.

'That was close,' I said.

'Too close.' Jasmine smoothed down her dress and straightened in her seat.

For the rest of the journey, we managed to keep our hands and mouths apart, but it was torture.

But the hardest part was when I walked Jasmine to her room and knew I would not be able to follow her inside.

'So...' I stood in front of her. 'Tomorrow, I guess we will be very busy with the management.'

'Yes,' she sighed.

We stood in silence again, neither of us knowing what to say. Eventually, I spoke.

'*Duerme bien* and I hope tomorrow is productive for you.'

'Hope you sleep well too and you enjoy working with the chef.'

I hated how everything was so formal and awkward. But we both knew that from now on, we had to be extra careful.

'*Hasta mañana*,' I said.

'See you tomorrow,' Jasmine replied and let herself in her room.

I opened my door then leant against it, wondering how I was going to survive the night without her.

31

JASMINE

My head was spinning. I'd spent the whole morning in meetings with Hortense, the Love Alchemist Empress (basically head of guest relations), going through all my observations and findings so far and trying to nail down which locations we both felt were best to add to the itinerary.

It was difficult because Hortense obviously knew a lot more about Jamaica than I did. But at the same time, my experience of the Love Hotel brand and the kinds of customers we attracted superseded hers. The way I saw it though, it wasn't a competition. The goal was to combine both of our strengths to come up with a formidable itinerary that our guests would enjoy and most importantly, that would help them fall in love.

Thankfully, she had another meeting to get to, so now I was in the office alone. But instead of grabbing lunch, I had to do the thing I'd been putting off for days: speak to Hazel.

I'd messaged first thing this morning to let her know I'd give her a call once my meeting had finished with Hortense to fill her in on the visit to Rick's Café.

I knew she would've expected me to call over the weekend,

but I was having too much of a good time and didn't want to leave our happy bubble.

It wasn't just the amazing sex that blew my mind. It was those other moments too. Walking hand in hand along Seven Mile Beach talking about everything and nothing and of course, the way he'd opened up to me.

I'd always wrongly assumed that because Alejandro was so gorgeous, he must be a ladies' man, taking advantage of his youth and good looks. But when he revealed he'd been in a committed relationship for three years, that shocked me.

My heart broke for him when I heard about how he'd tragically lost his girlfriend. Especially knowing that he'd also lost both his parents when he was still a teenager. To go through so many tragedies at such an early age must have been horrendous.

I imagined that kind of trauma forced him to grow up faster than most teenagers. Which could be why he seemed much older than his years. Then again, I wasn't a psychologist so I couldn't say for sure.

What I did know for certain though was that it couldn't have been easy to talk about or for him to even consider moving on, so it meant a lot that he trusted me enough to share something so personal.

And when he confessed that I was the first woman he'd been with since his girlfriend passed, I was stunned and honoured.

I hadn't been with anyone since my divorce, but that was completely different. Alejandro taking that step was a big deal. I was glad that I was able to help him get back into dating again.

Now that his desire had returned, no doubt once we went back to Spain, he'd be making up for lost time. Even though we had an amazing connection, I still had to be realistic. This could never be something serious.

Last night, I'd barely slept. I couldn't stop thinking about

Alejandro and wishing he was there in bed with me. I got myself so worked up that I'd used my vibrator and although it did the job, it couldn't even begin to compare to the countless spine-tingling orgasms Alejandro had effortlessly delivered.

It was clear.

Alejandro had ruined me.

Using a vibrator after having sex with him was like staying in a five-star hotel then being moved to a cockroach-infested, one-star hostel. There was no comparison.

But it was what it was. The weekend was fun, but now it was over between us.

There were a lot more staff buzzing around the hotel today. It wasn't deserted like last week, so we couldn't hook up without someone noticing.

My computer started ringing. When I glanced at the screen, Hazel was calling. And it was a video call.

Shit.

I should've phoned her straightaway instead of thinking about Alejandro.

'Hazel! Hi! I've just finished my meeting with Hortense and was about to call you!' I said as brightly as I could, despite the fact that my heart was thumping in my chest.

'I was starting to wonder if you were still alive,' she said solemnly. 'I was expecting you to call me back on Saturday when I called multiple times *and* messaged.'

'So sorry! I was having problems with my phone,' I lied, hoping I wouldn't be sent to hell. I was about to elaborate by adding something like the fact my battery had died because I wasn't expecting to be staying there overnight but Hazel knew as well as I did that all reputable hotels had spare phone chargers. Best to keep it simple.

'Really? What kinds of problems?'

Dammit. Why couldn't she just accept I had problems and leave it at that?

'Reception was patchy. And I wasn't sure if you had time off, so I didn't want to disturb you.'

'Hmmm,' she huffed. 'I was working all day. It's very unlike you not to get back to me straightaway. So? How was it?'

I filled her in on our trip to Rick's Café (minus the part about me rubbing my arse against Alejandro's cock on the dance floor of course).

'So as I mentioned to Hortense earlier, I think it would be a great addition to the itinerary. We'd need to check with legal regarding guests jumping and add something to state that they do so at their own risk.'

'Of course. But do you think it will stimulate romance?'

'Definitely!' I said as a flashback of my mouth pressed against Alejandro's jumped into my mind. 'The sunset is very romantic. And the atmosphere is very... charged,' I said diplomatically.

'How so?' She rested her finger on her chin.

'Well, there were lots of couples dancing closely and even the cocktails are named with togetherness in mind.'

Yes. *Closely* was one way of describing the provocative bumping and grinding people like me and Alejandro did.

And *togetherness* was a professional of way of avoiding going into detail about the 'Mating Season' drinks that were on offer.

She didn't need to know that Alejandro had researched the Jamaican Viagra cocktail personally, or that whilst I couldn't prove it was responsible for the after-effects, I *could* vouch for the fact that he was hard all night.

And I definitely wouldn't be stupid enough to add that I'd tried the Sex With Rick cocktail which had unrelatedly led to me having Sex With Alejandro several times over the weekend.

No. The less Hazel knew, the better.

'I see. And did *you* do any of this dancing?'

'Me?' My eyes widened as I tried to buy myself more time. 'I was there to observe. Most people were couples and I'm obviously single, so...' I shrugged, pleased that I'd answered the question without having to outright lie. 'I did however try the cliff jumping and it was thrilling!'

'Tell me more.' Hazel leant forward and I gave myself a mental high five for diverting her attention away from the dancing. 'Sounds great. And tell me about the sunset. Better still, send me some photos right now. I'd love to see it, especially as that's one of the main attractions.'

My stomach bottomed out.

Hazel wanted me to send photos of the sunset, but I just realised I didn't have any. Because although of course I'd watched it, briefly, I'd spent most of the time locking lips with Alejandro.

Shit.

Screwing Alejandro was bad enough, but at least I'd done it off the clock.

Hazel was right. The main reason for going to Rick's Café was to watch the romantic sunset, so of course she'd want to see photos.

I'd always prided myself on being good at my job, but I'd let myself down and Hazel.

'I tried taking some, but they came out blurry,' I said quickly, 'so I deleted them. The ones on the website are pretty accurate, though.'

'Is everything okay with you, Jasmine?' Hazel's face was more wrinkled than a frowning pug's.

'Yes!' My voice went up several octaves. 'Of course!'

'You don't seem yourself. Normally, you reply to my messages straightaway. And after every location you've visited, you've always sent me a barrage of photos afterwards, but not only were you MIA for an entire weekend, you've just told me that after taking a trip to the other side of the island, you don't have a single photo of the sunset: a key feature of the location!'

She had a point. A very, very valid point.

To be honest, I challenge anyone to even think about taking photos of the most beautiful sunset views in the world when they had the most beautiful man in the world's face in front of them.

And if she ever sampled his kisses, I could guarantee that Hazel wouldn't even remember her own name or have the ability to think clearly about anything.

But of course, I couldn't tell her that feeling his hard body pressed against me and the sensation of his delicious tongue flicking against mine had turned my brain to mush, so I had to think of something else to say.

Fast.

'You're right. I don't know what happened. I think I was so caught up in the beauty of it all that I didn't think to check how the photos had come out until it was too late. I'm sorry. It won't happen again.'

There.

Question answered.

In hindsight, there were loads of people taking photos so if I was thinking clearly, I could've asked a stranger to send me some images they'd taken and my problem would've been solved. But, like I said, it was impossible to think logically when Alejandro was nearby.

Hazel stayed silent for a few seconds before leaning back in her chair.

'Make sure it doesn't.'

Phew.

'Now.' She slammed her hand on the desk. 'Remind me why you felt the need to stay at a hotel?'

Looked like I wasn't out of the woods yet...

'Because our driver wasn't able to take us back.'

'Why not?'

Shit. I wasn't about to drop Bob in it by saying he was off his head.

'He seemed tired,' I said. 'And we couldn't locate another licensed taxi driver who would be willing to take the long journey back to our hotel. I know how much the Love Hotel values the safety of its Romance Rockstars, so staying at a hotel seemed like a small price to pay to guarantee our wellbeing.'

Boom.

That was a great answer even if I said so myself. If Hazel argued with me on that, she'd be saying she didn't care about our safety. And although what Alejandro and I ended up doing together was reckless, that wasn't our original intention.

'Very well. However, I noticed that there was only *one* hotel room on the credit-card bill. And that particular room type isn't large enough to accommodate a sofa. So where did you both sleep?'

'I'm sorry.' I frowned. 'When you say "that particular room type", what do you mean? And what led you to believe there wasn't a sofa?'

'I checked.' Hazel clasped her hands together.

She *checked*?

Jesus.

I wondered whether she'd actually called the hotel or researched the room online. Right now wasn't the time to think about how she'd done it, though.

Hazel was glaring at me. Clearly, she suspected that something was going on between me and Alejandro, so I needed to shut down her concerns.

Fast.

'You're right.' I nodded. 'The room was very small. Unfortunately, everywhere was fully booked at such short notice. There were several events on that weekend, so all that was available was the one room. That's why there is only one charge on the card.'

'You didn't answer my question: if there was only one room, then where did you *both* sleep?'

'I slept in the bed of course,' I said firmly.

'And your *underling*, Alejandro?' She raised her eyebrow. 'I'm sure I don't need to remind you how inappropriate it would be for a person in your position to share a hotel room with a subordinate, do I?'

'Of course not!' I scoffed, my heart now hammering so hard, I felt like I was about to pass out. 'I'm well aware of the rules. Alejandro made *other arrangements*,' I said, hoping she'd understand what I was trying to imply and leave it at that.

But of course, she didn't.

'Meaning?'

'Alejandro is a young man in a tropical paradise. I'm sure you've noticed that he attracts a lot of *attention* and it's no different here in Jamaica. But I'm his boss so it's not my place to ask questions about his personal life or whose bed he chooses to sleep in. His job was to accompany me to the café to research the food and refreshments there. And he did that. By the time it was clear that we couldn't return to Ocho Rios and there was an accommodation shortage, he was off the clock, so he wasn't obligated to answer to me.'

I finished my sentence and then zipped my mouth shut.

Despite the sweat pooling under my armpits and along my hairline, I had to act cooler than a cucumber.

I *had* to stay calm and confident.

The slightest stutter, the slightest sign of uncertainty could send this whole pack of lies crashing down and end my career.

'I see.' Hazel nodded. 'Well, now the staff are back in the hotel, be sure to keep an eye on him. Make sure he doesn't have any dalliances with our Jamaican Romance Rockstars. The last thing I need to deal with is another employee inappropriateness issue.'

'Understood.'

'Right, I have another meeting now. But let's speak again tomorrow so you can fill me in on what decisions you and Hortense have reached.'

'I'll add it to my calendar,' I said.

When I ended the call and put my computer screen to sleep, I leant on the desk and dropped my head in my hands.

That was close.

Dangerously close.

Hazel definitely suspected something. So if I wasn't sure before that I needed to shut things down with Alejandro, now I was certain.

It didn't matter that the man hadn't just rocked my world, he'd rocked my whole damn universe.

It didn't matter that I felt more connected to him than any other man in my life.

My career was everything to me. I couldn't lose it.

So as much as every part of my body ached for Alejandro, the fun was over.

There was no other option.

32

ALEJANDRO

It was now Wednesday. The last few days had been torture. Not just because I did not like working with the Dudley, the head chef, but also because I had not seen Jasmine.

When I had messaged her on Monday after work to see if she would like to meet, Jasmine replied saying she did not think it would be a good idea.

I knew that when we returned here, it would be difficult. There were more staff around. But that did not mean we could not arrange to meet somewhere away from the resort.

In just three days, we would start our journey back to Spain and return to our normal lives. Although we would be doing a stopover in Miami this time and not in London, so would have time alone, I could not wait until then to discuss what had happened. And what this could be.

Last weekend may have been something casual for Jasmine, but this meant something to me. I really felt like we had a chance for this to become a real relationship.

That was why I was not going to give up easily.

I dialled Bob's number.

'Hola, Bob! Qué tal?'

'Wah gwaan, bredrin?' I could feel his smile down the phone.

'Do you know somewhere private that I could take someone special, away from the hotel? Early in the morning, before work?'

'Yuh a luk fi sumweh tuh tek, Miss Jasmine?'

'Is it that obvious?' I said, pleased that I had understood that he was asking if I was looking for somewhere to take Jasmine.

'Mi did si dem sparks a fly fram daii wan. Mi happy fi yuh!'

I laughed. I supposed it would not take a genius to see the way that I looked at her, but I did not realise Bob had noticed sparks flying between us from the first day. It was a good thing management were not there to see them too.

Bob said he knew just the place that we could visit, but then said there was a problem.

'What is wrong?' I asked.

'Dem get rid ah mi.'

I frowned as I tried to work out what he meant.

'Somebody got rid of you?'

'Ya mon. Di management. Dem seh mi unprofessional.'

'No!' My mouth fell open. Bob was not like the chauffeurs the Love Hotel normally had, but he was not unprofessional. He always turned up when he was supposed to, he always put us at ease and when he had been drinking, he immediately said he was not fit to drive. Those were important qualities. 'So you cannot work for the hotel any more?'

'No mon.'

'I am sorry to hear that.' I really was. I needed to find out more about what had happened. Bob was a good man. 'But just because you do not work for the hotel, I can still book you if I pay for it myself, right?'

'Ya mon.'

'That is fine then!' The tension released in my shoulders. I trusted Bob. I had grown fond of him. I did not want to use anyone else.

Bob told me more about the location he had in mind for my surprise date with Jasmine, then we agreed on a plan. Everything was settled. All I had to do was one small thing: convince Jasmine to meet me, which would not be easy.

After sending Jasmine a text, I pulled on my shorts, put my phone in my pocket, then left my room to go for a run.

It was eight in the morning, so later than I normally ran, but what I had noticed from working with Dudley was that he was not an early riser. So as long as I was in the kitchen by ten, I was sure to be there before he was.

The beach was deserted which was just the way I liked it. As I sprinted along the shore, I took in the sight of the crystal-clear water. It was more translucent than the sea in Spain and I loved it. If I had time this afternoon, I would go for a swim.

As I ran, I tried to clear my mind of the frustration I felt about the whole situation with Jasmine. It all seemed so unfair. We had such a strong connection. Chemistry like that should not be ignored. I needed to find a way that we could be together. Hopefully, that was something we could discuss if she agreed to meet me tomorrow.

My phone rang and my heart instantly expanded, hoping that it was her calling after reading my text. But when I pulled it out of my pocket and glanced at the screen, I saw it was Lola.

'*Hola*,' I answered reluctantly. I still had not called since the weekend, choosing only to respond with texts.

'He speaks!' she said sarcastically. 'Are you avoiding me?'

'Why would I be avoiding you?' I said, trying to keep my voice level.

There was silence and when I looked down on the screen, she had sent a request to switch to a video call.

This was not good, but I had to accept.

'Wow. Beautiful!'

'*Gracias*,' I grinned, cheekily.

'I'm not talking about you! I'm talking about the beach.'

'I know!' I laughed, feeling more relaxed.

'So? Why haven't you called?'

Was I just saying I felt more relaxed? My shoulders tightened.

'Like I said in my messages, I have been very busy. The chef and the management are back at the hotel now so I am working night and day.'

'But I called you at the weekend. *Before* they came back. When you had time off...' She raised her eyebrow with suspicion.

'I was out.' My gaze dropped to the sand. I was not good at hiding things. I always liked to speak the truth.

'There's something you're not telling me.'

I dragged my hand over my face. I would have to tell Lola sooner or later, so there was no point in delaying the inevitable.

'I slept with Jasmine.'

'Ale!' Lola shouted. 'You promised you wouldn't!'

'I could not stop it.' I shrugged.

'But what about your career?'

'Everything is fine. We were careful. We were away from the hotel – on the other side of the island. No one saw us. And you will be happy to know that we have not seen each other since then.'

My chest tensed. I really hoped I could see her tomorrow.

'Good. You may have got away with it at the weekend, but you'd be an even bigger idiot to risk doing it again. Especially so close to when you're going back to Spain. Just keep your head down and focus.'

'That I can definitely do...' I smirked mischievously. Perhaps now was not a good time to joke, but I could not resist.

'Get your mind out of the gutter! I didn't mean like *that*. *Keep your head down* is an English saying for avoiding trouble. Keep your head away from between Jasmine's legs!'

'I am familiar with the saying.' I smiled. 'But I really think this could be something. It is not just about the sex.'

'Remember our last conversation about how many billions of women there are in the world?'

'I would not care if there were three trillion. Jasmine is the only one I want.'

'You're serious, aren't you?' Lola let out a loud sigh.

'*Sí.*'

'Bloody hell,' she said and hearing her say such a British phrase with her Spanish accent made me smile. 'And how does *she* feel?'

'I do not know. I have asked if we can meet to talk tomorrow. Away from the hotel.'

'Has she agreed?'

'I am still waiting for her to reply.'

'Keep me updated and be careful. Don't go to each other's rooms. Don't do anything at the hotel. No sneaking off to storerooms or hiding around corners. People always get caught doing that shit.'

'Sounds like you are speaking from experience.' I raised an eyebrow.

'I may or may not have hooked up with a waiter when I was working at a hotel in my early twenties. And getting caught *may* have been the reason I was asked to leave.'

'This is news to me!' I smiled.

'I was hardly going to share this information with my little brother, was I? Anyway, this isn't about me. This is about damage control. Before you get in any deeper, you need to make sure you're both on the same page. I don't want you to lose your job over this – especially if she doesn't feel the same.'

As much as I hated to admit it, Lola was right.

'Understood.'

'Anyway, I better go. I just wanted to check you were okay.'

'*Gracias*. And everything is good with you?'

'Yeah. Same old, same old. Not all of us can be having fun on a gorgeous tropical island. Some of us have to stare out of an office window and see grey skies in London.'

'You love it really!'

'I love London and my husband. But I don't love the weather.'

'You cannot have everything you want.'

'No. Remember that when you're thinking about shagging your boss again and throwing away your career.'

Touché.

'Point taken. Enjoy your day.'

I ended the call then looked at my messages.

My heart jumped.

Jasmine had read my text.

The *typing...* message flashed on the screen.

She was replying.

Now I just had to hope that I liked what she said...

33

JASMINE

I stared at my phone screen.

For the last ten minutes, I'd been trying to work out how best to reply to Alejandro's messages.

I read them again.

> How are you?
>
> I miss you. I really need to see you.
>
> Meet Bob tomorrow at reception at 5.45 in the morning (I know it is early but I promise it will be worth it).
>
> He will take you to meet me somewhere private where we will not be seen. You will be back in time to start work.

When I'd woken up and seen his messages, my heart had flipped. I'd missed him too.

I'd been playing the playlist he'd sent me non-stop. In the office, in my room... but always through my headphones. I didn't want to risk him hearing it through the bedroom wall or in the unlikely event he came into the office.

But like I'd said when he'd messaged yesterday and the day before, seeing each other wasn't a good idea.

I had to admit though, with every day that passed, my resolve weakened.

After seeing him every day last week and spending that magical weekend together, it was so hard to be apart. There were so many things I wanted to talk to him about.

I wanted to tell him how much I loved the artists that he'd introduced me to and tell him my favourite ¿Téo? songs.

I wanted to hear about how things were going with the chef. I'd been so busy that I either ordered food to eat in the office or the couple of times I'd eaten in the restaurant, I'd had to sit with Hortense and Alejandro was hidden away in the kitchen.

Sometimes, I'd heard him come in at night or leave in the morning. And when I heard the shower turn on through the bathroom wall, I wished I was there with him.

It was crazy to think that our rooms were right next door, but we'd managed to avoid seeing each other for almost three days. And I couldn't lie. I was at breaking point.

My fingers hovered over the phone keys.

I knew what I should write. I should just copy and paste my previous messages and remind him that it wasn't a good idea. Hazel already suspected something and Hortense seemed to be watching me like a hawk too. That was the sensible thing to do. So far, we'd gotten away with it, so we should quit whilst we were ahead.

But before I knew it, I'd typed out a reply that definitely wasn't a good idea and pressed send.

> Okay. See you tomorrow morning.

* * *

It was now Thursday morning and I was in the car with Bob, heading to the secret location to meet Alejandro.

My heart thundered in my chest. Partly with fear of getting caught, but mostly with excitement about seeing Alejandro again.

When I'd crept out of my room, I'd checked that the coast was clear and didn't see anyone around. Reception was empty too.

I'd subtly asked Nadine last night what time she started this morning and she'd said she'd be here at eleven, which was fine.

Hortense seemed to come to the office after ten, so as long as I was at my desk by nine-ish, I'd be fine. That gave me a clear three hours to spend with Alejandro. Not that we'd need that long of course. I was only going there to tell him in person that Hazel was suspicious and we couldn't continue, so depending on where this secret location was, I could be back in my room (alone) within the hour.

Yes. As soon as I'd explained the situation to Alejandro, I'd leave.

'How have you been, Bob?' I asked as Bob Marley's 'Three Little Birds' blared from the car speaker.

'Dem get rid ah mi.'

'Who got rid of you? The hotel?'

'Ya mon. Dem seh mi unprofessional.'

'No way!' I gasped. 'When did this happen?'

As Bob explained that he'd gotten a call on Monday evening to say his services would no longer be required, my stomach twisted.

Hazel.

She must've arranged for him to be sacked after our conversation. Yeah, he was drunk or stoned, but I know he wouldn't have tried to drive us home in that state. And anyway, I'd told Hazel he was tired. That wasn't a reason to fire him.

'That's not right.' I shook my head. 'Don't worry. I'll look into it and try and find a way to get you your job back. You're a good man.'

'Tanks, Miss Jasmine.'

About ten minutes later, Bob pulled over. The sky was lighter now and painted with orange and pink hues as the sun started to peek through on the horizon.

When I stepped out of the car, I spotted Alejandro.

God, he looked incredible. All I wanted to do was race over to him and sink my head in his chest as he wrapped his arms around me.

But I couldn't. I was only here to talk, tell him it was over, then leave.

'I won't be long,' I said to Bob, both to keep him informed and serve as a reminder to myself that I couldn't stay a minute longer than necessary.

'You came!' Alejandro smiled as I got closer.

'Yes, but I can't stay. I'm just here to talk.'

Alejandro didn't reply. Instead, he took my hand and led me down a pathway.

I knew I should pull away, but I couldn't. I loved the feeling of our fingers being intertwined; it was like his palm was a magnet and the force was too strong for me to break.

It was so peaceful here. All I could hear was the sound of the birds chirping and I think I heard water too, but couldn't be sure.

As we continued walking, the sound of water became louder. Were we near the sea? Alejandro had told me to bring swimwear so that would make sense. I didn't know why I was wearing the bikini Alejandro had bought me when we stayed in Negril under my dress when I already knew I wouldn't be staying for a swim.

But then when he led me around a corner and I saw a waterfall, I gasped.

It wasn't on the same scale as Dunn's River Falls, but it was still beautiful.

In the centre was a tall waterfall with water cascading down a rocky cliff, but on either side were two large, flat rocks where the flow of water was more gentle.

It wasn't just the beauty of the waterfall and the lush, green surroundings that caught my eye. It was the little table that had been set up on top of one of the rocks.

On top of the table was a beautiful spread of food.

'Wow!' I gasped. 'You made breakfast? What time did you get up to prepare all this?'

'Four.' He shrugged like it was no big deal.

'But you need your sleep!'

'Jasmine.' He took both my hands in his and I instantly melted. 'Even if I only slept for ten minutes, it would be worth it to see you. And since we got back, I have not been able to sleep, so I would prefer to do something more productive like cook for you.'

Alejandro looked into my eyes and the intensity of his gaze was like a laser burning through me. My stomach somersaulted and desire coursed through my veins.

If I continued looking at him and let him hold me with those soft, warm hands for a second longer, I'd want to kiss him and I couldn't let that happen.

'Thank you.' I pulled away. 'I'm starving!'

I headed to the table. It'd be better to sit on the wet rock in my bikini, so I pulled off my dress then put it in my waterproof bag on the driest area I could find.

It was funny. This time last week, I wouldn't have worn a bikini. I would've preferred to cover up in my swimming costume. But something had shifted. I felt more comfortable in my skin and judging by the way Alejandro was admiring me as he strode over to the rock, his eyes wide with desire, he approved too. Not that his opinion mattered any more.

As Alejandro peeled off his T-shirt, revealing his delicious, bare chest, I quickly diverted my gaze to the table.

He'd prepared slices of fresh mango, pineapple, banana and papaya and when I saw what was on the plate beside it, my mouth fell open.

'Are those saltfish fritters?' I asked.

'*Sí.*' He nodded. 'Dudley showed me how to make them yesterday. I remembered they were your favourite.'

'Thanks.' I smiled, warning my stomach to stop flipping. That was sweet of him to get up early to make them for me, though. 'Dudley's the Cuisine King, right?'

'*Sí*,' he repeated.

'How's it going with him?' I said, taking a bite of the fritter. It was delicious.

'Not good.'

'Why?'

'He is very... how do you say in English? Set in his ways? He is old fashioned. He does not like to try new things. He likes to remind me that he is the expert in Jamaican food, which of course is true. I told him that I already know this. I am not here to teach him how to cook Jamaican food. That would be stupid. I told him I am here to learn from him, to bring ideas back to the Spanish hotel, and to introduce him to some ideas which may complement his menu, but he says he does not need new ideas.'

'Oof.' I winced.

'And you? How is it with your manager here?'

'It's okay. We locked horns the first day or two but we're

making good progress on the itinerary. She wasn't sure about including Nadine's class or a visit to Rick's Café, but I said I thought it was good for fostering romance and creating a... connection between couples.'

'It worked for us.' Alejandro's mouth curved into a smile.

'About that.' I rested the fritter on the plate. 'I like you, but we can't see each other any more. Hazel already suspects something.'

Alejandro's eyes widened.

I explained the conversation I had and how I got around it. Now that I thought about it, we were lucky she didn't ask Alejandro to verify the story. I should've filled him in sooner on what I'd said.

'Even if she is suspicious, she does not have proof. We have been careful. We have not done anything at the hotel. We have not been in each other's rooms. She has nothing.'

'And the only way to make sure it stays that way is to end this. Before it's too late.'

'It is already too late.' He leant forward and brushed my cheek, setting my skin on fire. 'I have already fallen for you.'

I squeezed my eyes shut, savouring the sweet sensation of his hand on me. As the realisation of what he'd just said hit me, first I felt butterflies, then fear.

No, no, no. We couldn't afford to catch feelings. He probably just felt close to me because I was the first woman he'd slept with since Freya.

'Alejandro, I really appreciate you setting all of this up and making breakfast, but I've got to go.' I jumped up and raced forward.

'Jasmine!' he called out. Just as I reached the waterfall, he grabbed my arm and pulled me into him.

My head told me to resist and pull away, but I couldn't. My

body didn't want to. Alejandro tilted my chin upwards, then slammed his mouth onto mine. The kiss was a desperate collision of lips. It was hot, hungry and feral. Like we'd been told the world was about to end and we were determined to savour every last moment together.

As Alejandro's tongue swept through my mouth, I let out a groan of desire. Wetness pooled between my legs and it had nothing to do with the water streaming over us from the waterfall.

I knew Alejandro was overcome with desire too as his hardness pressed against me.

'I *need* you, Jasmine.'

'I need you too. But we can't. It's too risky.'

Alejandro slowly pulled away and when I opened my eyes, his pupils were the colour of charcoal.

Without saying a word, he scooped me up in his arms, carried me over to the other large flat rock, then laid me down.

'What are you...?' I looked up at him, my chest heaving with desire. 'You want to...? Here?'

He nodded. 'There is no one around. Bob said this place is quiet. People only start visiting later in the morning. We are all alone. I need you so much right now. Every part of me aches for you.'

'Me too.' I ran my hand over my pussy.

'Fuck, Jasmine. The sight of you touching yourself.' He winced like he was in agony. 'I... Please let me taste you. Let me bury myself inside you.'

Alejandro dropped to his knees and rested his hand on the sides of my bikini bottoms.

'Is it okay?' he asked.

'Yes.' I nodded.

'Tell me what you want,' he growled as he slid my bikini bottoms down my thighs, then past my legs and ankles until I was laid bare on the rock for him. 'Would you like me to eat you or fuck you?'

'I'd like both, but I'd also like not to get arrested and thrown into a Jamaican jail cell, so because we need to be quick, please just fuck me.'

Alejandro reached into the pocket of his trunks and pulled out a condom.

'Someone was confident.' I arched my eyebrow.

'I was not sure if this would happen, but I wanted to be prepared.'

He pulled his trunks down and as his enormous cock sprang free, I swallowed hard before running my hand down it. How was it possible that I'd missed it after just a few days when I'd gone without sex for years?

Anticipation raced through me and I spread my legs wide, ready for him.

Once he'd rolled the condom on, he lined himself up at my entrance.

'Sure?' he asked.

'Yes.'

Alejandro sunk inside me and I cried out. He'd only just started and it already felt amazing. I hooked my legs around his back, pushing him deeper.

'Are you okay?' he asked.

'*More* than okay,' I said, the sound of our bodies slapping together in the shallow water echoing around me.

I couldn't believe I was outside, my legs spread open whilst Alejandro fucked me at a waterfall. This definitely gave a new meaning to morning sex.

But as Alejandro looked down at me like I was the most incredible creature ever created and stroked my cheek, something felt different to the first night we had sex. Somehow this felt more... intimate?

'You are sure the rock is not too hard and cold for you?'

'A little.'

Alejandro froze.

'I will lift you up so you sit on my lap. *Vale?*'

'Okay,' I said.

A couple of swift moves later, I was straddling Alejandro's lap. I loved the feeling of being impaled on his dick. I started riding him, hard.

Alejandro groaned, then leant forward and kissed me.

'You are beautiful,' he groaned.

As our bodies moved together in perfect harmony, I was overcome not only with desire, but the sense that everything was just so... right.

It was like being stranded in the ocean and finally finding a stretch of safe land.

Like being reunited with a long-lost love after years apart.

Like travelling for months, sleeping in different shitty hotel beds, then finally coming home and sleeping on your own comfortable mattress.

Yes. That was it. When Alejandro was inside me, it felt like I'd come home.

Knowing that we were doing this outside where there was always a danger of getting caught should mean that we should be quick. But I felt so close to him right now, I never wanted this to end.

Alejandro unclipped the back of my bikini, leant forward and took my nipple in his mouth. I threw my head back, crying out with pleasure, just as he took the other nipple in his mouth.

'You are so... Jasmine, I...' He nuzzled his face in my chest as I continued riding him.

Just as I thought I had the build-up of my orgasm under control, Alejandro reached between my legs and started stroking my clit.

'Ohhhh! Oh God.' I rocked my hips faster. 'I'm going to... I'm close.'

As he peppered soft kisses along my neck and continued touching me, I knew I was about to lose control.

My orgasm erupted like a volcano. My blood felt like molten lava and despite the cool water gently lapping against our bare skin, every part of my body was on fire.

Alejandro continued thrusting, then several seconds later, his body stilled and he groaned as he emptied himself inside me.

My head dropped forward onto his shoulder and he wrapped his arms around me, our chests heaving as we struggled to catch our breath.

When I eventually had the energy to lift my head and open my eyes, Alejandro began trailing his fingers gently down my back. It was so soothing that I could fall asleep right here.

'Mmm,' I murmured. 'I wish we didn't have to go to work.'

'I know,' he sighed. 'I could stay like this, with you, here, forever.'

Alejandro traced circles on my back and a feeling of complete bliss and happiness washed over me.

I didn't remember ever feeling so at peace or experiencing such complete and utter satisfaction.

Last weekend was out of this world. I thought nothing could top it, but there was something about this morning that made me feel even more connected to Alejandro.

Knowing that we were supposed to be distancing ourselves,

not getting closer, should make me want to run for the hills right now. But I couldn't. I didn't want to.

And so I stayed.

When Alejandro gently pressed his lips on my mouth and kissed me tenderly, I didn't pull away.

Instead, I savoured every delicious moment. Hoping and praying it wouldn't be our last.

34

ALEJANDRO

I kissed Jasmine softly on the top of her head. She was currently resting on my shoulder, our arms wrapped around each other.

This felt like a dream.

That was...

I had no words. Well, that was not true. I had many words, but none came close to describing the enormity of emotions I felt when I was inside Jasmine.

Some of the sensations were familiar to me. The desire. The passion. The need. But the closeness? The connection? They were all new.

For two years, I had wandered through life with half a heart, half a body. But when Jasmine and I made love, it was like our bodies connected and I became whole.

Madre mía.

Listen to me.

My sister was a romantic, but even *she* would vomit if she knew the sentimental thoughts racing through my head right now.

It sounded corny, but it was how I felt.

And I almost told Jasmine.

When she straddled me, I nearly lost my mind and said out loud that I loved her. Luckily, I stopped myself just in time.

I did not want to scare her away. I knew she did not feel the same. And I knew that she would say it was too soon. But the truth was, these emotions did not start in Jamaica. My feelings for Jasmine had been growing for months. Being together at the weekend and again this morning just solidified what I always knew: that I was in love with her.

'What's the time?' Jasmine said lazily, her eyes still squeezed shut.

'Almost eight.'

'Already?' She groaned. 'I don't want to go to work! I just want to lie on this rock all day and let you make love to me over and over again.'

She felt it too.

Earlier, she said she wanted me to fuck her. I had offered to do the same. But now, she had said *make love*.

My heart swelled. Maybe there was hope.

'I meant, we could fuck... Not make love!' She bolted off my shoulder and laughed like the idea was ridiculous. 'Slip of the tongue. Stupid orgasm brain! We should get cleaned up and dressed. Just in case.'

Oh.

So she did not feel the same connection as I did.

For her, it really was just sex.

She scooped her bikini off the rock, then went and stood under the waterfall.

The sight of her beautiful body as the water trickled down her skin and she rinsed herself off was incredible. I was hypnotised by her beauty. It was only when she strode back over to the other side of the waterfall that I broke out of my trance.

After rolling off the condom and washing off, I joined Jasmine on the other rock with the food and put on my shorts just as she finished fastening her bikini top.

As we ate breakfast, my thoughts turned back to what she had just said.

It was clear. This was not serious for her.

Lola said I needed to find out how Jasmine felt before I fell for her so that I would not get hurt.

But now I knew we were not on the same page.

As for not falling for her and not getting hurt, it was too late.

Because it was clear that I had already done both.

35

JASMINE

I zipped up my suitcase and wheeled it towards my room door. I couldn't believe it was my last day in Jamaica. The time had flown by. Especially the last couple of days.

From dusk until dawn, I'd been locked inside the hotel's conference room training the Jamaican Love Alchemists and it'd been intense.

Originally, the plan was to space out the training sessions. But because so many key team members were ill during the first week, I had to cram everything into the second.

But the work I'd come here to do was done. I hoped I'd impressed Hortense enough that she'd rave about me to Hazel and that when I returned to Spain, the promotion would be mine.

The last few times I'd video called Hazel, she'd been fine, so thankfully, I was off the hook and all suspicions of Alejandro and I being involved had evaporated.

Shame I couldn't say the same for the situation in my brain.

That waterfall morning sex session still lived rent free in my head, playing on repeat day and night. And I could understand why. The feelings were unlike anything else I'd experienced in my whole life. Which was probably why I'd stupidly slipped up and called it *making love*.

I was glad I corrected myself quickly. I didn't want Alejandro to think I was some sappy almost forty-year-old falling in love with a toy boy just because he'd given her multiple orgasms.

Obviously, I liked Alejandro. A lot. In fact, I didn't think there was a man I'd ever liked more than him. But as much as wanted to continue seeing him, I just couldn't see where it could go.

The work issue alone was big enough. Especially as Hazel had made her thoughts on employee fraternisation very clear. But the age thing was an even bigger concern. Not because I thought Alejandro was immature. In many ways, he showed more maturity than my ex who was twenty years his senior. It was the future that concerned me.

Alejandro would want kids and I wasn't sure if that was something that I wanted or if it was even possible. I couldn't expect him to sacrifice becoming a father for me.

So that was that.

Plus, I'd already had one failed relationship with an age gap. And that was a nine-year difference, so I wasn't about to jump into another one with a man who was a whopping eleven years younger than me. *Nope. No way.*

Once we'd finished eating breakfast at the waterfall, I'd given him a long, slow kiss, thanked him again for an incredible morning and headed back to the hotel. And that was the last time I saw Alejandro.

Even if I'd wanted to see him, it wouldn't have been possible. Like I said, I'd been working non-stop and crashed out the second my head hit the pillow. He hadn't messaged, so I suspected it'd been the same for him too.

But now we'd be travelling back to Spain together. And that

included an overnight stopover in Miami. As tempting as it would be for something to happen there, this time, I really had to be strong.

I took one last look at my bedroom, then headed to reception. When I arrived, Nadine was there.

'Hey, girl!' She smiled. 'Can't believe you're leaving us! I've hardly seen you this week.'

'I know! It's been manic. How've you been?'

'Good! Hortense said she's interested in seeing my dance class, so thanks for recommending me.'

'You're welcome! I'll keep everything crossed for you. Let's keep in touch.'

Seconds after I'd given her my number, the hairs on my arms stood up and a gorgeous woody scent wafted through the air. When I turned around, I saw Alejandro a few feet away, looking ridiculously hot.

Did he ever look terrible? The idea of walking away from him in twenty-four hours would be so much easier if he didn't look like an Adonis.

Alejandro was kind, attentive, smart and an amazing cook. Why did he have to be outrageously attractive too? I felt sorry for all the single guys in the world. Age and work complications aside, he was the total package.

He smiled and my stomach flip-flopped.

Ugh.

'*Hola chicas!*' he greeted us.

'Hey, Alejandro!' Nadine beamed. 'I was just saying to Jasmine that it's been ages since I've seen you guys.'

'We have both been very busy.' He looked at me.

'So I heard! I hope you still got to do some bumping and whining during your time off?' She smirked.

Alejandro's eyes popped.

'She means practising the dance moves we learnt.'

'Oh...' His shoulders loosened.

'You thought I meant...' Nadine laughed. 'I hope you got some good, good lovin' too!' She looked between us then gave a knowing smile.

Did she know?

My heart raced, then I remembered that even if she suspected something, like Alejandro said when I told him about Hazel, she didn't have any proof. And I trusted Nadine. It was fine.

'I'm going to miss this place.' I changed the subject.

'Me too,' Alejandro said.

'Aww, you'll have to visit when it's open!'

'I might take you up on that,' I said.

I'd like to visit the hotel, but I'd also love to see my grandad. Despite trying to reach him several times on the phone this week during my short breaks, there was no answer. That was to be expected. He almost never answered. I wished I'd had more time here so I could've tried to visit again.

'Your driver's here.' Nadine signalled to a stiff-looking chauffeur in a smart, grey suit and hat, standing beside a shiny, black Mercedes.

My heart instantly sank. Although I'd given him a hug and said goodbye when he dropped me back to the hotel after my trip to the waterfall, I was still hoping to see Bob one last time.

I hadn't had a chance to look into his sacking yet, but I was making it a priority when I got back.

'Okay,' I said. 'We'd better get going. Thanks again for everything.'

'*Sí*,' Alejandro added. '*Muchas gracias.*' He stepped forward and gave Nadine two cheek kisses which instantly caused my brain to replay the memory of his mouth pressed on mine.

After I gave Nadine a hug, I headed over to the driver with Alejandro.

'Good morning, sir, madam. My name is Egbert and I will be your driver for today. Please, allow me to take care of your luggage.'

Egbert was perfectly polite and fitted the Love Hotel criteria perfectly. But he was formal and a bit robotic. He didn't have the same warm, energetic personality that Bob had.

'Nice to meet you, Egbert,' I said.

Just as we were about to get into the car, the sound of Bob Marley & The Wailers' 'Could You Be Loved?' boomed through the air. My head snapped up and I saw Bob's car racing towards us.

'He came!' Alejandro's face broke into a smile.

Bob parked haphazardly in the middle of the driveway, then casually got out of the car, the track still blaring.

'Tank jah mi ketch yuh!'

'I'm glad you caught us before we left too!' I raced over to him. 'Thanks for everything.'

'Yuh welcome! Walk good and memba fi call mi wen yuh reach.' He patted a frowning Alejandro on the shoulder.

'Bob said we need to remember to call him when we arrive home.'

'Ah, sí. Vale!'

We gave Bob a hug, waved to Nadine then set off to the airport.

'That was nice of Bob to come and see us off,' I said as the hotel grounds faded into the background.

'It was. He is a good man. They should give him a permanent job at the hotel.'

'I agree,' I said, hoping we hadn't offended the current driver. It was true, though. I reckoned he'd be a big hit with the guests.

Alejandro and I stared at each other in silence. My gaze dropped to his mouth. I wanted to kiss him so much. Perhaps we would've got away with it if Bob was taking us to the airport, but we couldn't risk it with this new driver. Anyway, it was over now. The waterfall was our goodbye.

'So,' I broke the silence. 'How have you been?'

We spent most of the journey exchanging stories about how full on it'd been. Like me, Alejandro had spent a lot of his time training. Walking the kitchen staff through the working methods that were unique to the Love Hotel and finalising the menu with the Cuisine King who, in the end, became more open to Alejandro's ideas.

Sounded like he'd accomplished what he'd set out to do in Jamaica too, so the trip could be declared a success. Now all that we both needed was to secure the promotions we so desperately wanted.

* * *

The flight to Miami was short, so it wasn't long before we were in a taxi and checking into our hotel for the night.

'This is my room.' Alejandro stopped outside a door in the hallway.

'I think I'm further down.' I pointed.

'Would you like me to walk you there?' he asked.

'I'm f...' I was about to say I was fine. It couldn't be more than fifty metres away. But travelling for hours together without being able to kiss him had been torture and my resolve had weakened. *Again.*

He might just literally mean that he was going to walk me to my room. But there was a chance he was asking for more.

'That would be... yes, please.'

When I got to my door, I tapped the keycard on the reader and stepped inside. 'Would you... like to come in. For a... drink?'

Clearly, I'd left my willpower and common sense in Jamaica because I had promised myself approximately ten million times that we were over and yet here I was inviting Alejandro into my room for *a drink*, knowing full well that it wasn't a glass I wanted to feel against my lips; it was him.

'Sure,' he said.

Alejandro closed the door and we just stood there in front of each other, staring. I bit my lip, then leant in towards him. He dipped his head and held my gaze.

I could've tried playing it cool, but I wanted him too much. I quickly closed the gap between us, pressing my mouth onto his.

Instead of being crazed and feral like our first kisses, this time, it was slow and gentle. Alejandro scooped me up and carried me over to the bed.

He undressed me slowly in silence before making love to me. And this time, there could be no mistake. It wasn't hard, fast fucking. It was slow, sensual lovemaking.

Afterwards, I lay on his chest and we fell asleep wrapped in each other's arms.

And it was, without doubt, the best sleep I'd had all week.

How well I'd sleep once I was back in Spain and things were really over between us was a different story.

36

ALEJANDRO

'So are we going to talk about what will happen when we return to work tomorrow?'

I rolled over in bed to face Jasmine, then propped my head up on my elbow, waiting for her response.

We had avoided talking about our future for too long. We did not discuss it after we made love in her hotel room in Miami.

We did not raise it during the flight back to Spain, which was understandable because it was something to discuss in private.

And when we landed and got a taxi back to her apartment, we did not talk about it either, because we could not stop kissing. Instead, we made love, showered together, made love again, then fell asleep.

But tomorrow, we would return to work and I needed to know for sure if this really was just sex for her. Because it definitely was not for me.

'You're right.' She let out a heavy sigh. 'We should talk. I just wanted to stay in this bubble for as long as possible. These past two weeks with you have been... magical. But I just can't see how we can continue.'

'We can talk to human resources,' I suggested. 'Tell them we've fallen in love.'

Her eyes widened. I did not care if my statement shocked her. She needed to know the truth.

'I love you, Jasmine. And after you left the waterfall, I was not sure that you felt the same. But now, I *feel* it. *Here.*' I tapped my heart. 'I know you love me too.'

Jasmine opened her mouth then closed it again. Eventually, she spoke.

'I *like* you a *lot*. But it's too soon to put such a big label on those feelings. We agreed from the start that it was just sex.'

'No!' I raised my voice and sat up. 'You cannot tell me you do not feel that now, it is more. What we did last night, in Miami, and under the waterfall was not just fucking.' My nostrils flared. 'You are lying to me and to yourself.'

She swallowed hard and her gaze dropped. She knew I was right.

'It won't work.' Jasmine blew out a breath. 'Even if Hazel had a personality transplant and gave us her blessing, which she wouldn't, there's still the age thing.'

'*Fuck* the age difference!' I ground my jaw. 'I have told you a hundred times it does not matter to me!'

'Right *now*, it doesn't. But what about in a few years when you've achieved more of your professional goals and want to focus on having a family? What *then*?'

'It is *you* that I want! I have always been indifferent about having children. Having you will be enough.'

'Things change. I can't afford to throw away my career and risk you breaking my heart when you wake up one day and decide you want to be a father and I can't give you a child. It's best to avoid all that pain and make a clean break now. I'm sorry, Alejandro.'

Frustration raged through me. She really did not understand how I felt about her. She did not believe that she was enough for me all on her own. I had tried to reassure her, so many times, but it seemed like there was nothing I could say to convince her.

As much as I wanted Jasmine, I should not have to beg for her to declare her true feelings.

I jumped off the bed, dragged on my clothes, grabbed my suitcase then stormed out of Jasmine's apartment.

And out of her life.

37

JASMINE

It took approximately thirty seconds after Alejandro walked out and slammed the door of my apartment for the first fat, salty tear to roll down my cheek.

I'd lost him.

I saw the anger and frustration in his eyes when he bolted off the bed. And I couldn't blame him.

He'd put his heart and his pride on the line by declaring his feelings and telling me he loved me. But I'd been too chicken to reciprocate.

Not because I didn't feel the same, because he was right: I loved him. More than I'd ever loved anyone in my life. But I was scared: genuinely terrified of getting my heart crushed.

There were plenty of examples of age-gap relationships where the man was older and the woman was younger. I mean, look at my ex and his new squeeze for starters.

But the other way around? My brain highlighted countless female celebrities who'd *dared* to date younger men and it had ended in tears.

And that was exactly how I saw things going with me and Alejandro.

The pain was already excruciating. But imagine how much worse it'd be if we moved in together and started sharing a life.

My stomach clenched as memories of my painful divorce came flooding back. Including the way my ex argued over stupid things like who got to keep the crystal glasses and I kid you not, the salad bowl. A fucking salad bowl! It wasn't even anything special. Of course I told him he could keep it. The point was, I couldn't go through all that crap again.

That was why like I'd said it was better to make a clean break now.

I'd considered what Alejandro had said about going to Hazel or HR and telling them about our relationship. I'd also thought about suggesting we put things on hold for a few months until we both hopefully got our promotions and then we could go to HR. But it wouldn't be fair to ask him to wait and it only addressed one of the main barriers, so I'd dismissed it.

And now here I was. Alone.

I wiped away another tear, pulled the bedsheet over my head and continued crying into my pillow.

* * *

After dragging myself to the bathroom to get ready for work, I took my concealer out of my make-up bag. I was going to need to use the whole tube to try and disguise my puffy eyes.

I rarely cried. I always considered it a waste of time because it didn't solve anything. Whatever problems that caused the tears in the first place didn't miraculously disappear once you'd used up an entire box of tissues, so it was pointless.

Normally, I found that if I threw myself into work or another project, it helped take my mind off things. *Keep calm and carry on* was the motto I swore by.

But so far, it wasn't working. I'd spent the whole day and night sobbing and feeling sorry for myself. I'd tried cleaning my apartment, doing the washing and even reading, but none of them stopped me from feeling upset about how things had ended with Alejandro.

Every time I pictured a happy memory from Jamaica, I was reminded of what I'd let slip out of my fingers.

Today would be better, though. Work was all I needed. I'd be fine.

* * *

Thankfully, the first few days back at the hotel went smoothly. I was rushed off my feet catching up with everything that had happened whilst I was away, welcoming new guests and preparing my final report on Jamaica for Hazel which I'd submitted two days ago.

She'd replied yesterday to confirm she'd received it and would have a proper look at it soon, but had added that so far, she was very impressed with what she'd read and the feedback she'd received from Hortense, so she hoped to have good news for me soon.

Hearing that made me do a happy dance. I'd done it. The promotion I'd wanted for so long was finally about to become mine.

Luckily, I'd avoided seeing Alejandro too. I had access to his schedule so had carefully co-ordinated any kitchen visits for when he wasn't working.

That didn't mean I hadn't spent almost every waking moment thinking about him, though.

My phone rang and when I saw it was Stella, I smiled.

'Hi!' I said, getting up from behind my desk. I hadn't spoken to her since I'd returned to Spain so I decided to head out for a walk along the beach to make sure no one could eavesdrop on our conversation.

I slid off my sandals and let my feet sink into the soft, golden sand. It was different to the whiter sand in Jamaica, but still beautiful.

'Hey! Are you back in Spain?'

'Yes. Got back a few days ago.'

'So... how are things with Hottie-Andro?'

'Hottie-Andro?'

'Alejandro! Thought he deserved a nickname. Chief Orgasm Giver was also a contender. So was Orgasm Oracle, but then I remembered Max already held those titles so I settled on Hottie-Andro. You're welcome!' She laughed and my gut twisted.

'It's over,' I sighed.

'Oh no!'

I filled her in on what happened and she seemed genuinely sad.

'So that's that. Back to reality.'

'I'm so sorry. You sure you can't work it out?'

'No.' I shook my head, now my stomach was churning so much, I felt sick. I didn't understand why I was still finding it so hard. I'd been at work for days. I should be feeling better. 'It was great whilst it lasted.' I could feel the tears building again. I needed to change the subject. 'My love life isn't great but things are looking up professionally!'

'Oh yeah? What's happened?'

'I sent Hazel my report and she seemed enthusiastic. Said she should have some good news for me soon.'

'Sounds like you're getting that promotion!'

'I hope so!'

'That means you're in the clear! You're so lucky you two got to enjoy yourselves in Jamaica without it causing any issues at work.'

'Yes. It was a combination of luck and being careful. The staff that got caught made the mistake of hooking up on the hotel grounds. But Alejandro never slept in my room or vice versa. And we didn't kiss at the resort either.'

'Smart. Maybe you should offer a course on how to get away with fucking your co-worker without your boss finding out!'

'I think I'll pass.' I smiled.

'Hi!' I heard Stella call out to someone. 'It's Sammie. We're just about to go for afternoon tea.'

'Very fancy!' I said.

'It's for work. I've got a new client that wants me to design some marketing materials for their new themed afternoon-tea menu, so obviously I said it was important that I try it out. Purely for market research, of course!'

'Of course!'

'Hey, Jasmine!' Sammie called out. 'How was Jamaica?'

'Amazing, thanks.'

'When's the resort opening? Do you think you could hook me up? I'm fed up with the dating apps and watching Stella and Max suck each other's faces whenever we go out. I'm happy for them, but I need to find my own face sucker!'

'Face sucker?' I laughed. 'That's an interesting name for your future soulmate!'

'So what d'you reckon? Can you pull some strings? Get me a spot in the Love Hotel Jamaica ASAP? Pretty please?'

'I wish I could,' I replied. 'But the Jamaican resort will be predominately targeted at the North American market. You'll have better luck with our Spanish resort or the new one in Italy.

And they only contact applicants when they find a perfect match, so I have no influence over that, I'm afraid. But the fact they're opening more hotels means there's more chance of getting selected.'

'I'm not fussed about the location! They all sound amazing, so I'll go wherever my dream man is!'

'You should definitely apply. Like the saying goes, *you have to be in it to win it!*'

Just as I was about to ask how Max was, my phone buzzed with a message. When I looked at the screen, I saw a text from Hazel asking me to come to her office.

'Sorry but I've got to go! Hazel's just messaged! I think this is it!'

'Yay!' They both cheered.

'So happy for you!' Stella added. 'Make sure you ask for a shitload of money to reflect how brilliant you are at your job. And the use of a gorgeous villa so me and Max can come back and visit!'

'I'll do my best!' I chuckled, feeling a surge of happiness flood my heart for the first time in days. I was so glad Stella and I were friends.

After saying our goodbyes, I literally sprinted to Hazel's office, my heart pumping with excitement.

I knocked on the door.

'Come in,' she called out.

I pushed the door open, brimming with anticipation. My hard work was finally about to pay off.

But when I stepped inside, my eyes widened with shock because Hazel wasn't alone.

Sat in front of her desk was Alejandro.

Panic ripped through me.

He wasn't due at work for another three hours. I'd checked

and Alejandro was definitely on the late shift, so why was he in Hazel's office?

Bile rose in my throat.

Had he reported me for misconduct, because I'd ended things?

No.

As angry as he was, that wasn't Alejandro's style. He was a good man.

I had to play it cool. Act like I wasn't affected and that everything was fine. She probably wanted to discuss my report and thought it was easier to have us both here because we'd attended the activities together.

'Hello, Alejandro.' I nodded in acknowledgement. 'You wanted to see me, Hazel?'

'Yes,' she said solemnly. 'I wanted to discuss your report.'

Phew.

My shoulders instantly loosened. See? I'd worried over nothing.

'Of course! No problem! How can I help?'

'I was particularly interested in Rick's Café...' She paused.

'I know Hortense was unsure,' I jumped in, 'but I really feel it would be good for stimulating romance.'

'Yes.' Hazel raised an eyebrow. 'You said that during our conversation. You also said there was a *beautiful* sunset, but you didn't have a single photo.'

'Apologies again about that.'

'So you suggested I look for some online.'

'Yes. They have some great ones on their website.'

'Indeed. But you see, I wanted something more recent, so I searched online. They tend to have lots of different photos for places like this on TripAdvisor, social media and whatnot...'

'Oh, I'm sure they have,' I said calmly, wondering why she was giving so much importance to these bloody photos.

'And they even have *videos* which are even better, because it makes you feel like you're there: right in the middle of the action. I found this one which was recently uploaded that I thought you'd be interested to see.'

I swallowed hard. Why didn't I like the direction this conversation was taking?

Hazel swivelled her computer screen around to face me and Alejandro and when I saw the video, my stomach plummeted a thousand metres below the earth.

Alejandro dragged his hands down his face.

The footage didn't just show the sunset.

It was a video of me.

With Alejandro.

Not just standing next to Alejandro.

Kissing Alejandro.

Fuck.

38

JASMINE

On a scale of one to ten of how bad this video was, with one being harmless and ten being very bad, this was at least ten billion.

It wasn't just *very bad*. It was a total and utter clusterfuck.

So fucking terrible, there weren't enough adjectives in the dictionary to even begin to describe it.

Alejandro and I weren't just kissing, we were *devouring* each other like starving wild animals that'd just killed their prey and were gorging on a tasty meal.

My hands were roaming all over his arse. And if that wasn't damning enough, I pushed him into me and... God, this was so embarrassing... then hooked my leg around him as if we're about to start fucking in public.

Jesus.

I didn't even remember doing that.

The very kind person who filmed this pornographic public display, then decided to zoom in, giving me (and now the whole internet) an even closer view of our tongues tangling and hands wandering.

This was mortifying.

I squeezed my eyes shut, not sure I could handle any more. When I peeked again, Hazel's face was scarlet and steam poured from her ears. From the corner of my eye, I saw Alejandro's head in his hands.

Thankfully, the video then flicked back to the sunset before roaming around the rest of the café, but it was irrelevant. We'd all seen enough to know that Alejandro and I were totally screwed.

There was nothing I could do or say to fix this. I couldn't claim the video was fake. It was very obvious that it was us. I'd fucked up, so I just had to woman up and own it.

'Hazel, I'm sorry. I take full responsibility for—'

'No!' Alejandro jumped up. 'It was me. I pursued her. I begged her to kiss me. She said it was not a good idea, but I did not let it go.'

'And I'm assuming that you two didn't just stop at kissing?' Hazel slammed her hand on the desk, then paused the video. Neither I nor Alejandro said a word. 'So this was why you conveniently had to get a hotel room!'

'No! It wasn't like that!' I protested.

'As well as acting inappropriately on company time, you used company money to pay for a night in a hotel so that the two of you could fuck! I'm *so* disappointed in you, Jasmine. Not only is this a blatant abuse of power, taking advantage of a younger employee under your care; it's also a fraudulent use of expenses, which I'm sure is a criminal offence.'

My eyes bulged and my stomach bottomed out. This was even worse than I thought. But she was wrong. I had to defend myself.

'What you're saying isn't true! I didn't take advantage of Alejandro! And we didn't get a hotel room so that we could fu—'

'I don't want to hear it!' she snapped. 'Jasmine, you're fired. Pack your things and leave. Immediately!'

'But—'

'No!' she barked. 'I'll be launching a full investigation, so you'll hear from legal in due course. Clear out your desk now before I call security!'

'Enough!' Alejandro stood up, his nostrils flaring. 'Do not speak to Jasmine like that!'

'It's okay.' I went to touch his shoulder, grateful that he'd stood up for me, but then pulled back. Given the situation, any form of physical contact wasn't a good idea. 'I'm leaving.'

As I got up, I tried to stop my bottom lip from quivering, then left the room, my head hung low and my shoulders slumped.

I was so close to having everything.

And now, thanks to my own stupidity, I'd lost it all.

39

ALEJANDRO

Puta madre.

We were fucked.

I was still standing in front of Hazel's desk, my jaw tense and anger consuming every part of my body.

Jasmine must be devastated.

She had done such good work in Jamaica and was probably expecting Hazel to promote her. That was what I had hoped too when I got the message to come in earlier. But I could not have been more wrong.

When Hazel had started asking me questions about our visit to the café and the hotel we stayed in, I knew something was wrong. I wanted to message Jasmine to warn her, but then she walked into the office.

Although things had ended badly between us, it did not mean the way I felt about Jasmine had changed. Unfortunately, love was not an emotion that could be shut off in just a few days.

I had not seen her at all for days, which was unusual, so I knew she must have been avoiding the restaurant when I was working. I wished I could say I had been happy about that because she hurt me and I did not want to see her again, but that was not true. I still longed for her. I still wanted her. I missed her. And when she walked into the office, all of my feelings flooded back to the surface.

Which was why right now, I wanted to run to Jasmine and take care of her.

'Sit down!' Hazel snapped.

Reluctantly, I did as she asked.

'Now I'm going to need you to tell me how Jasmine took advantage of you so I can file a report.'

'I already told you!' I shouted, anger bubbling in my chest. 'Jasmine did not take advantage of me. *I* pursued *her*. I have liked her for months.'

'Alejandro, you are a very talented chef and you're doing great work here. If you tell me how Jasmine, a manager in a position of power, took advantage of you, forced herself on you during a work assignment, which let's be honest, is obvious from the way she's shamefully mauling you in that video, then pressured you into staying over at a hotel so that she could lure you into her bed, then I can launch a formal investigation and press criminal charges. We will of course organise any counselling and support you may need to help you through this trauma.' She softened her voice, like she gave a shit about me.

'For the last time, Jasmine did not force herself on me, or *lure me* into her bed! I am a grown man. I make my own decisions and everything was mutual and consensual. You made a mistake firing her. She is fantastic at her job and a good, honest woman.'

'I don't think you realise what you're saying. If you are telling me that you willingly had sexual relations with your superior, that will be gross misconduct and I will have no option but to let you go.'

I swallowed hard. I had been so focused on worrying about

Jasmine that my mind had blocked out the ramifications for my own life.

Hazel was going to fire me. Losing my job didn't just affect me. It meant I would no longer be able to help Evita.

This was very, very, bad.

But there was no way I could let Jasmine take the blame.

'If that is what you feel you must do,' I leant forward to let her know I was not afraid of her, 'then do it.'

'Such a shame,' she sighed. 'I was about to suggest you were promoted to Cuisine King, but, like every man, you had to ruin a good thing because you couldn't keep your cock in your pants. You're fired! Get out!' she shouted dramatically.

I shook my head, got up and strode out the door, wondering how the hell I was going to fix this.

40

JASMINE

My phone rang for the third time. I should've switched it off. I wasn't in the mood to speak to anyone right now. I didn't know if I'd ever be.

The sound of 'Hopelessly in Love,' by a British reggae artist called Carroll Thompson, that Bob had played in Jamaica, vibrated around the room. It instantly brought memories of my time with Alejandro flooding back.

For the past two days, I'd been in bed, buried under the sheets, only dragging myself out to go to the toilet, get some water or to pick at the scraps of food in the fridge.

Last night, I had a grape sandwich for dinner. I kid you not. I didn't have anything to put inside the last bit of stale bread I'd toasted except for fruit. And a grape sandwich seemed like a better option than an orange one.

When I reached over to pick up my phone, I caught a whiff of my armpits. Ugh. I needed to shower.

It was Stella again.

Every time the phone rang, I'd wished it was Alejandro, but I knew it wouldn't be. I'd ruined his life.

First, I crushed his heart by not admitting my true feelings. Then I got him fired, ripping the job he loved so much from him and jeopardising his sister's education, all because I couldn't keep my libido in check. Because I'd given into temptation.

So fucking stupid.

'Hi,' I answered solemnly. If I didn't answer, Stella would just keep calling. I was lucky to have such a good friend who cared.

'Thank God!' She exhaled. 'I've been calling for days and you didn't answer. So I called the hotel and they said you didn't work there any more. What the fuck?'

'That's right.' I dragged myself upright and propped the pillow behind my head. 'Hazel found out about me and Alejandro. She wasn't calling me to her office to promote me. She called to fire me.'

'Nooooo!' Stella gasped. 'I don't understand. How'd she find out? You were so careful?'

'There was a video online. Someone filmed the sunset at a place we visited and there I was dry humping Alejandro in public.'

'Oh my God!' Stella fell silent. 'Shit.'

'That's a polite way of describing the situation.'

'Have you spoken to Alejandro?'

'No. But one of my co-workers messaged because they'd heard we'd both been fired and asked what happened, so I know Hazel let him go too.'

'But this is all so fucked up! You're both *amazing* at your jobs! *That's* the most important thing. Whether you two decide to screw or not should be irrelevant as long as you do what's asked of you during working hours!'

'I agree.'

'So what are you going to do?'

'Not sure yet. I have to try and do something to at least get

Alejandro's job back. And I promised Bob, a taxi driver there that I'd help him too, but...'

'But what?'

'I'm just... I'm struggling. I've been in bed since it happened. I'm just so embarrassed. So disappointed in myself. I've let so many people down. Alejandro, his sister, my team, my guests.' A tear rolled down my cheek, rapidly followed by another one.

'Stop that, right now! You haven't let anyone down. If you ask me, you did nothing wrong! And you are Jasmine freaking Palmer! You are strong, you are brilliant and you excel at getting shit done. So you're gonna get your fine arse out of bed, shower, have breakfast then make a kickass plan for how you're going to get not just Alejandro and Bob their jobs back, but also your *own* job back. There are loads of singletons that need you back at the Love Hotel! They need you to work your sneaky, brilliant alchemy magic to help them find the love of their lives, just like you did for me and Max and so many other happy couples. The only way you'll be disappointing anyone is if you give up without a fight!'

Hearing Stella's words of encouragement made me tear up for a different reason. I was so happy to hear that despite how I'd screwed up, she still believed in me.

I wiped away my tears and blew out a breath.

'Thank you. I agree. I have to fight this.'

'Damn right! Me and Max will be behind you all the way. You've got this!'

A warm sensation flooded my stomach. A fire had now been lit inside me.

I was great at my job.

I didn't deserve to be fired for falling in love.

'I've got to go.' I swung my legs out of the bed. 'I need to shower, eat, then prepare to battle.'

'That's the spirit!' Stella said. 'Go get 'em, tiger!'

41

ALEJANDRO

'Any news?' Lola's face appeared on the phone screen.

'Not yet.' I shook my head.

When I told her I had been fired, naturally, she called me every bad name under the sun and reminded me that she had warned me something like this would happen. But when I explained that I loved Jasmine, and gave her more details about all of the things that had happened, she was much calmer and understanding.

I had told her that I was not giving up. That I would fight to get Jasmine her job back and if possible, save mine too.

In the meantime, I had been looking for whatever kitchen jobs I could find, determined to earn enough to continue my monthly payments to Evita.

When I told Evita, she immediately said she would work some extra shifts which I was against because she needed to study and Lola said she would have another look at her finances and see if she could help out too. It would be tough, but we would find a way to get through this.

I had also sent an email to Celine, the founder of the Love

Hotel. The more I thought about it, the more I believed that it was Hazel, not me and Jasmine, that had acted inappropriately.

Hazel seemed to get some strange joy from firing people. Like she was drunk on the power she had over us. And ironically, she accused Jasmine of coercing me, when if anyone was pressuring or coercing me to do something against my will, it was Hazel, when she encouraged me to say that Jasmine had taken advantage of me.

It was wrong and making false claims like that undermined the progress that was being made in the world to try and bring the real work predators to justice.

I had said this to Lola and she had agreed and insisted that I gave her the founder's email so she could contact her too.

'I haven't heard anything back yet either. Have you ever met the founder?'

'*Sí*. A few times. She was always nice. The hotel is founded on her kind, caring, positive values. I do not think that if she was at the hotel, this would have happened. My gut tells me she is a decent woman.'

'Good. I suppose all we can do is keep our fingers crossed. What about Jasmine? Have you spoken to her?'

'No.' I hung my head. 'I want to, but she must hate me. Like you, she said this would happen but I did not listen and now she has lost her job because of me.'

'What you both did was reckless and irresponsible, but sometimes, we're drawn to people and the force is so powerful, there's nothing you can do to stop it. Whenever you spoke about Jasmine, your face lit up in a way I haven't seen since Freya. It's like Jasmine brought you back to life. That kind of love is rare. One of the biggest barriers to the two of you getting together was losing your jobs, right?'

'*Sí*.'

'Well now you've both been fired, problem solved!' She laughed.

'Jasmine is also worried about the age difference. She thinks one day, I will wake up and want children and she will not be able to give them to me.'

'So go and get the snip! Film it and show her the video!' She laughed again.

'*En serio?*' I raised my eyebrow. I was not averse to the idea, though. I loved Jasmine so much, I would do anything for her.

'I was joking... sort of! I don't know how, but think of a way to win her back. It's not too late.'

Maybe there was still a chance.

I had never been one to give up easily, and I was not going to start now.

Right then, I decided I was going to find a way to win Jasmine over.

I loved her and did not want to let her go.

But first, I needed to get her job back.

42

JASMINE

The oven timer sounded, interrupting the music playing in the background. I'd lost count of how often I'd listened to this playlist today.

After what happened, I'd stopped playing it because it brought back too many memories of my time in Jamaica. But today was a new day. I didn't want to forget those memories. I wanted to look back on them fondly, no matter how painful it was to be reminded of what I'd lost.

As I opened the door and slid the baking tin out, I held my breath.

This was my fourth attempt at trying to bake the pineapple and coconut cake. Because I didn't have a recipe, I had to try and guess the ingredients and quantities.

I used too much oil in the first one. The second one tasted awful I *think* because I was over enthusiastic with the amount of flour and I burned the third one, so I had everything crossed that it'd be fourth time lucky.

It actually didn't look too bad and the scent of pineapple and coconut flooded my kitchen, which looked like a bomb had hit it.

Although I wasn't looking forward to cleaning up, as I rested the tin on the hob, I felt a sense of pride. Baking a cake wouldn't be a big achievement for most people. But for someone who'd been repeatedly told for years that they were rubbish at anything cooking-related, it felt good.

I knew I was supposed to wait for it to cool down, but I was anxious to know if it was any good, so I sliced a small piece off the edge.

Fingers crossed...

That actually tasted really good!

Alejandro would be proud of me. At least I hoped he would, seeing as I'd baked it for him.

It'd been an interesting week. After my chat with Stella, I'd showered, gone shopping, prepared some pasta and cleaned my apartment from top to bottom. Then I'd started working on my email to Celine: the founder of the Love Hotel.

I explained everything. How apprehensive I was about being sent away with Alejandro to Jamaica knowing I had feelings for him. How determined I was to keep things professional. How hard we both fought to keep our distance. And how much I'd fallen in love with him.

I'd also stressed that whilst battling through all of those emotions, I'd still delivered what was asked of me and gone above and beyond the call of duty. Like I'd always done at the Love Hotel.

As well as pleading my own case, I'd spent hours creating a separate presentation on Alejandro. I detailed all the hard work he'd done on the trip, spoken about how much the guests raved about his food and why he was an asset to the Love Hotel brand. I'd even included a gallery of photos I'd taken of his food.

I inserted screenshots and photos of the many messages and

cards I'd received from happy guests, plus listed dozens of testimonials.

And I also added a document on our experiences with Bob and why I felt he was worthy of a permanent role at the Jamaican resort.

I threw everything at that email. Poured my heart and soul into it. I'd lost count of how many hours I'd spent overall, but when I'd hit send at three in the morning, I felt like a weight had been lifted off my shoulders.

I'd sent it a week ago and hadn't received a reply yet, but I wasn't going to give up. If I hadn't heard from her in a few more days, I'd visit the head office and try and set up a face-to-face appointment. I'd met Celine before and she seemed lovely and down to earth, so I was sure I could find a way to get her to see me. And if I couldn't, I'd try another approach. I wasn't giving up until I'd exhausted every possible avenue.

After pouring the pineapple juice over the cake, I picked up my attempt at a peace-making sign which read *I'm so sorry* in big, red letters. I'd drawn it out onto some card earlier, coloured it in, cut it out, then attached it to two toothpicks ready to insert into the cake.

All week, I'd been wracking my brain, trying to think of a way to get in touch with Alejandro to apologise and the idea finally hit me last night.

Cooking and baking weren't my forte. But Alejandro loved food. It was his passion and the way to his heart. I wasn't expecting a sponge cake to make him forgive all the mistakes I'd made and I knew he must hate me, but I needed him to know how sorry I was. And I hoped that by doing something outside of my comfort zone, like baking, just because I knew he'd like it, it'd show him that I was trying to make an effort.

I hoped that the gesture would be one small step towards a long path of forgiveness.

It was probably too late to salvage any hope of a relationship with him, but I had to try. Men like Alejandro didn't come around every day and I was a fool to let him slip through my fingers.

I'd had a lot of time to think this past week and I'd realised a lot of things.

I'd been worried about the age gap thing, but Alejandro had displayed a more mature attitude than me. None of us knew what would happen in the future. All we could do was live for now.

I'd been worried about whether Alejandro would wake up one day and want children, by which point, it'd be much harder for me to fall pregnant. But who's to say that I wouldn't wake up in six months' time and decide that I wanted children?

It was impossible for anyone to predict the future. I didn't know what was in store. All I knew was how I felt right now. And as much as I'd tried to deny it, I loved Alejandro with all my heart. I was scared to admit it before, but now I wanted the world to know.

There were billions of women in the world and I was the one he wanted to be with. And even if every single man on earth offered themselves on a platter to me, I knew without a shadow of a doubt that there was only one man that I wanted: Alejandro.

He had everything I wanted in a man and more. He was so loyal, so kind, so caring, so loving. And whether we got to spend five years together or forever like I hoped, I wanted to treasure every single second.

Once I'd transferred the cake to the box I'd bought, I ordered a taxi to drop me at Alejandro's apartment. I had to send a package to his place from the hotel a few months ago, so I still had his address on an old email.

Luckily, when I arrived, someone was just leaving the building, so I was able to get inside without ringing the buzzer.

When I found his door, I placed the box on the floor, knocked the door, then left.

It wasn't fair to just turn up unannounced and expect him to talk to me. I'd left the cake; now I had to leave it to him to decide whether he wanted to contact me.

As the taxi pulled up back outside my building, I spotted a large, black Mercedes parked in front of the main door.

I took out my key and just as I put it in the lock, I heard my name being called.

'Jasmine?'

I spun around, then my eyes popped as I saw a tall woman with short, dark hair.

'Oh my goodness, Celine. What are you doing here?'

'I got your email. Can we talk?'

'Oh! Great! Yes! Of course!' I stuttered, opening the door and leading her up to my apartment. It was only when I opened the door that I remembered that the open-plan kitchen was a tip. 'Sorry about the mess.' I winced. 'I'd just finished baking.'

'No problem.' She waved her hand. 'You have a lovely home.'

'Thank you.' I exhaled. It was a modern and minimalist style apartment with simple décor. Plain white walls with some paintings I'd bought when I'd moved to Spain lining the walls, oak wooden floors and neutral-coloured furniture. 'Would you like something to drink?'

'Water would be lovely.'

Once I poured two glasses, I joined her on the sofa.

'So, you said you read my email?'

'I did. And Alejandro's.'

'He emailed?' I frowned.

'He did. So did his sister. And several former guests including Stella and Max. Multiple times...'

'Oh,' I said, unsure whether she was annoyed that she'd been bombarded.

'And it made me really angry,' she said. My stomach twisted with dread, but then just as I was about to protest and stand my ground, she continued. 'When I first set up the Love Hotel, I wanted it to be a place of positivity, love and happiness. An idyllic retreat where couples could find love and somewhere the best people in the business would enjoy working. I always wanted it to have a family vibe. A warm, welcoming atmosphere.'

'That's exactly what I've always tried to create too.'

'I know. I always hoped it'd be successful, but I never expected it to take off so quickly and on such a large scale. I'm grateful for that, but one of the challenges with growth is that it's impossible to oversee everything. You have to delegate and hope that others will share the same vision. But we made a mistake by hiring Hazel and innocent people like you and Alejandro have suffered because of it. So I wanted to apologise for that and thank you for bringing the situation to my attention.'

'Oh!' I didn't know what I was expecting her to say, but it wasn't that.

'The company is called the *Love* Hotel. It's supposed to inspire love. And to me, the fact that two of our very best Romance Rockstars have fallen in love isn't something that should be punished. It should be celebrated!' A wide grin spread across her face. 'You're both single, consenting adults and I love that the atmosphere is so romantic, magical and infectious that even our Rockstars can't resist falling in love too! It proves that what we're doing at the hotel works! That's why I'm here to ask if you'd consider coming back to join our family as our newly appointed Love Alchemist Empress?'

'What?' I gasped. 'You'd like me to come back? And you're giving me a promotion?'

'Yes!' She nodded. 'Your presentation was powerful. So was Alejandro's. What impressed me was that he said very little about why he should get his job back. He spoke more about you and how amazing *you* were. And I noticed that you did the same. The majority of your presentation focused on Alejandro and Bob. Jasmine, you epitomise everything I wanted to create with the Love Hotel. You've gone above and beyond. So if you come back, you'll also receive an extra raise on top of your new salary, as a small token of my gratitude.'

'That's... wow! Thank you!' Relief and happiness washed over me, but then my chest tightened. 'What about Alejandro?' I didn't want to go back without him. It wouldn't feel right.

'We'd love him to come back too, but as our Cuisine King!'

'Yes!' I jumped off the sofa and punched the air with joy. 'That's amazing! He deserves it so much.'

'I know. I've tried his food several times and have always been impressed. I'm going to visit him next, so thought maybe you'd like to come with me, to tell him the good news?'

'Um...' My brain froze. 'Perhaps it's best if you tell him. I know he'd appreciate it. I'm just happy he got his job back.'

'But what about your *relationship*?' Her face creased with concern.

'I'm still hoping we have a chance, but right now, I'd like to give him some space. See if it's still something he wants. But don't worry; whatever happens, or doesn't, it won't affect our work. We'll still be professional and won't let it create an awkward atmosphere or anything. I promise.'

'Right. I see. Don't give up on each other, though. Love is special. It's not something you want to let slip through your fingers.'

'I'm not throwing in the towel just yet. I'm still hoping he'll forgive me.'

'Good. Well, I wanted to tell you the good news in person, so now I've done that, I'll let you get on with your day.'

'Thank you.'

'Oh, and in case you hadn't already guessed, Hazel no longer works at the Love Hotel.'

Thank God for that.

'That's good,' I said diplomatically. Calling it *good* was an understatement. I considered doing a victory dance, but decided that would be unprofessional, so gave a gentle nod instead.

Celine turned to leave.

'Oh,' I called out, 'I forgot to ask whether you'd considered Bob's position?'

'I did. I called him myself and he's quite a character! You're right. He'd be a fantastic addition to the Jamaican team.'

'Brilliant!' I grinned.

'I should head off to Alejandro's. Sure you don't want to come?'

Every fibre in my body was screaming, *Yes, yes yes! Go and get your man*, but I had to be patient. Hopefully, he'd got the cake and my message. When the time was right, he'd get in touch. If I hadn't heard from in a few days, I'd try again.

'I'm sure,' I said.

'Okay. So we look forward to seeing you back at work tomorrow!'

'Yes!' My stomach flipped with excitement. 'Thanks so much again for everything.'

'No problem.'

I shut the door, switched on Alejandro's playlist, then danced around the room. I did an honorary wiggle of my hips to mark the fact that Alejandro had not only got his job back, but had finally secured his dream position.

Then, when the track switched to Lucy Pearl's 'Dance Tonight', I gave my booty several extra celebratory shakes in honour of Bob getting a role at the hotel too. I was so happy!

It was a shame I couldn't share the news with Alejandro. He'd probably be more thrilled to hear about me and Bob than he would himself. He was always so selfless. God, I missed him so much.

I was just about to call Stella to tell her the good news and thank her and Max for pestering Celine's PA when there was a knock at the door.

Celine must've forgotten something.

I skipped over to the door, still buzzing with joy. But when I opened it, it wasn't Celine standing there.

It was Alejandro.

43

ALEJANDRO

When Jasmine opened the door, my breath caught in my throat and every nerve ending in my body came alive.

Madre mía.

She was breathtaking.

I knew I had missed Jasmine, but my reaction to seeing her for the first time in a week showed that I'd missed her more than I'd realised.

The urge to throw my arms around her and hold her tight was overwhelming. I wanted to hold her. I wanted to kiss her. I wanted to stroke her soft skin. Inhale her sweet scent. I just wanted her.

But I had to go slowly. I could not mess this up.

'Hi!' she said, her eyes like saucers and her mouth wide with shock. 'You're here! I mean, obviously you're here. It's just, I wasn't expecting you. I thought... Did you see Celine?'

Jasmine was always so cool and composed, so it was reassuring to know that just like me, she was nervous.

'*Sí*. She was leaving just as I was about to ring your doorbell. I came to thank you for the cake.'

I was in the kitchen testing a new recipe when I heard my buzzer. By the time I went to the door, there was no one there. I was about to go back inside when I looked down and saw the box.

When I opened it up and saw that Jasmine had made an apology cake, my heart swelled so much, I thought it would burst.

Jasmine was a confident woman, but I knew baking was something she was not comfortable with. So for her to take the time to do something she knew would mean a lot to me was a big deal.

I planned to come and see her anyway, once I had found a way to get her job back, but as soon as I received her thoughtful gift, I knew I did not want to put it off any longer.

'You're welcome!'

Music was playing in the background. I had not noticed it before because seeing Jasmine again had scrambled my brain.

'You are listening to the playlist!' I smiled.

'Yes! I love it! Especially this song.'

It was ¿Téo?'s 'In Your Body'.

'I am glad. That is one of my favourites. And "Part of Me".'

'Same!' She grinned. Our eyes locked for a few beats, then Jasmine cleared her throat. 'So, did Celine tell you the news?'

'No.' I shook my head. 'She thanked me for my email and said she would leave you to update me.'

'We've got our jobs back!' Jasmine jumped up and down excitedly.

'*Qué?*' My eyebrows shot up.

'She came to tell us we can go back to work at the hotel!'

'That is amazing!' I threw my arms around Jasmine and squeezed her tight. It felt so good to hold her close. I breathed in her scent and closed my eyes. I had dreamt about this moment for so long. Then I realised I had not checked she was fine with a hug, so pulled away. 'I am sorry.'

'No need to apologise!' She smiled. 'I've missed having your arms around me.'

'I have too. So much. I have also missed kissing you,' I looked into her beautiful eyes.

'Really?' She smiled.

'*Sí*. Want me to show you how much?'

'That would be a *very* good idea.' She bit her lip.

After cupping her face, I leant down and pressed my lips onto hers.

As our mouths connected, it was like everything made sense in the world again. Our lips moved hungrily, desperate to make up for all of the time they were apart. But even if I kissed her for a week, it would never be enough.

I could feel myself getting hard and knew that if we continued, I would be carrying her to the bedroom.

'Jasmine.' I reluctantly removed my mouth from hers. 'I want to make love to you, but we still have some things to discuss.'

'You're right.' She slowly opened her eyes. 'But first, I have to tell you the good news!' She took my hand and pulled me over to sit with her on the sofa.

'You already told me!' That kiss must have pureed her brain like it had done to mine.

'No! There were *two* pieces of good news. Actually, no. *Four* other pieces of good news.'

'Four?' My eyes widened. 'Tell me!'

'Well, extra-good news number one: they're hiring Bob.'

'*Genial!*'

'Two: they've got rid of Hazel.'

'*Bien*. She deserved to be fired.'

'And three: there's a new Cuisine King at the hotel.'

'Oh.' My heart sank. Under different circumstances, I would have hoped to have been considered, but I knew it was only a matter of time. I would make head chef one day. For now, I was just grateful to have my job back. 'Have you heard anything about him?'

'I have. He is very talented. And kind. And smart and very sexy.'

I frowned, then as the realisation of what she had said hit me, my mouth dropped open.

'In case it isn't obvious, the new Cuisine King is you!'

'*En serio?*' I jumped off the sofa.

'*Sí!*' Jasmine said. 'I'm totally serious! Congratulations!'

I picked her up off the sofa and span her around, almost knocking over the vase on her coffee table.

'I cannot believe it.' I shook my head. My pulse raced, my heart thumped and I was not ashamed to say that I even felt a tear come to my eye. I had waited so long for this moment.

'You'd better, because it's happening! Your dream has finally come true!'

'Wow. Lola and Evita will be so happy.'

'And proud. Just like I am. You did it! Just like we all knew you would.'

Now two tears came to my eyes. Freya would have been proud of me too.

'*Gracias.*'

'No need to thank me. You're the one that did all the hard work.'

'Celine also told me that you had emailed her?' I said.

'I did. I told her you were amazing and she'd basically be an idiot not to get you back and promote you.'

'Ha!' I smiled. 'I told her the same in my email. But I did not call her an idiot!'

'No? You missed out. It was strangely effective!' She laughed and the sound made my chest swell.

'And us?' I said, bringing it back to the most important part of our conversation.

She took my hands in hers and as we both sat back on the sofa, I prepared myself for her response.

'I did a lot of thinking and you're right: the fact that we work together and the age difference don't matter. The fact is, I love you, Alejandro. More than anything. And I don't want to waste time worrying about the future and what may or may not happen. I know we'll be great together. So I'd love to go all in, if you'll still have me?'

'There is nothing I would want more.' I leant over to kiss her. Getting my job back was fantastic. Finally becoming Cuisine King was incredible news too. But hearing that Jasmine loved me and wanted us to be together was the greatest news of all.

'That's a relief!' She laughed when we came up for air for a few seconds before kissing again.

When we had finally lasted more than thirty seconds without our lips fused together, I remembered something.

'I do not mean to question your maths.' I stroked her cheek. 'But you said there were four pieces of good news, but you only mentioned three extra things?'

'Oh yeah!' She smiled. 'I got promoted too!'

I bolted upright, my eyes wide.

'Why did you not tell me that as the first piece of news? That is amazing!' I pulled her in for a hug and then gave her another long, slow kiss.

'You're now looking at the new Love Alchemist Empress.'

'Congratulations! I am so happy for you. You deserve this!' I squeezed her tight.

'Thanks.' She smiled. 'I'm so excited!'

'I know how much this means to you. You're going to be the best Love Alchemist Empress in the universe!' I said and meant every word. 'Actually, you are not the only person with extra good news.'

'Oh?'

'*Sí*. Your cake. I tried it and once again, it was delicious. So I am officially declaring you a Dessert Doyenne.'

'Dessert Doyenne?' She laughed again.

'Well, as we are employees, sorry, Romance Rockstars, of the Love Hotel once again, it is only right that I give you a crazy job title, no?'

'Very true! So you really liked it?'

'I loved it!'

'I'm glad. It was my fourth attempt and it wasn't as fun baking it by myself as it was with you.'

'Next time, we can bake it together.'

'That would be great! Maybe you could teach me a few more dishes too?'

'*Por supuesto*,' I confirmed. 'I want to do everything with you: cook, travel... enjoy all that life has to offer. Whatever comes our way, as long as we are together, I know it will be wonderful.'

'Agreed!' She kissed me again. 'Seeing as we both have work tomorrow in our new big fancy roles, this might be the most relaxing day we have off for a while, so we should get started on enjoying ourselves.'

'What would you suggest we do first?'

'I was about to clear up the kitchen then make a start on lunch, but perhaps we could skip straight to dessert?' She raised her eyebrow suggestively.

'Well, you are the newly crowned Dessert Doyenne.' I stood up, took her hand and led her to the bedroom. 'And as the English like to say, dessert is *always* a good idea.'

EPILOGUE
JASMINE

Three months later

'Make a wish!' Evita called out as everyone gathered around the table with my giant birthday cake.

We were at Lola's house in South London where we'd come to celebrate my fortieth with our closest friends and family.

As well as Alejandro, or Ale as I now called him, his sisters and their partners, I'd invited Stella, Max, Sammie and Max's friends Colton, Natalie their adorable daughter, Betty and my family: not just my parents, but my grandad and his wife Lorna too.

I still couldn't believe we'd been reunited.

Ale could see how disappointed I was that I didn't get to see Grandad in Jamaica, so he'd secretly liaised with Bob to visit him. It took a few attempts, but when Bob finally got to speak to him, he'd video called me and let's just say, it was a very emotional call.

When I knew I'd be in London for my birthday, I asked

Grandad if he'd like to visit and when he accepted, I organised the flights for him and Lorna.

Telling Mum was hard and when they'd first reunited, it was awkward, but they were slowly working through things and Mum even thanked me for bringing him over, which was progress.

'Happy birthday, half pint!' Grandad smiled, then blew me a kiss. I was so happy he was here to share my special day with me.

'*Gwaan,* Miss Jasmine!' Bob's voice boomed from my phone. He'd video called from Jamaica because he didn't want to miss out on my celebrations.

I blew out the candles and tried to think of a wish.

'What did you ask for?' Betty asked innocently.

'It's a secret,' Max said sweetly, pressing his finger on his lip.

'The truth is,' I said, wrapping my arm around Ale's waist, 'it was hard to find something to wish for, because I already have everything I could ever want. I'm surrounded by people I adore, including my grandad, I have my dream job and the most incredible partner a woman could ask for.'

Before I went to Jamaica, I was dreading my fortieth birthday. But now, as clichéd as it sounded, I honestly felt like my life was only just beginning. I had so much to look forward to.

Ale leant forward and gave me one of his amazing kisses that I loved so much.

I'd thought the time we'd spent in Jamaica was magical, but the last few months were even better.

After the first month, it was clearer than ever that we were madly in love, so we started looking for a bigger place together. It took a few weeks, but eventually, we found a house near the beach. It wasn't cheap, but with our increased salaries, we were both able to afford the rent and still have enough to put aside for holidays and enjoying life.

Work was going brilliantly for both of us. I was loving my new role. I still got to work closely with our guests, plus I was developing a training programme for Love Alchemists in the hotel's rapidly expanding international locations which was so exciting. And my new boss was much nicer than Hazel. I felt supported and valued.

Ale was thriving too. There wasn't a day that went by that I didn't receive comments from our guests about how amazing his food was. He was building a talented team too and I loved seeing how much he enjoyed sharing his knowledge.

He'd been sharing his knowledge with me too. He'd kept his promise to help teach me some more dishes. One of my new favourite things was dancing around our kitchen on our days off together whilst he showed me how to cook or bake something new. Even if my attempts to recreate the dishes weren't perfect, he always had encouraging words to say and still insisted on licking the plate clean.

And it turned out that that there were many benefits to working with your partner. When we had the same shifts, we travelled into work together. We got to see each other throughout the day and steal kisses and hugs in the stockroom or occasionally, have private *meetings* in our offices at lunch or after work... We made sure we always locked the door, though.

It was a relief that everything was out in the open and we didn't have to sneak around. All of our fellow Romance Rockstars were happy for us. Most said they had seen the sparks flying for months. What Celine had said was right: true love was something to be celebrated, not hidden away.

When the investigation was launched into Hazel's conduct, it came out that her husband had had an affair with a co-worker, so she was particularly sensitive about work relationships. Given what happened with my ex, I understood the pain she went through. But she let her personal experiences affect the way she treated others and the way she did her job.

With the exception of the married employee, everyone else she'd fired for 'inappropriate behaviour' was single, so she'd blown everything way out of proportion.

I used to be angry with my ex. And although I still knew what he did was wrong, I no longer cared. If we didn't break up, I wouldn't have taken the job at the Love Hotel and I never would've met the love of my life. I hoped that one day, Hazel would find happiness with the right person too.

'I am a very lucky man,' Ale announced to the room. 'I had to work hard to convince her to date me, but the battle was worth it!'

Everyone erupted into laughter.

'We're happy for you both!' Lola said.

'Here, here!' Stella added.

'Thanks!' I said as Ale took more photos of me in front of the cake. He held up his phone to take another, but then paused.

'Everything okay?' I asked.

'It's a message from Celine with a preview of the article!' He stood beside me and everyone gathered around the screen to have a look.

Workplace Romance

You've heard about the single guests that have found love at the famous Love Hotel. But the hotel's magic is so powerful that several employees have fallen for each other on the job too. We spoke to the co-working couples that have fallen under the luxury resorts' romantic spell.

When I saw the large photo of me and Ale together, a huge

grin spread across my face. We were gazing into each other's eyes on the beach with the sunset behind us.

'That is a beautiful photo,' Ale said.

'I love it!'

When it came out that there were two other couples secretly dating at our hotel, Celine was thrilled. The marketing department then came up with the idea that it was something that could be celebrated publicly.

After talking it through, Ale and I said we'd be happy to take part in the article. If it helped to promote the hotel and encourage people to visit the hotel to find their match, then it was a positive thing. I'd never been happier in my life and I wished everyone could experience the feeling of true love that I had.

Once I'd cut the cake, I loaded the slices onto a plate and started doing the rounds.

'Cake, Sammie?'

'I'd love some. By the way, thanks for inviting me.'

'No problem!' I smiled. 'And a little birdy told me you'd applied for the Love Hotel...'

'Stella told you?'

'No... I have my sources. And let's just say my sources may be currently assessing some potential matches...'

'Oh my God!' she squealed. 'No way! So do I have a place? Am I going to get the call?'

'Like I said before, I can't promise anything, but I'm keeping everything crossed for you.'

'Thank you!' She beamed.

After I handed out all the cake, I headed back to my amazing man who'd just selected a reggae song that now blared through the speaker.

'Remind you of anything?' I asked, snaking my arms around his neck.

'*Sí.*' A grin spread across his face. 'Our first dance lesson and you rubbing against me on the dance floor at Rick's Café.'

'Oh sweet memories.' I kissed him softly.

'Shall we make some more right now?'

'Definitely!'

As Ale wrapped his arms around me, I finally thought of something to wish for: I wished that moments like these would last forever.

And when Ale looked into my eyes, I knew that the best memories were yet to come.

* * *

MORE FROM OLIVIA SPRING

Want to know what happens when Sammie visits The Love Hotel in gorgeous Italy? Find out in book three in the series!

In case you missed the previous gorgeous and hilarious romantic comedy in The Love Hotel series from Olivia Spring, *The One That Got Away*, is also available to order now here:
www.mybook.to/GotAwayBackAd

ACKNOWLEDGEMENTS

Hi there! Thanks so much for reading *What Happens in Paradise*. I hope you enjoyed Jasmine and Alejandro's romantic adventures in Jamaica and Spain.

If you've read any of my other fifteen books, then you'll know that I absolutely LOVE writing the acknowledgements page, because I get to say thank-you to the amazing people who helped me create this story.

First of all, I'd like to say a massive *gracias* to my fantastic husband. Thanks for your constant support, for celebrating the highs, giving the best hugs when I'm feeling low and for listening when I yabber on about my characters. Love you to the moon and back!

Mum, thanks for diligently reading over this book, giving helpful feedback and for being one of my biggest cheerleaders.

I'd like to 'big up' my dad: thanks for the great reggae recommendations and for taking me to Jamaica to show me my roots. I'll remember those trips forever and they gave me so much inspiration for this book.

To my brilliant beta reader, Emma Grocott: thank you for taking the time to read this book and helping to spread the word on social media. You're amazing!

Jas: Thanks for all of your enthusiasm for this book and all of my others. I appreciate you SO much!

To my lovely niece: thanks for reading over this novel so meticulously with your excellent eagle eyes.

Shout-out to my awesome author friend, Fiona Zedde. I'm so glad we met! Thanks for all of the advice, encouragement and for checking over the Patois.

Huge thanks to my editor Megan Haslam and the brilliant Boldwood team for your hard work and helping me to bring my books to a bigger audience.

To my incredible cover designer, Rachel Lawston: I can't believe this is the sixteenth cover you've created for me! Thanks for being so talented.

Thanks to copyeditor Emily Reader and proofreader Rachel Sargeant for helping my words shine and to my website designer Dawn for the updates.

I'm so incredibly grateful for all of the brilliant bloggers, Bookstagrammers, ARC readers and BookTokers who have shown this story so much love. Thank you for taking time out of your busy days to read my book, then write such gorgeous reviews. Your wonderful social media posts and videos are invaluable in helping me spread the word.

And a ginormous thank-you, to *you*, dear reader. I know that there are a gazillion books available, so the fact that you chose to buy and read one of mine, really means the world. Sending you a big, warm, squishy virtual hug!

Right, I'm off to continue writing book three in the Love Hotel series, which will be Sammie's story. Look forward to sharing it with you soon...

Lots of love,

Olivia x

PLAYLIST FOR WHAT HAPPENS IN PARADISE

Single – Natasha Bedingfield
Independent Women Part I – Destiny's Child
Three Little Birds – Bob Marley & The Wailers
Tempted to Touch – Beres Hammond
Light My Fire – Sean Paul (feat. Gwen Stefani & Shenseea)
Belong in the Sun – ¿Téo (feat. Lido)
Close To You – Maxi Priest
Who Knows – Protoje (feat. Chronixx)
Can't Take My Eyes Off of You – Lauryn Hill
Good Day – Sean Paul
You Bring Me Joy – Mary J. Blige
Could You Be Loved – Bob Marley & The Wailers
I Need Your Love – Beres Hammond
Good Love – Lucy Pearl
Missing You – Soul II Soul
Hopelessly in Love – Carroll Thompson
Everything – Mary J. Blige
Dance Tonight – Lucy Pearl

In Your Body – ¿Téo?
Part of Me – ¿Téo?
Love Has Found Its Way – Dennis Brown
One Love/People Get Ready – Bob Marley & The Wailers

ABOUT THE AUTHOR

Olivia Spring is a bestselling author of contemporary women's fiction and romantic comedies, now writing spicy romance for Boldwood.

Sign up to Olivia's mailing list for news, competitions and updates on future books.

Visit Olivia's website: www.oliviaspring.com

Follow Olivia on social media here:

- facebook.com/ospringauthor
- x.com/ospringauthor
- instagram.com/ospringauthor
- bookbub.com/authors/olivia-spring

ALSO BY OLIVIA SPRING

The Love Hotel Series
The One That Got Away
What Happens in Paradise

LOVE NOTES
LOVE IN EVERY CHAPTER

WHERE ALL YOUR ROMANCE
DREAMS COME TRUE!

THE HOME OF BESTSELLING
ROMANCE AND WOMEN'S
FICTION

WARNING:
MAY CONTAIN SPICE

SIGN UP TO OUR
NEWSLETTER

https://bit.ly/Lovenotesnows

Boldwood

Boldwood Books is an award-winning fiction publishing company seeking out the best stories from around the world.

Find out more at www.boldwoodbooks.com

Join our reader community for brilliant books, competitions and offers!

Follow us

@BoldwoodBooks

@TheBoldBookClub

Sign up to our weekly deals newsletter

https://bit.ly/BoldwoodBNewsletter

Printed in Great Britain
by Amazon